Christmas
at the Inn on
Bluebell Lane

BOOKS BY KATE HEWITT

FAR HORIZONS TRILOGY
The Heart Goes On
Her Rebel Heart
This Fragile Heart

AMHERST ISLAND SERIES
The Orphan's Island
Dreams of the Island
Return to the Island
The Island We Left Behind
An Island Far from Home
The Last Orphan

THE GOSWELL QUARTET
The Wife's Promise
The Daughter's Garden
The Bride's Sister
The Widow's Secret

THE INN ON BLUEBELL LANE SERIES
The Inn on Bluebell Lane

STANDALONE NOVELS
A Mother's Goodbye
The Secrets We Keep

KATE HEWITT

Christmas
at the Inn on
Bluebell Lane

bookouture

Published by Bookouture in 2023

An imprint of Storyfire Ltd.
Carmelite House
50 Victoria Embankment
London EC4Y 0DZ

www.bookouture.com

ISBN: 978-1-83790-297-2
eBook ISBN: 978-1-83790-296-5

To the lovely people of Monmouth,
who welcomed this American family to Wales!

CHAPTER 1

ELLIE

OCTOBER

"I'm afraid it's not good news."

"Wh—what?" Ellie Davies stared at her sister-in-law, trying not to show how nervous she felt. She'd been delaying this financial reckoning of the inn for a couple of months, it was true, but she hadn't expected Sarah to sound quite so *grim*. Admittedly, they'd all known more or less that the finances of the place weren't tip-top, but they were *managing*. Mostly. Weren't they?

"The books," Sarah stated, thumping the ledger that she'd placed on the kitchen table in front of them like some sacred tome, "they don't balance."

"They... don't?" Ellie took a sip of tea as she avoided Sarah's censorious gaze, looking out the window of the Bluebell Inn, into the garden beyond. A few chickens pecked in the long grass, under the low-hanging boughs of a gnarled, old apple tree, a wooden swing hanging from one of its thick branches. It was a lovely sight, encompassing exactly the kind of quaint coziness that this inn had to offer the discerning guest. Could Sarah really be implying it might all be at risk? "Are you sure?" Ellie asked Sarah, turning back to look at her, hoping for some caveat or consideration, but her sister-in-law looked down her long, patrician nose as she pursed her lips.

"Yes, I'm sure, Ellie. The inn has been operating at a loss basically since it began, as everyone should know, since it's what I've been saying from the beginning—"

"Yes, I know, but we've still *managed*," Ellie cut across her, trying to smile, as if she could simply jolly her sister-in-law along. "We were always going to be on a shoestring, weren't we?"

"Well, we're now running out of string," Sarah replied flatly. She flicked her long, auburn braid over one shoulder as she flipped open the ledger to show Ellie exactly what she meant.

Two years ago, Ellie and her husband Matthew, along with their four young children, had moved from suburban Connecticut to the tiny village of Llandrigg in South Wales, to help Matthew's mother, Gwen, renovate the family bed and breakfast, known as the Bluebell Inn. The move had been prompted by Matthew's redundancy, which had hit him—and the whole family—hard. They'd needed a change, a chance to reset, recalibrate, re-everything.

Life in the little village had been challenging at first, trying to make ends meet, but also, more significantly, learning to adjust to an entirely new way of living, so different from the comforts, conveniences, and familiarity of life back in the United States. Matthew might have been born and raised in Wales, but after twenty years in the US, he'd become used to American living, and it had been all Ellie or any of their four children had ever known.

Two years on, Ellie could acknowledge that *she* might have been the one who'd had the most trouble adapting at first, but they'd all managed to learn to embrace life here, and even to love it, and they'd transformed this ramshackle, rather homely inn. Now, instead of your common-or-garden B&B, it was a "family inn," offering families of all shapes and sizes a unique getaway, and an opportunity to experience all the aspects of rural, community life—from weeding the veg patch and collecting eggs, to family-style meals, craft afternoons and game nights. Ellie had thought it had been, if not a roaring, then at least a modest, success, with solid bookings throughout the summer and most holidays. But it appeared she'd been wrong, based on what Sarah, who was the company's accountant as well as her husband's sister, was now saying.

"Look, Ellie," Sarah indicated, running a finger down the ledger, but as Ellie leaned forward to scan the neatly written columns, the figures simply swam before her eyes. Math had never been her strong suit.

"Can you explain it to me?" she asked. "Because I'm not sure I can make heads or tails of all that."

Sarah sighed and closed the book. "I can explain it easily enough," she told her as Ellie's gaze moved inexorably back to the window and the comforting view. The wooden swing six-year-old Ava loved to play on moved gently in the autumn breeze. They'd built something *good* here, she thought, taking refuge in that. It couldn't slip away from them simply because of figures in a ledger. "But can you pay attention, please?" Sarah continued, an edge of impatience sharpening her voice. "This is important, you know."

"I'm sorry." Ellie turned back once more, repentant. They might have built something good here, but it appeared now to be at risk. She needed to understand why, and her sister-in-law certainly seemed to think so, too.

When she'd first moved to Llandrigg, Ellie and Sarah had rubbed each other the wrong way. Sarah had seemed so confident and accomplished, striding through life with elegant aplomb, while Ellie had felt more of a mess, mired in doubts about the move, as well as her own potential place in Llandrigg

—and in the family business. Sometimes she'd felt as if Sarah had been turning her nose up at her, and Sarah, in turn, had felt excluded from the goings-on with the inn.

They had come a long way from those first uneasy months, but the truth remained that they were very different people, as evidenced right now by the way Ellie was tempted to avoid this conversation, while Sarah was grimly determined to have it. If only Sarah could sound a little more *optimistic*, Ellie thought as she took a reassuring sip of tea to steady herself; over the last two years, she'd come to love the quintessentially British drink.

"I'm listening," she assured her sister-in-law. "So, explain it to me, please. Why don't the books balance, exactly?"

"Because they generally don't when you're spending more money than you make," Sarah replied rather tartly. "That's how it works. More *out* than *in* tends to be a recipe for eventual bankruptcy, whether it's in a few weeks, or months or years."

Bankruptcy? Ellie's stomach hollowed at the thought. The move to Llandrigg had been prompted, in part, by their own family's brush with bankruptcy, after Matthew's redundancy. They'd had to sell their home in a fire sale and money had been very tight for a while. The last thing Ellie wanted was for her family to experience that kind of disappointment and upheaval again.

"But are we, really?" she pressed, still unable to believe it could be as cut and dried as that. "I mean, I know money has been tight, of course I do, and we've always had to cut things pretty close to the bone, but we've been fully booked nearly every—"

"Holiday, yes," Sarah cut her off, her tone gentling yet still intractable. "But there are only about thirteen holiday weeks in a year, and thirty-nine that aren't. It's those thirty-nine weeks we need to worry about."

"There have been *some* school-term bookings," Ellie protested.

Not nearly as many, it was true; for the month or so on either side of a school holiday, the inn might be half or even fully booked, but for the rest of the year, it tended to be pretty sparse. Ellie hadn't actually minded that much; the truth was, life was busy enough, and when you had a house full of guests, many of them young and noisy, and your own family besides, she'd enjoyed having a bit of a break in between. Maybe she *should* have minded, all things considered.

Sarah *had* been asking to go over the books with her and Matthew since the end of the summer, Ellie acknowledged uncomfortably. Matt would normally have been at this meeting, but he'd had a last-minute opportunity to scout out some Welsh blue slate roof tiles at a reclamation yard in Abergavenny. She didn't think he'd been all that worried about the inn's finances, but maybe he should have been. Maybe they all should have been.

"So... what are you saying?" Ellie asked, adopting what she hoped was a cheerfully pragmatic tone. This was a solvable problem. At least, it could be. It *had* to be. "We need to increase our bookings? Maybe up our marketing budget a bit, get the word out again?" She raised her eyebrows in expectation, only to have Sarah sigh and shake her head slowly.

"Ellie, it's not that simple. We haven't got the money to do any of that. The truth is, we never really did. You're right when you say we've been running this place on a shoestring. It doesn't give us anything to play with now, I'm afraid." She paused before stating resolutely, "Running the inn as it is is just about all we can manage, and even then not for very long."

Ellie reached for her teacup once again and took a much-needed sip. She wasn't liking the sound of this, at all.

"If we go on as we are," Sarah continued matter-of-factly, "with the bookings we currently have, we'll be just about completely out of money by the end of March."

"By March!" Ellie stared at her in dismay. "But that's less than six months away."

"I know."

How could this have happened? How could she have let it? The truth was, Ellie knew, she'd been a bit head-in-the-sand about it all, letting Sarah be in charge without thinking much more about it. Gwen and Matthew, she suspected, had been the same. They'd all preferred the practical work of making sure their guests had a good time. And then there had been their own family life. At fifteen, her oldest, Jess, was having a seemingly never-ending round of friendship dramas and boy crises. Ben, at thirteen, was in possession of a tireless amount of energy, and needed a fair amount of redirecting, as well as support and encouragement, to make sure he stayed on top of his schoolwork as well as out of trouble. Ten-year-old Josh was in his last year at the local primary and they'd been touring the comprehensive in Abergavenny as well as a few other schools, to figure out the best fit for his interests and quiet disposition. Then there was Ava, at only six, who still liked cuddles and stories and elaborate bedtime rituals. There simply hadn't been *time* to worry about the state of Bluebell Inn's finances, especially as whenever Ellie turned around, there was another booking... if only one, admittedly, or maybe two.

"So, if we don't have the money to up our marketing," Ellie asked, still trying to be pragmatic, "what do you think we should do?"

"I don't know." Sarah frowned. To her credit, she'd been diligent about the inn's accounts, and this wasn't the first warning Ellie had been given, so she knew it shouldn't come as so much of a shock. Last spring, Sarah had suggested increasing their prices, but Ellie's mother-in-law, Gwen, had insisted she wanted the inn to be an affordable holiday for everyone. This summer, Sarah had cautioned against their plans to turn the old pond at the bottom of the garden into a swimming hole, insisting there wasn't enough money to install a pump and filtration system, or a pool liner, and so Matthew had reluctantly put those plans on hold.

No, Ellie acknowledged with a sigh, this shouldn't have come as a surprise. It was just her blithe determination to tackle what was right in front of her and nothing else that had made her ignore all the warning signs her sister-in-law had so dutifully given.

"There must be something, Sarah," she insisted now. "We can't just... *end* things." Not after all the work they'd done, all the energy and emotion they'd invested in this place, this *life*.

"We can raise prices," Sarah suggested, "like I've said before, or find a way to increase bookings without increasing our budget. Those are the only options I can think of, and they have to be enacted sharpish." She paused. "If you'd taken my advice a few months ago—"

"I know, and we didn't," Ellie replied quickly. "We should have, absolutely. But those are two good suggestions." She tried to smile, although anxiety was now churning her insides. If the inn went bust, what would happen to them? To Gwen? As much as Ellie had initially resisted the move to Llandrigg, she knew she was now just as resistant to the idea of leaving it. The children were settled, she was settled, Matthew loved being the inn's maintenance man and general director. They'd all found a purpose as well as a happiness here. They simply had to find a way to make this work. "I could go on social media a bit more," she suggested. "Post about it on various sites and blogs and things." She'd done that at the beginning, to drum up business, and it had seemed to work; their first summer, they'd been fully booked every single week. But, Ellie supposed, she'd trailed off because she'd felt as if the inn was established, and life had, inevitably, become busy. "I'll contact some magazines, as well," she added, "maybe ask them to run some features."

Sarah looked decidedly dubious. "I'm not sure why they

would run a feature on an inn that has been quietly running for two years already," she remarked. "But I suppose it's worth a try."

"You don't want it to close, do you, Sarah?" Ellie asked impulsively.

Although she didn't think she'd ever be best friends with her sister-in-law, for their temperaments were simply too different, they had come to respect and even like each other. At least, she hoped they had. Sarah had certainly become more involved in the running of the inn; she was here several times a week, checking in on things, chatting to guests, taking part. Her two children, sixteen-year-old Mairi and fourteen-year-old Owen, had also often come along; Mairi was one of Jess's best friends and Owen loved to kick a ball around with Ben. The inn really had been a family endeavor.

"Of course, I don't want it to close!" Sarah looked affronted, and even a little hurt. "I'm just trying to be *realistic*, Ellie. I suppose, like you, part of me was hoping we could just trundle along for a while longer, but it really is time to face facts. If we don't do something fairly drastic soon, I don't think we'll have much choice in the matter, and we might just have to shut our doors."

"Have you spoken to your mother about this?" Although the inn had originally been Gwen's idea, back when her husband David had been alive, she'd taken more of a back seat in its operational running and decision-making since Ellie and her family had arrived. Gwen was happy to bake treats for the family teas and manage the garden, but the bigger decisions she left to Matthew, Ellie, and Sarah, with seeming gratitude and relief. Still, it was her house, her dream, and Ellie knew she would need to be informed... and involved.

"I've tried," Sarah replied, "but, like you and Matt, she's been a bit tricky to pin down." She sighed, her face drawn into somber lines. "I know it's not easy to face something like this, and to be honest, I haven't wanted to face it, either. Perhaps I should have a been more diligent about getting us all to face the music a bit sooner, as it were, but here we are. It's time."

"Yes, here we are," Ellie echoed. And it wasn't a very good place to be. She knew Sarah had her doubts about how a few Facebook posts might help, but Ellie was determined to try. "Maybe we should have a meeting," she suggested. "A family conference, of sorts. Everyone can pitch in with ideas about how to help."

"Maybe," Sarah allowed, sounding skeptical, "but we'd better do it soon." She glanced at her watch. "I'm sorry, but I need to get to work." She worked part-time for an accountancy firm in Abergavenny, in addition to her work for the inn. "Let me know if you schedule a meeting."

"All right." Ellie stood up, following Sarah to the door. "Thank you for your hard work, anyway," she said, and Sarah gave her a fleeting smile.

"Sorry it's not better news."

As Ellie watched her sister-in-law walk briskly to the car, she couldn't help but think that while Sarah might not want Bluebell Inn to close, such an event wouldn't affect her nearly as much as it would Ellie and her family. Sarah lived in a smart executive-style home in Llandarth, the next village over, and her husband Nathan had an important, corporate job in Cardiff. She did the inn's books as a kindness, and she and her children wouldn't suffer *too* much if the place went under.

But what would she and Matthew do? How would they manage for money? Since they'd moved to the Bluebell Inn, they'd muddled along, managing their expenses with a combination of savings from the sale of their house—which hadn't gone for nearly as much as they hoped—and chipping in with Gwen for groceries and bills, without worrying too much about who paid for what. They hadn't drawn an actual salary from the business yet, and it hadn't seemed to matter too much, because, so far, their expenses had been minimal. But, Ellie acknowledged, that wouldn't always be the case. Her parents had come to visit last summer, but she'd been hoping to travel to see them in the States the week after Christmas—six airline tickets would not be cheap. Now she wondered if they even had the money for such a trip.

She took a deep breath. If the inn went under, she told herself, still trying to be pragmatic, it wouldn't be the absolute end of the world. Matthew could look for a job in Cardiff or even Birmingham, which was only a little over an hour away. She could find work too. As for their plans to buy a house in the village, to make more space for guests and give themselves some breathing room... well, they would just have to be put on hold. That wasn't the end of the world, either. They'd been living in the inn's attic for the last two years. They could keep doing it, even if Ellie sometimes dreamed of having her own kitchen, an ensuite bathroom, a house that didn't need fire doors or signs reminding guests of the Wi-Fi passcode.

No, Ellie realized as she turned away from the door, it wasn't the loss of their livelihood, such as it was, that was bothering her. It was the loss of the inn itself, as a functioning business, a way of life. The dream she and Matthew had made together, along with Gwen and Sarah and the children. The dream she'd cherished.

Slowly she walked through the downstairs rooms they'd transformed over the last two years—the little games nook with its shelves of board games and puzzles and a few squashy armchairs; the cozy sitting room with its deep sofas framing the fireplace, the comforting scent of woodsmoke lingering in the air; the dining room with its table that seated sixteen, the glass-fronted cabinets with Gwen's family silver and porcelain. All of it felt so familiar and beloved now, even though it had been strange when she'd first moved in here.

The whole family had pitched in and worked hard—Jess

with her American-style treats and traditions; Ava as chief egg collector; Ben running the children's assault course in the garden with Matt; and Josh organizing the games room with its assortment of games. Ellie had managed social activities and Gwen had planned the menus, while they'd both chipped in with the cooking. Really, everything about this place had been a joyful, joint effort, and one that had been Ellie's brainchild, something she was inordinately proud of, simply because it had been hers. It *couldn't* go under just two years in. Ellie wouldn't let it.

Filled with determination, she marched back to the kitchen and started clearing the tea things from the big, rectangular table of scrubbed oak, moving around the cozy, cluttered space as she had a thousand times before, and yet somehow finding everything precious—the ancient Aga, the Welsh dresser full of china, the big, battered tins of flour and sugar that Gwen used just about every day.

"Was Sarah here?" Gwen asked as she came into the kitchen, still wearing her gardening gloves, her silver hair tucked back in a neat bob, her blue eyes crinkled in query. Petite and trim, she looked younger than her sixty-nine years. "I was just trying to tidy up the flower beds... you have to keep on top of them, even at this time of year, or everything looks too rampant." She shook her head ruefully, smiling, and Ellie managed to smile back. The inn's garden was a delightful jumble of flowers and shrubs, raised beds and wild spaces for children to explore, welly boots required.

"Yes, she just left," Ellie replied. "Cup of tea? I'm afraid the pot's gone cold, but I can brew another."

"That would be lovely, Ellie. Thank you."

Her relationship with her mother-in-law had certainly benefitted from working on the inn together, Ellie reflected as she went to switch on the kettle. When she'd first moved to the Bluebell Inn, she and Gwen had stepped cautiously around each other, both of them seeming to be in a constant state of prickly self-defense, always misunderstanding each other, despite their good intentions.

But Gwen's cancer diagnosis just a few weeks after they'd moved had changed things, and Ellie had been both glad and honored to help her mother-in-law through her chemotherapy and its debilitating after-effects. When Gwen had been well enough, they'd settled into a symbiotic working relationship, bouncing ideas off each other, each acceding to the other's area of expertise. Ellie would be sorry to lose that, if they had to close their doors. She thought Gwen would be, as well.

"What did Sarah want?" her mother-in-law asked in a voice of only mild curiosity.

Ellie kept her back to her as she bustled around, making tea.

"She wanted to go over the inn's accounts."

"Ah, yes." Gwen let out a sigh. "She's been asking me to do that for ages, and I just haven't had the heart to face it. I don't suppose the numbers are all that inspiring."

Ellie turned around and placed a cup of tea in front of her mother-in-law. Like her, Gwen had clearly had suspicions that things hadn't been going as well as they'd wanted them to.

"The way Sarah said it..." Gwen made a face as she picked up her cup of tea. "I knew it couldn't be good news. Thank you for this, Ellie."

"It's no trouble."

"The inn hasn't had that many bookings since the summer holidays," Gwen remarked on a sigh.

"We are fully booked for half-term in two weeks," Ellie couldn't help but protest, even though she knew her mother-in-law was right, just as Sarah was.

"Yes..." Gwen let out another small sigh. "But a week here and there isn't going to do it, is it? That seemed to be what Sarah was implying, anyway. I just haven't wanted to think about it, to be honest."

"That is essentially what Sarah said," Ellie admitted.

For the first time, Gwen looked more alarmed than merely resigned. Her heart and soul were bound up in this place, Ellie knew. As practical as she was trying to be, losing the inn would be hard, indeed, for her as well as Ellie. "So how bad is it?" she asked. "Did Sarah tell you, exactly?"

"She said..." Ellie took a deep breath. "She said unless things changed fairly drastically, then... we'd run out of money in just under six months."

"*Six months!*" Gwen looked truly shocked. "Completely? As in... *bankrupt?*"

Ellie nodded. "I haven't looked at the actual amount in the account, but that's what Sarah said."

"Goodness." Gwen took a sip of tea, her expression dazed. "I must admit, I didn't realize it was as quite as bad as that. I assumed we could muddle along for a while longer yet."

"I thought the same."

They were both silent for a moment, absorbing the gloomy import of the news.

"But there are things we can do, Gwen," Ellie finally said, doing her best to rally. "We don't have to take this lying down. I told Sarah I'd get more active on social media again, maybe contact a few magazines..." She trailed off because Gwen was looking almost as skeptical as Sarah had.

"Will that really be enough?" she asked dubiously.

"Well, it's a start." And the truth was, Ellie couldn't think what else to do.

"I don't suppose it would be the absolute end of the world, if we had to close," Gwen mused slowly, echoing Ellie's earlier thoughts. "David and I paid off the mortgage on this place ages ago, and our bills are minimal. We could manage on my pension and savings—"

"And Matthew and I could work," Ellie said quickly. "Of course you wouldn't have to support us, Gwen, if it came to that." The last thing she wanted was her mother-in-law worrying about finances on their account.

"I know." Gwen smiled sadly. "But I would be sad to close our doors as an inn, especially when you've managed to turn it into something I could really believe in."

"You were a part of that, too," Ellie insisted. "Sometimes I feel like I just took the idea you and David originally had and embroidered it a bit."

"And such lovely embroidery it was," Gwen replied with a smile.

For a second, they simply gazed mistily at one another, and then Ellie straightened as she gave a little clap. "Right, well, it's not over yet," she stated firmly. "I know this is a blow, but I really do believe we can turn things around with a little effort and energy and maybe also a little luck." She gave her mother-in-law a bracing smile, more determined than ever to banish Sarah's bad news with practical steps. Together, they could do it. She'd make sure of it. "The Bluebell Inn," she stated grandly, "won't close on our watch!"

CHAPTER 2

SARAH

No one ever liked giving bad news, Sarah thought with a sigh as she drove away from the Bluebell Inn, bumping down the rutted track with a slight wince. She knew they needed to re-gravel the drive, but that was yet another thing that the budget didn't stretch to. There was homely, she thought, and then there was just plain shabby, or even rundown, and as of late, the inn was definitely veering toward the latter, despite the changes Ellie and Matthew had made—the friendly-looking sign of white-painted wood at the end of the lane, with 'The Bluebell Inn' written in curly gold script, the neatly tended flower beds by the old wrought iron gate.

Sarah appreciated Ellie's determination to do something, but at this point, she couldn't help but wonder if anything could save the inn, a thought that tore at her heart. Over the last two years, she'd been spending more and more time there, recon-necting with her brother and mother, as well as Ellie and her nieces and nephews, treasuring those newfound relationships, even if she'd never quite been able to say as much. Sarah knew she'd never been much of an *emoter*, but she would miss the busyness of the inn, the guests she'd been able to meet and chat

to, the sense of welcome and friendship that had been fostered...
especially when her own home currently felt so unwelcoming.

Her stomach cramped as she thought about last night—
Nathan hadn't returned from his job as an investment manager
in Cardiff until past ten o'clock. Both Mairi and Owen had
already been in bed, Owen having been moping because his
father had promised to play football with him after work.
Nathan hadn't even sent a text to warn Sarah that he'd be late,
at least not until she'd texted first, when it had gone seven and
dinner was already on the table. When he finally had come
home, he'd been tired and irritable, waving Sarah away even
though she had barely said a word.

"Don't give me that, please, Sarah," he'd told her wearily,
despite having only said hello. "I'm sorry I'm late, but you know
things are really busy at work."

Sarah had been amazed to hear a slightly accusing note in
his voice; did he actually blame her for something that was
entirely up to him? And why didn't she call him out on it?
Because she didn't, and hadn't for months. Even when he'd
seemed so irritable last night, she hadn't come back swinging,
the way she once might have, or even offered a pointed reply.
No, last night she'd just heated up his supper in the microwave,
and murmured something about how, yes, she knew it was a
busy time.

How *pathetic* she was, she thought with a grimace, oblivious
to the verdant green hills that rolled onto the horizon as she
drove toward Abergavenny. It wasn't like her, or at least it
hadn't been in the past. She'd always prided herself on being
strong, self-assured, striding through life with confidence. She
knew it was off-putting to some—even to Ellie, at least when
she'd first moved here—but it had felt like a kind of armor to
Sarah, a way to face and indeed combat the world. But somehow, over the last year, she'd become this placating and even

cringing creature when it came to her husband... because, she feared, that was the only way to keep her marriage alive.

Sarah pushed away that unpalatable thought before it could fully form and focused on the road as she came to the outskirts of Abergavenny, a quaint market town at the foot of three gentle mountains—the Skirrid, the Blorenge, and the Sugarloaf. Sarah had hiked them all.

Ellie wasn't the only one who could bury her head in the sand about the difficult parts of life, she acknowledged wryly. She hadn't pushed too hard about talking about the inn's finances because she hadn't wanted to confront them herself— just as she'd didn't push Nathan too hard, either, on why he came home so late many evenings, or what had been making him so tense. She hadn't taken him to task about letting Owen down about the football, and last week she'd said nothing when he'd missed a family dinner on Friday night, even though he'd told her that morning he'd be home, and she'd made a roast dinner specially. It was cowardly of her, and it wasn't fair to her children, and yet some instinct for self-preservation continued to keep her silent. If she challenged him, the way she usually did, what would happen?

It was a question Sarah didn't want to ask, never mind answer.

A long, low breath escaped her. At some point, she knew, just like with the inn's finances, there would have to be a facing up to reality... and a reckoning. But, she thought with a rather grim smile, not today.

Twenty minutes after leaving the inn, she reached the building on the edge of Abergavenny where the accountancy firm where she worked had its office. Sarah had been working there for over ten years, since the children had been small; she'd liked the part-time hours, earning her own wage, and having something to do besides bake cupcakes or read to reception years—*that*, she realized suddenly, stopping mid-thought, was Nathan's voice, not hers.

Back then, she actually wouldn't have minded staying at home for a few more years, for the children's sake as much as her own, but Nathan hadn't really seen the point of it. He'd always been ambitious, and she'd matched him, as best as she could. It was futile to engage in some revisionist history, Sarah told herself rather crossly as she headed up to the office. She'd been glad to go back to work, eager for the new challenge... hadn't she?

Sometimes she felt as if her current uncertainty—*and*, she thought, *let's face it, unhappiness*—colored everything about the way she viewed her life, past, present, and future. It was like every photograph of her life had been washed in sepia. She needed to get a grip, get her *self* back.

"All right, Sarah?" the receptionist, Rhiannon, asked cheerfully as Sarah came into the office.

Sarah forced her usual brightly determined smile onto her face. "Yes, absolutely fine," she assured the receptionist, with perhaps just a bit too much force.

Rhiannon's cheerfulness faltered as she glanced at Sarah striding so swiftly by.

"Glad to hear it," she replied, and Sarah thought she sounded a bit dubious. She certainly felt more than a bit dubious herself.

It was a relief to enter her office and get down to work, not worry about what was going wrong in her life. When she had a column of numbers in front of her, her mind was able to empty everything else out and she felt as if she could breathe easier. The formless doubts and worries that had been plaguing her faded away, and she enjoyed being able to focus. There was nothing quite as satisfying as a string of figures that added up, a spreadsheet that made sense. A few hours in and Sarah felt her sense of equilibrium, fragile as it was, return.

Unfortunately, those doubts and worries crowded in the moment she let them, and they started to take alarming shape when she went to make herself a coffee in the office's little kitchenette, or when she ate a sandwich at her desk, skimming news and struggling to push back the black cloud that kept threatening to hover over her, subsume her completely.

Get a grip, Sarah. This isn't you. This isn't you at all.

Except right now, it was.

When had she started to doubt Nathan? To fear her marriage wasn't as solid or strong as she'd believed—assumed, really— that it was?

She and Nathan had met in the university's debating society; they'd taken each other on, arguing for and against "This House would put corporate profits before individual privacy." Sarah had lost, by only a point; Nathan had argued for the motion, she against.

He'd good-naturedly gloated about his victory and asked her out in the same breath. Now, Sarah found herself wondering what would have happened if *she'd* won the debate. Would Nathan have even asked her out? He'd always liked to win, but then, she had, too. They'd matched each other, in so many ways... so why did she feel so *mis*matched now? Was it all in her mind, and Nathan had just had a few late nights, or was something bigger going on?

Fortunately, Sarah thought, she had enough to distract her from her own unhappy thoughts. She left at three on a Wednesday, so she could pick up Mairi and take her to the stables outside Llandarth to groom and ride her horse, Mabel. Sarah had fallen in love with horse riding as a child, and although she didn't get the opportunity to ride too much now, she loved being able to encourage the same passion in her daughter, who, until recently, had been absolutely horse-mad, with posters on the walls, pony books adorning her shelves, the whole lot. Then the teenaged years had struck, and Mairi sometimes seemed as if she'd rather do anything else than groom or ride Mabel. Sarah kept hoping her daughter would fall back in love with the pursuit, as well as the beloved animal she'd been taking care of for the last eight years.

"Good day at school?" she asked brightly as Mairi flung herself into the front seat; Owen had football practice and would be coming home on a later bus.

"I got a fifty-four on my maths test," Mairi replied, leaning her head against the seat and closing her eyes. "I'm going to *fail* my GCSEs."

"It's only October," Sarah replied mildly, "and your exams aren't for another six months. You've got time, sweetheart, I wouldn't worry just yet."

"You don't know how stressed I am, Mum!" Mairi declared in an injured tone, and Sarah managed to hold her tongue. It wasn't as if *she* hadn't taken the state exams in ten subjects that every student had to sit at the end of year eleven, or done her A levels two years later, or sat university exams three years after that, not to mention the four accounting exams she'd had to take to qualify as a CPA. *Oh, no.* She couldn't possibly understand what that sort of pressure was like.

"I'm sorry you're stressed," she replied diplomatically, and pulled out onto the road.

"I don't have time to deal with Mabel," Mairi continued, "be there every single day, brushing and feeding and all that." She let out a theatrical groan that would have made Sarah smile if she didn't already feel so tense.

"Mabel is a commitment, Mairi," she reminded her daughter, trying not to sound as if she were giving her a lecture when she knew she basically was. This was far from the first time they'd had this conversation, and Sarah doubted it would be the last. "One you agreed to, quite happily."

"Yeah, when I was *eight*," Mairi retorted. "What, I'm never allowed to change my mind?"

"Is that what you really want to do?" Sarah tried not to sound too censorious, too *hurt*. Mabel had been a present to Mairi and she'd been in love with that horse, riding her every day, taking hours to groom her, thrilled that Mabel was really hers, always asking to go to the stables, wishing they could keep Mabel in their back garden. And now she just wanted to walk away?

Her daughter was stressed, Sarah reminded herself, which was understandable, considering this was an important exam year, and Mairi had always been competitive about her academics. Sarah knew she needed to be a steadying presence, even if right now, she felt far from steady herself.

Mairi let out another groan as she slouched further down in her seat. "I mean, I *like* Mabel," she said, "but it's a lot, you know? Every single day after school, and before school, too..."

"I've been checking on Mabel in the mornings," Sarah reminded her, making sure to keep her voice mild. And she had been doing so for years. Mairi hadn't taken care of Mabel in the mornings except on weekends since she'd started secondary school over three years ago.

"Yeah, but *weekends*..." Mairi protested.

Clearly, she wanted an argument. And, in truth, Sarah felt frayed enough to think about giving her one. She already tiptoed around her husband; did she have to tiptoe around her daughter, too? Yet she knew she shouldn't take her frustrations out on her daughter, who had her own troubles to deal with.

"If you really feel like it's too much," Sarah stated calmly, "we can think about selling her." Even if the prospect of doing such a thing tore at her heart. Mabel would fetch several thousand pounds at least, but Sarah felt as if she were part of the family. A Welsh cob, Mabel was a deep, russet brown, with a gleaming coat and the softest, loveliest eyes you could imagine. She was gentle and loving, but could jump like a champion.

Mairi looked startled, and then a bit alarmed. "I don't want to *sell* her—"

Sarah raised her eyebrows. "I thought that's where you were going with this."

"No, I just..." Her daughter blew out her breath. "I just want some *help*, Mum."

"Ah." Sarah nodded slowly. "I see. Well, I'll certainly help you feed and groom her today," she replied, but Mairi let out a little sigh.

"Thanks," she said, a bit of an afterthought, but Sarah decided it was better than nothing.

Sarah always enjoyed being at the stables, run by Trina, a cheerful woman in her fifties whom she'd counted as a friend for many years.

"All right there, Sarah? Mairi?" Trina called in a friendly voice as Sarah and Mairi headed across the yard, toward Mabel's stall. "Lovely day, isn't it, for October? So warm!"

Sarah glanced up at the pale blue sky, the balmy air indeed holding a summery warmth even though it was well into the month, the leaves only just starting to change color. "Yes, lovely and warm," she agreed. Hard to believe Christmas was just two months away.

Mairi went to make Mabel's feed, while Sarah started grooming the Welsh cob, drawing the curry comb from the top of the horse's head, down her back in long, smooth strokes, making her coat gleam a deep brown with touches of gold. There was something incredibly soothing about the repeated motion, Mabel's soft nickering, the smell of hay and horse. For a second, Sarah closed her eyes and rested her forehead against Mabel's warm flank, letting herself enjoy the sweet simplicity of the moment, Mabel's easy acceptance of her. There was no love, she thought, like the love of an animal—warm and uncomplicated.

Right now, she wouldn't think about Nathan's frostiness, or the fact that the Bluebell Inn was practically teetering on the verge of collapse, or how she'd started waking up in the night, eyes straining in the darkness, heart thundering as if she'd had a nightmare she couldn't remember.

Anxiety attacks, she'd discovered when she'd looked up her symptoms online. Common to women in perimenopause, but although she was forty-six, Sarah didn't think that was it. Her anxiety was from another source, from the events of her life that felt as if they were slipping out of her control, no matter how hard she tried to hold onto them.

But she wasn't thinking about any of that, she reminded herself wryly as she opened her eyes and lifted her head, even if she actually was.

She pressed her hand against Mabel's flank. "Good girl," she murmured, and the horse nickered softly in return.

"Do I have time to go for a ride?" Mairi asked once they'd finished with the feeding and grooming. She'd clearly gotten over her mini tantrum in the car.

"I think Mabel would like that very much," Sarah replied, smiling as Mairi went to saddle her horse.

A few minutes later, daughter and horse were cantering down one of the trails that led from the stables to the surrounding countryside.

"Coffee?" Trina asked as Sarah wandered over to the comfortably cluttered main office that made up one side of the stable yard.

"Thanks, that would be great." She'd shared many a cup of coffee with Trina while Mairi was out riding, and she was grateful for the offer now.

"Mairi starting to resist coming a bit?" Trina surmised shrewdly as she switched on the kettle in the kitchenette in one corner of the office and Sarah managed a wry smile of acknowledgement.

"How did you guess?"

"Because she's sixteen, and girls go one way or another around that age. They either become absolutely horse-mad, or they lose interest completely."

"I don't think Mairi is losing interest completely, at least not yet," Sarah replied. Her daughter had certainly not appreciated her suggestion to sell poor old Mabel. "She's stressed about exams," she told Trina.

The other woman nodded in sympathy as she handed Sarah a mug of coffee. "It's so hard on kids these days, with so much pressure," she remarked. "But what about you?"

Sarah raised her eyebrows as she cradled the cup against her chest. "What about me?" she asked, hearing the prickle of defensiveness creep into her voice. Had Trina noticed something about her, how tense she was?

Her friend shrugged, looking bemused by Sarah's spiky response. "Just asking how you are."

"Oh. Right." Sarah let out a slightly wobbly laugh. Clearly, she was a bit sensitive, to the point of paranoia, to respond that way to a simple question. "Sorry."

"But... *are* you okay?" Trina asked in concern. "Because that's not the normal response to a how-are-you-doing sort of question."

"No, I don't suppose it is."

Sarah took a sip of her coffee, mostly to stall for time. Did she really want to tell Trina what was going on in her life, or, really, what she *feared* was going on in her life, because she didn't actually know. They were friends, yes, but their conversation tended to be innocuous chitchat about horses and weather, nothing more, and Sarah hated admitting weakness to anyone.

She was the kind of woman who always had it together, who answered emails as soon as they hit her inbox; whose fridge and pantry were filled with neatly labelled Tupperware; who reminded every other mum in her child's class about school photographs. She was proud of being that kind of mother, that kind of person, even if it all sounded a little pathetic to her right now. She wasn't ready to admit anything, not yet, and in point of fact, she didn't even know what she would admit.

"Just, you know," she finally hedged. "Life. It gets... busy."

"Yes, it does."

Trina gave her a rather beady look, and Sarah suspected she saw right through her prevarication, yet she found she didn't regret it. What was she supposed to say? *My family's business is going under, and my husband keeps coming home late, and I'm really starting to worry about it.*

No. She didn't want to talk about any of that—not to Trina, not to anyone. She did not want to give voice to the fears she hadn't let herself entertain, not properly, even in the privacy of her own mind.

"Well, let me know if I can help with anything," Trina replied lightly, and she heaved herself up from her chair to head back out to the stables, while Sarah drank the rest of her coffee alone.

By the time they got home, it was after six, the sunny afternoon turning dark and chilly, that hint of summery warmth having vanished, reminding Sarah that it really was autumn, and soon it would be winter, with darker nights, frosty mornings, the to-do list that Christmas entailed needing to be ticked off.

Sarah could tell by the clutter of trainers and sports kit by the front door that Owen was already home; a jar of peanut butter, a loaf of bread, and a pint of milk all left out on the pristine counter told its own familiar story.

"Tea's in ten minutes," she called to Mairi, who had disappeared upstairs, as she tidied everything away. At least the chili she'd made that morning in the slow cooker was bubbling away nicely, filling the kitchen with its spicy scent. She grabbed a pack of instant rice from the cupboard and put it in the microwave.

Nathan clearly hadn't come home yet, and when Sarah checked her phone—again—there was no message from him to say when he'd be back. Months ago, she would have expected him for dinner just about every night, by half past six at the latest. If he'd been running late, he would have called or texted to say so, but not anymore, it seemed. When had that changed? When had her husband started seeming annoyed by the obligations of family life, of marriage?

She debated texting him to ask him his ETA but then decided against it. She feared it would just annoy him—and it would annoy *her*, when he invariably replied to tell her he was having another late night. *Don't know when I'll be back so don't wait up*. It always came across like a warning, or even a scold.

Nathan hadn't started working late until recently, and while Sarah knew the employees of the wealth management company where he worked were always under pressure to perform, she wasn't entirely convinced that was the reason for Nathan's late nights. When she'd asked him what he was working on that was creating such demands, he'd mumbled something rather vague about clients and accounts. Sarah understood his work, had discussed it with him in the past, but he'd seemed reluctant to part with any details of what client or account was giving him so much grief. Was he hiding something, or did he just not want to talk to her?

There was still no word from her husband when she called Mairi and Owen down to tea, and they all ate in silence until Owen asked, a bit sulkily, "Where's Dad?"

"At work," Sarah replied in that mild voice she used that she had come to loathe; it felt like a form of denial, of gaslighting her children as well as herself. As if it were reasonable for Nathan to be at work every night until nine or ten, without any credible excuse besides simply being busy, when he'd never been so busy before.

"Again?" Owen complained unhappily. "He's *always* at work."

"It's a busy time," Sarah murmured, even though she didn't know whether to believe Nathan's excuse or not. "Anyway." She tried to brighten her voice, her mood. "He'll be home soon, I'm sure. Tell me about your day. How was football club?"

Somehow, she managed to carry the conversation along, as Owen talked about football, and Mairi worried about failing maths again, and Sarah promised to go over her homework with her after they finished the meal.

She was just loading the dishes in the dishwasher while Owen went to change out of his muddy football kit and Mairi to get her homework, when her phone pinged with a text. Sarah's heart lifted with hope that it was from Nathan, but it wasn't. It was from Ellie.

Been on social media all afternoon and will contact some magazines tomorrow. We can do this!!!

Underneath were several thumbs up and smiley face emojis that made Sarah feel a contradictory mixture of exasperation and amusement. It was typical of Ellie to exude such enthusiasm, maybe it was part of her American sense of optimism, and while it lifted everyone's spirits it also sometimes felt like denying reality. She knew how much Ellie wanted to save the Bluebell Inn, maybe even singlehandedly since it had been her idea, but Sarah just wasn't sure if that was possible. Or was her own dark mood coloring the inn's prospects?

"Mum? Can you help me?" Mairi asked, clutching her text-books to her chest as she stood in the doorway of the kitchen.

"Of course, darling. Let me just wipe the table and then we'll have a look at what you're finding difficult."

"Quadratic equations are going to be the *death* of me," Mairi exclaimed dramatically as she dumped her books on the table before Sarah had had time to wipe it.

"I've never known a quadratic equation to be lethal," Sarah teased as she quickly wiped the table before they sat down, handing the books back to Mairi, who took them with a drawn-out sigh. Smiling, she reached for one of the textbooks in her daughter's arms. "Dangerous, maybe, though..."

She was rewarded with a small, answering smile from her daughter, and improbably, considering how many cares were currently burdening her, Sarah felt her heart lift a little. It was possible to make things better, even if just a little.

She would talk to Nathan, she decided, and get to the bottom of what was going on, whatever it was. It was futile to keep burying her head in the sand this way; it was time to take action. Maybe she'd arrange a date night; the kids were certainly old enough to manage on their own for an evening. She'd make a reservation at that gastropub on the edge of Llandrigg, and wear something slinky and sophisticated. It was, perhaps, an obvious and clichéd ploy to woo her husband back, and it certainly wasn't her usual MO, but maybe that was a good thing. She knew Nathan wouldn't be expecting it, so maybe it could work? And even if it didn't, at least they'd be able to talk honestly, however much that might hurt.

Ellie might be on a mission to save Bluebell Inn, Sarah thought, but as she studied a page of inexplicable algebra, she realized she was now on a mission, too—to save her marriage.

CHAPTER 3

GWEN

Gwen stared at the name of the sender of the email in her inbox with blank bemusement. John McCardell! She hadn't heard from him in decades, hadn't even really thought of him in years. He'd been a friend of David's during university in Swansea, and also his best man during their wedding, with David acting as John's best man when he married Michelle.

Early on in their marriages, they'd seen more of each other —caravan holidays when the children were little; Gwen recalled a hazy montage of wet afternoons stuck inside and windy days on the beach, trying to barbecue. They'd had the occasional evening out when they were in each other's neighborhoods, although, as John and Michelle lived in the East Midlands, that hadn't happened all that often. As the children had grown older and life had become busier, they'd seen each other less, although they'd always stayed in touch. It had dropped off, however, after David had died over twenty years ago, dwindling to Christmas cards, and in recent years not even that. She wasn't sure whether it had been John and Michelle who had lost touch or if she had, but somehow the years had slipped by without much contact. Why on earth was John emailing her now?

The subject heading was simply "Hello!"; Gwen couldn't help but note the exclamation point. She didn't think she was really an exclamation point sort of person; it felt a little bit like shouting, or letting out one of those booming laughs that made her wince. Not that she was against booming laughs, of course, and, in any case, she didn't remember John as being a loud or brash sort of person. He had a keen sense of humor, as she recalled, a dry, quiet wit that David had enjoyed, as well as a natural enthusiasm for life. So why the exclamation point now?

Clearly, she was overthinking this. After the upheaval of the last few years, with Matthew and his family moving in, the renovation of the inn, and her own cancer diagnosis and treatment, then finally the hoped-for remission, which felt both wonderful and fragile... well, she supposed she'd been enjoying the *expectedness* of life lately. But it was only an email, after all.

Somewhat apprehensively, Gwen clicked open. It took a few seconds to load on her ancient laptop—Matthew kept insisting she needed a new one, but since he and Ellie both had more modern ones, Gwen hadn't really seen the point. She only used her laptop to browse the internet, do a bit of online shopping, and check her email once in a blue moon—in fact, she realized as she looked at the date, John had sent this email over a week ago. Hopefully it didn't contain anything time-sensitive... but then, why would it?

Finally, the email loaded—several paragraphs!

Gwen started reading.

Dear Gwen,

I hope this missive finds you well! I know it's been many years since we've been in touch properly. I'm afraid I haven't been the best correspondent as of late.

Michelle was always the one who managed our social calendar, as well as the Christmas cards, and I'm very sorry to tell you she passed away two years ago, after a brief battle with pancreatic cancer. I'm learning to manage on my own, although if you remember from our holidays of old, I was never the most competent in the kitchen. Still, I've learned to master a curry and the full English breakfast—what more do you need??

I hope you're well—hard to believe it's been over twenty years since David died. I still miss him and think of him often. The reason I'm writing is because I'm going to be heading your way fairly soon, assuming you still live in Llandrigg, which I think you do. I did a cheeky google of Bluebell Inn and saw it had had something of an exciting rebrand! Assuming it's not under new ownership, I guess you've been busy?!

Anyway, Izzy and Mike are expecting a baby—they moved to Monmouth a couple of months ago, which isn't too far from Llandrigg, as far as I can tell from the map. Would you be willing to meet an old friend for coffee or even a meal? I don't know many people in the area, if any, and old friends, as you know, are gold.

Kind regards, as always,

John

Gwen sat back in her chair, her mind whirling. Poor Michelle! She hadn't even known she'd had cancer, and of course John and Michelle hadn't known about hers. They really had fallen out of touch, she acknowledged sadly, something that was so easy to do without even realizing, as the years slid by, one after another. She hadn't known their daughter, Izzy, and her husband, Mike, had moved to Monmouth, either; that was only half an hour from Llandrigg. She remembered going to their wedding ten or so years ago, feeling slightly lonely at the occasion, without David. It had been lovely to see John and Michelle briefly, but as parents of the bride they'd been understandably busy, and Gwen had barely spoken to them. She had been seated at a table with distant relatives of theirs that she didn't know. Still, she was glad to hear about Izzy. She had a hazy recollection that she'd been having some trouble conceiving, so it was certainly good news now.

Gwen straightened, her fingers poised over the laptop's keyboard. Since the email was a week old, she really should reply as soon as possible. And yet what should she say? Of course, she'd be happy to have a coffee or, yes, maybe even a meal, with John. He was an old friend, and she didn't have all that many of those anymore. But at the same time, the prospect filled her with an uneasy apprehension, after all these years. What on earth would they talk about? And, really, John had been David's friend, not hers, although they'd got along well enough. She and Michelle had got on, as well, although Gwen wasn't entirely sure they would have been friends apart from their husbands. Michelle had been one of those rather terrifyingly athletic people—doing half-marathons every other weekend, up at five in the morning for her daily run, downing protein shakes and being very careful about her weight. When she'd been younger, Gwen had been rather intimidated by it all.

But now David and Michelle were both gone, and it was just her and John left. It caused a sweep of sorrow to blow through Gwen, like a chilly wind. She was only sixty-nine; John a year or two older. It was a time of life, she supposed, when one should get used to loss, but then again loss never felt natural or right.

"Gwen?"

Gwen looked up from her laptop, grateful for the interruption. "Hi, Ellie." She smiled at her daughter-in-law, who had been looking rather stressed, dark circles under her blue eyes and lines of strain from her nose to mouth, since Sarah had come over three days ago, with the news about the dire state of the inn's finances. Ellie seemed to be on a one-woman mission to save the place, while Matthew had been a bit less concerned by Sarah's grim warnings.

"Sarah's always been a bit of a doomsayer, hasn't she?" he'd said.

Gwen had felt compelled to murmur, "She's practical, certainly, and errs on the side of caution, perhaps, but I wouldn't call her a *doomsayer*."

"Does any business these days have more than six months' budget in the bank?" Matthew had countered. "It's just not the way the world works anymore. I'll cut costs as much as I can on the operating side of things, of course, and we won't make any big investments in the property anytime soon, but I don't think things are about to fall off a cliff. Not just yet, anyway."

Gwen had wanted to be reassured by his confidence, but Ellie had seemed less convinced, and she was determined to drum up more business. She'd been posting all over social media, Gwen knew, on various tourist and community sites and pages, mentioning the inn. They hadn't had any further book-ings, though, as far as she was aware.

"I wondered if you wanted a cuppa," Ellie said, smiling back. She looked tired but determined, her dark blond hair pulled up in a ponytail, her hands planted on her hips. "And I had a few ideas to run by you."

"A cup of tea would be lovely." She needed a few more moments to absorb John's email, and then to think about how to reply. She didn't know why it had got her in such a tizzy; he was only asking to meet up, after all.

She followed Ellie into the kitchen and sat at the table of scrubbed oak, while Daisy, the springer spaniel puppy Matthew had got the children last Christmas, trotted over to curl at her feet. Poor old Toby, who had been with her for fourteen years, had passed away peacefully last spring. Gwen still missed him. Daisy was a lovely little bundle of pure joy, but she wasn't *her* dog, that old, faithful friend, trotting by her side, resting his grizzled head on her knee.

"So, I've gone a bit crazy and absolutely plastered social media with posts advertising the inn," Ellie announced with wry briskness as she boiled the kettle and began making the tea. "Maybe a bit too much. You can put people off, I know, if you keep spamming them with advertisements, but I did my best to make it more organic and interesting." She gave a small sigh. "We'll see." She smiled ruefully as she handed Gwen a cup and then sat at the table opposite her with her own.

"Any luck with the magazines and newspapers you were hoping to try?" Gwen asked as she took a sip of her tea, and Ellie grimaced.

"Unfortunately, no. It seems there's no incentive for them to do some kind of feature or spread on Bluebell, because nothing has really changed. If we were offering something new or different, they said they might be interested. But, right now, we don't have an 'angle,' and we need one, if we want to be featured in the press."

"That's too bad," Gwen murmured. "But understandable, I suppose."

"Yes..." Ellie frowned. "I don't want to just leave it, though. I know there's *something* we can do."

"Yes..." Gwen knew she sounded dubious. She understood Ellie's frustration—of course she did—but she was honest enough to acknowledge to herself that she didn't actually share it, at least not completely. Ever since Matthew and Ellie had moved to Llandrigg, Gwen had been easing away from the bed and breakfast, gratefully handing it on to the next generation. Admittedly, she'd been a little alarmed at her son's original plans for the business—marble ensuite bathrooms, infinity showers, and a fitness center in the barn—but he'd backed off those, and then Ellie had suggested turning it into a family-style farmhouse instead, warm and welcoming, cozy and casual. Gwen had been entirely on board with that idea, but she'd also been on board with her son and his wife managing the lion's share of the work. As long as she could bake her Welsh cakes and keep her chickens, she was happy.

And she could do that, guests or not. Besides, she would be seventy next year. Did she really want to be helping to manage a business at that age? It was a question she had started to ask herself, if only in the quiet of her own mind. Still, she didn't want to say as much now, especially when she felt the need to be supportive of Ellie. She knew how much keeping the inn going meant to her.

"Some of the magazines did say if we were doing something unique, offering some kind of deal, they might be interested in doing a feature," Ellie continued. "Maybe we could even offer a giveaway—a three-night stay or something, to one lucky winner?"

Gwen frowned thoughtfully. "That wouldn't exactly fill the coffers, though, would it?"

"No, but the publicity could be amazing." Ellie leaned her elbows on the table, her expression now positively alight. "And then I was thinking... what about Christmas? If we get cracking with an idea now, and ring the magazines ASAP, it could work..."

"Christmas?" Gwen repeated uncertainly. They usually closed for the week of Christmas, assuming families wanted to be at home for the holidays, or away visiting their own family. And, by then, they were all usually ready for some downtime, anyway.

"Yes, Christmas. I know we usually close that week, but what if we didn't? What if we offered a week-long holiday to order, the kind of Christmas everyone dreams about but doesn't want to have to make happen themselves?"

"What would that look like?" Gwen asked, genuinely curious.

"Well, I haven't worked out all the details," Ellie admitted, ducking her head, "more just a vague plan. We could go with a sort of Dickens *Christmas Carol* theme... old-fashioned parlor games, the massive roast dinner with all the trimmings, Christmas crackers, a huge tree in the sitting room..." She shrugged, spreading her hands. "I'm sure there are a million ways we could make it magical."

It sounded wonderful, Gwen thought, but like an awful lot of work, although she knew Ellie and Matthew would probably do most of it. And yet... at *Christmas*. Already she could imagine the stress and strain of pulling off a huge event at that time of year, especially when it was usually the only opportunity they all got to relax. Still, it might be worth it, especially if Ellie were so determined.

"It does sound magical," Gwen told Ellie. 'But I don't want you to have to take on a load of work that could put you under enormous stress, especially at that time of year—"

"The *real* stress," Ellie replied, "is thinking this place might go under. Making a splash at Christmas seems like a good way to get noticed—and it might actually be fun." Ellie's mouth tilted up at the corners again as the sparkle returned to her eyes. "We can create the kind of Christmas we all really want, the kind you see in magazine spreads and Disney films, something really wondrous and magical, with loads of decorations, and food, and presents and games. It will be amazing!"

The kind of Christmas Gwen usually had wouldn't be found in either magazines or films, she thought ruefully. Generally, she was content with her family all around her, a somewhat chaotic opening of presents and a meal that was rushed onto the table despite military-level planning and then consumed in just a few minutes, amidst the detritus of dirty dishes, congealed gravy and turkey bones. She traditionally ended the evening with her feet up and the telly on, a large tin of Cadbury Roses, and maybe a small sherry nearby. Presumably their guests would want a slightly different experience, but if Ellie had some ideas...

"Why don't we have a family meeting?" Gwen suggested. "Get everyone involved with the idea. Figure out how to make it work. Even if the inn is going under, one last big push is surely worth it?"

"Exactly what I was thinking!" Ellie beamed at her. "I wanted to check with you, though, because it will mean a busy Christmas for all of us, getting the place ready, doing everything in style..."

Style? That had never really part of the Bluebell Inn's appeal, but Gwen could appreciate why Ellie wanted to go for it now. If people were going to book for Christmas, they'd want something special. That was certainly understandable.

"All right, then," she agreed. Ellie was already getting out her phone.

"I'll put a message on the family WhatsApp group," she said. "A call to arms! We can meet next Saturday afternoon, hammer out all the details, get everyone's input. I'm sure the kids will have some good ideas, especially to appeal to the younger generation. Maybe Jess can make some TikTok videos for advertising or something."

TikTok? Gwen had no idea what that was, but she decided now was the time to be enthusiastic. "Sounds wonderful," she told Ellie warmly. She was glad her daughter-in-law had far more get-up-and-go than she did, certainly. "Thank you, Ellie, for thinking of all this. I am very grateful for your determination."

"Well... let's hope it pays off." For a second, Ellie's smile wobbled, and underneath her determined enthusiasm, she looked uncertain and afraid.

So much was riding on this for her, Gwen reflected with

sympathy. Her daughter-in-law had poured her heart and soul into this inn over the last two years, so it was understandable why she'd feel so strongly about saving it, more strongly than anyone else, perhaps.

Gwen knew she had been relinquishing it slowly, over time, so the possibility of it closing now felt sad, but not overwhelmingly so... just another chapter in a long and varied book. She was proud of what she and David had accomplished, and then what she'd managed on her own, but she also felt the weight of her years, the possibility of something different.

"I'm sure it will pay off," she stated with as much conviction as she could muster. She patted Ellie's hand and finished the last of her tea before rising from her seat. "I'm afraid I need to finish an email I was about to send."

"An email?" Ellie raised her eyebrows, clearly intrigued because Gwen was not the most tech-savvy person—far from it; she was often asking Ellie for help on how to do something online. "Anything interesting?"

"Just... an old friend, who got in touch quite unexpectedly. We might meet up."

"That's nice," Ellie replied with her usual easy warmth. "Is she someone you knew from before moving to Llandrigg?"

"A friend of David's, actually," Gwen replied, and realized, to her horror, she was blushing. What on *earth* for? "From university. We haven't seen each other in a decade, though, so..." She shrugged and she saw the curiosity brighten in her daughter-in-law's eyes, although she just nodded.

With another murmured thanks, Gwen hurried from the room.

Back at her laptop, she stared once more at her screen. What to write? John had sounded so warmly enthusiastic, and she wanted to match his tone, at least a little.

After a few minutes' reflection, she started to type.

Dear John,

How lovely to hear from you, and I am so very sorry to hear about Michelle. Grief always feels unexpected, in my view, as well as unnatural. I hope you are coping all right; I'm sure the prospect of a grandchild helps.

I'd argue (or at least David would) that you need a full English breakfast, a curry, and a Sunday roast in your repertoire. Maybe also a pudding—jam tart or treacle sponge?

I am trundling along well enough at the Bluebell—Matthew and his family moved to Llandrigg two years ago, and are doing the day-to-day running while I chip in with a bit of baking—see above!

It would be lovely to catch up over a coffee—I'll give you my mobile number and we can arrange a time.

Kind regards,

Gwen

Was the "kind regards" too stuffy? She had managed a bit of banter, and included a dreaded exclamation point, which she was now wondering if she should take out. You could never really tell the tone of an email, but an exclamation point seemed to soften things a bit. She'd keep it in, she decided, and pressed send.

CHAPTER 4

ELLIE

A WEEK LATER

Ellie scanned the ream of sheets she'd printed out as she took a deep breath and let it out slowly, to steady herself. They were about to have their important, emergency family meeting, and she wanted to be on the front foot. It was already past the middle of October, with their half-term guests arriving in just over a week, and there was absolutely no time to spare. Outside, in the garden, the leaves were tinged with yellow and red, windfall apples, turning soft and brown, littering the long grass. Even though the days were still fairly warm, the nights were drawing in earlier, and in the morning, every leaf and branch was tipped with frost, riming the world in white

Gwen had said there might be snow soon, dusting the hills that overlooked the little village, its few narrow lanes and rectangle of green touched with frost. Christmas felt ages away, but it really wasn't—just over two months until the actual day, and hardly enough time to get ready for what Ellie was planning, and yet somehow they would have to. Ellie was determined to make this work, but she still wasn't sure how committed everyone else was to her cause.

She'd only seen Sarah once since they'd had that chat, and her sister-in-law had seemed a bit dubious about her potential plans.

"If you want to try some last, big push, by all means, go ahead," she'd told Ellie. "I'm just not sure what we need right now is to be spending more money."

"You've got to *spend* money to *make* money," Ellie had replied with an attempt at breezy insouciance, and Sarah had given her one of her very dry, Sarah-like looks.

"Said no accountant, ever."

Matthew hadn't been much better. Unlike Sarah, he hadn't been gloomily predicting the end of everything—quite the opposite. He'd been somewhat breezily dismissive, insisting that most outfits like theirs ran on a shoestring, cutting everything close to the bone. Having very little in the bank was, he insisted, a pretty normal state of affairs, and since their bills were minimal, his mum's mortgage paid off, they really didn't need to worry too much.

Ellie had been rather surprised by his carefree attitude, considering that they'd been running things rather *close to the bone* back in Connecticut, when Matthew had been made redundant and they'd been so behind on mortgage payments they'd almost had to hand their house back to the bank. They'd done a fire sale instead, but it had left them with very little, and Matthew had certainly taken it to heart at the time.

Of course, that thankfully wasn't the danger this time around—Gwen owned the Bluebell Inn free and clear, and, like Matthew had said, their bills were minimal. The only danger they were in was not being able to afford to run the bed and breakfast anymore. Matthew could get a job elsewhere easily enough—or so he seemed to think—and Ellie thought she could probably pick up something, as well. She'd worked part-time for a literacy charity back in Connecticut, and when she'd been feeling low about the inn's chances last week, she'd had a quick peruse of online job sites, and found several she was pretty sure she was qualified for. Now that her visa had come through, she was allowed to work, so nothing was stopping her from sending out her CV, just in case.

Nothing, of course, except the Bluebell Inn. The truth was, she didn't *want* to get another job. She wanted, quite desperately, for the inn to survive, for them to keep running it the way they had been, for everything to go on the same. She just hoped everyone else wanted that, too. Hence, this emergency meeting —her, Matthew, Gwen, Sarah and Nathan, and all the kids. The inn was a family affair, and so saving it would be, as well, or so Ellie hoped.

She glanced in the mirror above the hall table, trying for a determined smile, but her eyes looked tired, and her dirty blond hair definitely needed a cut and color. She'd make sure to do it before Christmas; she wanted to look her best for the big event... Assuming there *was* a big event, and that everybody agreed to her plan.

"Mum?" Jess came out of the kitchen, sounding far more British than she had two years ago, back when Ellie had still been "Mom" and they'd all struggled with the unfamiliar British terms—car park instead of parking lot, lesson instead of class, pavement instead of sidewalk, and what felt like a million other words and phrases that marked them out as foreigners, despite the shared language. Then, of course, there had been the Welsh street signs and names to grapple with, and mandatory Welsh lessons in school. Even Ava knew more Welsh than she did, Ellie acknowledged wryly.

"Yes, sweetheart?" she asked, smiling.

"I think the blueberry muffins are done. Do you want me to take them out?"

"Yes thanks, Jess. That would be great." Ellie gave her

daughter a grateful but distracted smile before she met her gaze in the mirror once more, gave herself a quick, bracing nod, and then followed her daughter into the kitchen.

"What is this all about, anyway?" Jess asked as she took the muffins out of the Aga and placed them on a cooling rack, her lips pursed into a frown, her dark hair pulled up into a ponytail. She'd grown up so much in the last two years—now fifteen, she was tall and willowy, the coltishness of youth already turning into the grace of young womanhood. It made Ellie feel sad and proud at the same time. How had her oldest child become so grown-up? "Why is everyone coming over, exactly?"

"To have a family meeting," Ellie replied rather grandly. She reached for the big teapot decorated with roses that rested on a shelf above the Aga and started spooning loose tea in. "To talk about the inn."

"The inn isn't really in *trouble*, though, is it?" Jess's frown deepened, a shadow of worry in her hazel eyes.

A few days ago, Ellie had mentioned, fleetingly, that the inn was experiencing a bit of a hiccup, money-wise, but that they just needed some strategies to sort it out. She hadn't wanted to worry the children, and she'd thought she'd been successful in that aim—Ben had merely shrugged, Josh had nodded slowly, and Ava had skipped off to play. But now Jess cocked her head, her eyes narrowing.

"*Mum?*"

"Financially, things *are* a little tight," Ellie admitted carefully. She wanted to talk about the inn's money troubles in the context of a possible solution. "So, this morning we need to brainstorm a way to make things even out."

"And if we can't? Brainstorm a way?"

"Let's cross that bridge when we come to it," Ellie replied lightly. "I'm sure between all of us, we can think of some good ideas. We have before."

"But... we won't have to *leave*, will we?" Jess pressed, a trace of genuine alarm in her voice.

Eighteen months ago, when Jess had been having such a hard time at school and had even tried to run away, managing to get all the way to Heathrow Airport, hoping to fly back to America, Ellie could never have imagined that her daughter might one day be worried that they'd have to leave Llandrigg. All she'd wanted was to return home to Connecticut; it was heartening that she now wanted to stay here with the same depth of feeling.

"We won't have to leave," Ellie promised. At least, she hoped not.

Once, she'd missed their old life in Connecticut with nearly the same fervor as her daughter, but those days had gone. She was proud of what they'd built at the Bluebell, and she was glad of the friends she'd made, the life they'd carved out for themselves. But the inn was a big part of all that. Would she feel the same about Llandrigg if it failed? If *she* failed?

"Muffins!" Ben exclaimed, loping into the kitchen and grabbing two off the cooling rack before Ellie could ask him not to.

"Ben—" she began, only to find her thirteen-year-old had already stuffed an entire muffin into his mouth. "*Ben.*" She shook her head, exasperation warring with affection. "Those are for our meeting."

Ben gave her his puppy-dog look, blue eyes wide with appeal underneath his shaggy mane of light brown hair. He'd had a growth spurt recently and was now taller than she was by a good few inches; like Jess, the round softness of childhood was turning into something more grown-up. "But I haven't had breakfast," he protested. "And I'm starving."

"Then pour yourself a bowl of Shreddies or something," Ellie replied tartly, rescuing the second muffin from his hand, and putting it back on the rack. "And don't steal any more, please!"

Grumbling theatrically under his breath, Ben grabbed a

bowl and the cereal box, trailing Shreddies all across the newly wiped counter.

Briefly, Ellie closed her eyes and prayed for patience. This was going to go well, she told herself, not for the first time. It had to.

Just then, the front door opened, and Sarah came into the kitchen, followed by Owen and Mairi. Owen slouched, his hands in his pockets, looking around for Ben, and Mairi, Ellie thought, looked a little drawn and anxious, one finger twirling a strand of her strawberry blond hair.

"No Nathan?" she asked in surprise, only to see her sister-in-law's expression tighten.

"He's busy with work."

On a Saturday morning? Ellie just nodded her understanding, not wanting to pry. Come to think of it, she reflected as she poured boiling water into the teapot, Nathan hadn't really been part of the Bluebell Inn lately. At the start, he'd seemed as enthusiastic as Sarah, offering his business and marketing expertise, helping with some of their initial advertising, but in the last six months or so his interest—and his presence—had both dropped off, although Ellie hadn't actually noticed until now.

"Work is very busy, I suppose?" she asked, realizing she was going to press, after all, just a little.

"Yes," Sarah said flatly, and that seemed to be very much the end of the conversation.

"Hopefully it'll ease up soon," Ellie replied—a peace offering to which her sister-in-law gave a jerky nod. "Coffee?" she asked. "Or tea?"

Sarah's expression softened slightly, and Ellie didn't miss the flicker of relief that passed over her face, like a shadow, when she realized Ellie wasn't going to ask any more questions. "Coffee, please, thanks."

Ben and Owen had gone to play football outside, Ben leaving his bowl of sodden Shreddies barely touched by the sink, despite his insistence he'd been starving, and Mairi and Jess had already slipped out of the room, as well. Ellie could hear their giggles as they disappeared upstairs. She was grateful the cousins had learned to get along; at the beginning, as with so much else about their move, it had been difficult. Mairi had seemed standoffish and Jess had been insecure, but they'd managed to sort out their differences and were now close friends.

She focused on making Sarah a cup of coffee, and not asking about Nathan. "Gwen and Matthew should be down any sec," she said. "And we can call the kids all back—"

"Do you really want them to be involved?" Sarah cut across her. "It might create a certain amount of chaos."

"This has always been a family effort," Ellie replied firmly. "And they might have some good ideas. They have before."

A few minutes later, Gwen and Matthew both made an appearance, and then Ava came skipping in, followed by Josh. Ellie hollered for the girls upstairs, and Matthew went to get the boys from outside, and after another few minutes of cheerful chaos, chairs being scraped across the floor, all ten of them were gathered around the kitchen table with cups of tea or coffee, the plate of blueberry muffins in the middle.

"So, I've called this meeting," Ellie began, "because we need to figure out a way to make the Bluebell Inn survive financially. And I *know* we can do it," she continued quickly, before anyone could make a protest or ask a question, "because we already know the idea is sound and the people who have come here on holiday have absolutely loved it. We have the reviews in the guest book to prove it, along with a great rating on Tripadvisor."

"Except for that family who said they didn't realize they'd be put to work like skivvies, and left after the first day, asking for a full refund," Ben chimed in helpfully as he grabbed a muffin.

"Except them," Ellie agreed, holding onto her determined smile. "But they were definitely an aberration."

"What's an aberration, Mummy?" Ava asked, her blond curls bouncing as she cocked her head, her face screwed up in concentration. ·

"Something different from anything else," Jess supplied, with a questioning glance for Ellie. "Right?"

"Yes, pretty much," Ellie agreed.

Gwen asked, wrinkling her nose, "Were they the couple with that little chihuahua? He was absolutely *frightful*—"

"No, that was another family." The inn had always operated a friendly dog policy, although it had caused a bit of stress every so often. "Anyway." It was amazing, Ellie thought, how quickly the conversation could spin off into a tangent. She supposed that was par for the course when you had ten people involved, and six of them were children. Maybe they should have kept it to adults, but she'd been hoping for an all-together-now vibe that wasn't happening quite yet. But it would.

"Is the inn really in trouble?" Josh asked in concern, his dark eyes narrowed, his silky hair sliding into his face. "Because you never said anything."

"It's not in *trouble*," Matthew replied kindly. "Not *per se*. It just needs a little help."

Josh did not seem particularly reassured. "But Mum said something about *surviving*, and you only say you need to survive if you might *die* or something—"

"Is the inn *dead*?" Ava asked in a tone of excited interest.

Ellie felt the conversation slipping away from her again. "Look," she interjected, "let's not worry too much about all that. Yes, we need to make ends meet a bit better than they are currently, but the point is, they *can*. They will."

"How?" Sarah asked, rather pointedly.

"Well, I've got an idea," Ellie replied, glad to get to the crux of it. She reached for the sheets she'd printed out earlier—mood boards cribbed from Pinterest, online articles about other bed and breakfasts and hotels, and her own attempts at creative brainstorming. Hopefully it would be enough to inspire her crew. "*Christmas*," she exclaimed, injecting her voice with an overdose of enthusiasm. "A very special holiday week for very special guests, giving them the kind of Christmas we all dream of—a huge tree, decorations, carols, mince pies, presents, snowmen—"

"We can't exactly provide snow on demand..." Matthew interjected mildly.

"I know, but it's the *mood*," Ellie persisted. "Look at what I've printed out—some other hotels have done a similar kind of thing, and they've been really successful." She'd fallen in love with the photos of cozy sitting rooms with Christmas trees and roaring log fires; dining room tables laden with fine linen and china, and, of course, a massive, gleaming roast turkey. Personal touches in every bedroom, mince pies and hot toddies in the evening, parlor games straight out of Dickens, Christmas-themed crafts for children, carol singing around the piano...

It would be *amazing*. It had to be.

"It does look nice," Gwen said slowly, a smile softening her features as she gazed down at one of the photos Ellie had printed out. "And I've always loved decorating for Christmas. It would be nice to do it up properly..."

"What's the ultimate aim, though, really?" Sarah interjected. She held up her hand, palm facing outward. "I'm not trying to rain on your parade, Ellie, really, I'm not, but one week's extra booking isn't going to transform the inn's prospects, I'm afraid. The situation is more serious than that."

"It is?" Josh exclaimed, looking properly alarmed.

"It might," Ellie replied calmly, even though her heart was starting to hammer, "because I've managed to get the interest of a national Sunday supplement, and they're willing to do a feature on the inn's Christmas week!" She couldn't keep the triumph from her voice; it had felt like a major coup, and had taken her hours of calling, cajoling, and downright begging.

Plus, the newspaper had had a spot they needed to fill at the last minute. Ellie had decided it was providential.

"Really?" Matthew looked impressed. "You've been keeping that quiet!"

"I was waiting for the right moment," Ellie replied with, admittedly, rather false modesty. She glanced at Sarah, who looked surprised but not nearly as impressed as Matthew.

"Even so," Sarah said, and Ellie struggled not to grind her teeth.

"It's a big deal, Sarah," Matthew protested. "That kind of publicity is like gold dust—"

"I'm assuming we'll have to have the place decked out to the nines for when this newspaper comes out here," Sarah continued in her relentlessly pragmatic way. She'd seemed unusually gloomy this morning; Ellie wondered if something else was going on. Something, perhaps, to do with Nathan? Was that why he wasn't here?

"Well, yes, that's true," Ellie admitted. "They'll want to take photos of everything, so we'll have to have it all ready."

"When?"

"In two weeks," she admitted, "and even that is pushing it, to get the feature into the papers in time. But they were willing to rush it—"

"And you really think we'll have this place photo-shoot ready in *two weeks*?" Sarah asked, sounding incredulous.

Ellie glanced around at her family; everyone was looking at her with various degrees of skepticism, uncertainty, and only a little hope. Even Ava looked like she doubted her.

"We can do it if we all work together," she said firmly. "Come on, everyone! This is a challenge—let's rise to it! Together!" Her voice was rising, at any rate, and rather shrilly.

"It's not that we don't want to, Mum," Jess replied quietly. "It's just... it will cost a lot of money to get everything ready in that amount of time, and what if it doesn't work?"

Trust her daughter to be so level-headed, Ellie thought. She didn't approach her bad hair days or being left on read by her friends with the same kind of reasonableness.

"We have to try," she insisted. "And we don't have to have every single room completely ready for the photo shoot—it's just staging, really. If we deck out a bedroom and the sitting room—"

"But we'll need to put up a Christmas tree," Sarah pointed out, as if that were insurmountable.

"Yes, and we *can*," Ellie vowed. "Even if it's a fake one. Look, the newspaper *wants* to sell this. They're not looking to rake us over the coals. They want us to explain our vision, give them a little taste of it—"

"It could work," Matthew remarked, his eyes crinkled up in a smile, enthusiasm kindling in his voice at last. "We're selling them a vision, like you said. It doesn't have to be completely in place."

"Exactly," Ellie said with relief, sagging back in her chair. She reached for her cup of tea and took a sip of the now lukewarm brew.

"I could do some baking," Gwen offered. "Mince pies and my iced gingerbread—it won first prize in the WI competition, back in the day."

"Yes, wonderful," Ellie enthused. She turned to the children with a hopeful smile. "What about thinking up some parlor games and crafts for the kids? Christmas-themed, of course—"

"We could decorate paper snowflakes with glitter?" Mairi suggested. "And make ornaments for the tree? The craft shop in Abergavenny sells baubles you can paint yourself. Then the kids could hang them on the tree themselves, too."

"Wonderful," Ellie replied warmly. "That sounds absolutely fantastic, Mairi."

Soon, the ideas were flying, if not precisely thick and fast, at least at a fairly good clip. Cookie decorating, carol singing, a visit from Santa Claus, a local Christmas market in the inn's garden, homemade or locally sourced gifts for every guest.

An hour flew by almost without her realizing, and when the ideas finally slowed to a trickle, and then a silence, the cups of tea and coffee drunk and the plate of muffins sporting nothing but a few crumbs, Ellie finally put down her pen.

"Phew," she said, smiling at everyone. "I think we have enough to be getting on with for now. Matthew, can you source a Christmas tree for the photo shoot? Mairi and Jess, do you want to be in charge of crafts? If you could knock up a few samples to show the people from the paper, that would be great. Josh, I'm putting you in charge of games and puzzles—the more Christmassy, the better. Ava, you can help with Josh, can't you? Ben, you can work with Dad and Owen to handle the outside— I'm thinking fairy lights on the evergreens, maybe a bit of decoration on the assault course?"

"And a Santa's grotto, naturally," Matthew added with a smile. "I was thinking beneath the willow tree."

"Perfect!" Ellie turned to Gwen. "Can you bake a few samples like you suggested, and maybe do a Christmas menu?"

"Yes, of course." Gwen was smiling, seeming to catch her enthusiasm.

Now there was only Sarah to deal with. Ellie turned to her sister-in-law as she stiffened her spine.

"Sarah—"

"I can make a budget," Sarah offered. "And make sure we all keep to it!" She smiled to soften her words, and Ellie let out a little laugh.

"Wonderful, thank you, Sarah."

Everyone had a job, she thought with satisfaction. They really could make this work. She held her empty teacup aloft in a toast.

"Here's to the Bluebell Inn's first ever Christmas Week!"

CHAPTER 5

SARAH

As they drove away from the Bluebell Inn, Mairi and Owen chattered away in the backseat, clearly buzzing with ideas. Owen wanted to create an ice-skating rink in the pond that had once been touted as a potential swimming hole.

"But what if it's not below freezing?" Mairi asked, and Owen started googling how to freeze your own ice rink.

"We could rent a chiller and a compressor," he read off his phone. "Or you can get an *eco* rink, where it's not actually ice at all, but you can still skate on it."

Both options sounded ridiculously and prohibitively expensive, Sarah thought, but chose not to say. She didn't want to dampen her kids' enthusiasm, or pour any more cold water over Ellie's big idea, even if she still had her doubts. She would do her best to enter into the spirit of the thing, although her own spirits were flagging. It would be good to have a project, and like Ellie, she really did want the inn to succeed, even if there were other, more personal matters on her mind

Yesterday, she'd suggested a meal out to Nathan, and he'd agreed to go to a nearby pub together tonight. It wasn't the fancy meal Sarah had been hoping for, but at least it would be a chance to talk, after another week of him arriving home late most nights. It could be the restart they both needed, she told herself as she drove to the football pitch where Ben had his Saturday practice, dropping him off before taking Mairi to the stables.

"I don't have a lot of time," her daughter warned her as Sarah parked. "I've got *so* much revision to do."

While she was glad Mairi was intent on studying, Sarah had noticed that her daughter seemed to have plenty of time to watch TikTok videos or message her friends. She held her tongue, though, hoping that once Mairi had groomed Mabel, she'd want to ride her.

Sure enough, Mairi decided she had time for a quick ride while Sarah went in search of Trina, determined to present a brighter front than she had last week. When she found Trina, however, her friend looked so harried that Sarah forgot all about wanting to seem put together herself.

"Trina?" she asked. "Is everything okay?"

"Yes, I suppose," Trina replied, blowing out a breath as she swept her curly gray hair from her eyes. "Just trying to keep everything afloat, and sometimes that gets a bit tricky."

"Does it?" The stable yard had always seemed a busy, bustling place to Sarah. "What's the problem?"

"A few clients have withdrawn their horses," Trina told her on a sigh. "Not because of anything I've done, mind, but, as you know, circumstances change. One family's moving, another one has decided to sell their horse because of the expense. You know how it is." She gave a little shrug of her shoulders. "I've also lost one of my instructors for the Riding for the Disabled program, so I'm going to have stop running it, which is a real shame. They were understanding about it, but the nearest program is in Chepstow."

"That's miles away," Sarah replied in sympathy. She'd seen the program in session when she'd come to the stables some afternoons; the look of joy on the children's faces when they sat astride a horse, feeling powerful and fast, often for the first time, had been wonderful to see, and, in Sarah's mind, an important part of the yard. "I'm so sorry, Trina."

Trina shrugged, determined to be philosophical. "Well, easy come, easy go. You've got to be flexible in this business, always ready to think of something new."

"I think you need to be flexible in most businesses, these days," Sarah remarked wryly, thinking of the inn. The only constant in life, she thought, was change.

"In any case..." Trina paused. "I'm thinking of retiring. I'm not getting any younger, and I don't have anyone to take over the stables. I might have to close, but it's been a good run, hasn't it?" She gave a rather crooked smile.

"Close?" Sarah looked at her in deep dismay. She'd been coming to this stables ever since she was a little girl—first to ride herself, and then with Mairi. Trina's mother had run it before her.

"I know it would be disappointing, but there are plenty of farms around that would be willing to stable a horse. You shouldn't have to worry about Mabel."

"Yes, but—"

"Anyway." Trina spoke firmly, clearly as loath to talk about what was wrong, just as Sarah had been last week. "How are you? Things looking up since last week?" Her smile was kind, her gaze shrewd.

"Well... yes." Sarah gave her friend a determined smile as she thought of tonight's dinner with Nathan. "Yes, I think they are."

Just after seven that evening, Sarah was changing into a silky top and her nicest pair of jeans while Nathan waited downstairs. She glanced in the mirror in ruthless inspection—was that a strand of gray in her auburn hair? Actually, Sarah realized as she peered closer to study her reflection, it was more like two or three strands, or maybe even four or five. She'd always been a bit proud of her hair—a long, thick mane of auburn waves that fell halfway to her waist and hadn't had a bit of gray—until now. Well, she told herself in pragmatic resignation, it had to happen sometime. She'd been lucky to escape the inevitable thus far.

Otherwise, she still looked pretty good for forty-six—a trim figure, a few crow's feet by her blue eyes, but nothing too much to worry about yet. She kept herself in good shape, which she knew Nathan liked.

A sudden shaft of annoyance had her stilling. Why was she thinking like this, as if she had to impress her husband just to keep him interested? As if it was all up to her? It was the kind of attitude she would normally have derided, and yet she found herself falling into it now without even realizing, simply out of fear.

And what exactly are you afraid of, Sarah?

"Sarah?" Nathan's voice floated up the stairs, mild enough, but Sarah thought she heard a slight edge of impatience to it. "Are you ready? Our reservation is in ten minutes."

"Yes, coming!" She spritzed a bit of perfume on her throat and wrists and ran her fingers through her hair.

You can do this, she told herself, giving her reflection a final once-over, steely smile in place.

Nathan was standing by the front door, jangling the keys in his pocket as Sarah came downstairs. His gaze flicked over her once, but he made no comment, and she told herself not to be disappointed. She hadn't made that much of an effort, after all.

"Let me just say goodbye to the kids," she said brightly, and Nathan shrugged his assent.

Owen was in the family room, fingers jabbing at a game controller while the TV screen was a blur of animated movement.

"Only half an hour more," Sarah told him, to which he grunted in reply.

She turned to Mairi, who was sitting at the kitchen, a mountain of textbooks and revision guides surrounding her.

"Mairi, you've been going at it for a couple of hours now," Sarah said gently, resting one hand on her daughter's shoulder. "Maybe give yourself a bit of a break?"

"I still have my maths homework," Mairi replied with a shake of her head, twitching her shoulders so Sarah's hand fell away. "And we have our mock exams next *month*, Mum."

"I know, but there is all of half-term—"

"Jess and I are running crafts every afternoon at the inn for half-term," Mairi cut her off. "I'm not going to have *any* time."

"Sarah!" Nathan called again.

"All right, then," Sarah told her daughter as mildly as she could. "I'm just worried for you, that's all."

Mairi didn't reply, and Sarah decided to leave it for now.

She hurried back to Nathan, giving him a smile that he returned, at least, although it was little more than a lip curl. Never mind. They'd reconnect in the pub, over a bottle of wine and a shared brie en croute, the fire crackling away, the lights low, the mood intimate.

"I'm worried Mairi's hitting the books too hard," she confided once they were driving toward Llandrigg. "She's studying all the time, and she seems so stressed about it. More than she usually is."

Nathan shrugged, his gaze on the road. "A little stress doesn't hurt anyone, and it will motivate her to do well."

"But it's only October," Sarah protested, keeping her voice mild. "She can't keep up that level of anxiety for another seven or eight months, can she?"

"Maybe she won't."

He sounded so unconcerned that Sarah struggled not to feel stung. When had he stopped seeming interested in his own children? Or was she being too harsh? Nathan had a point, after all; stress had motivated Mairi in the past. She was, like her parents, a high achiever. Sarah had always been proud of that, as had Nathan, so why was it now giving her cause for concern?

"I can't remember the last time we went out," she remarked, deciding to change the subject.

Nathan's mouth tightened. "You know I've been busy."

Briefly, Sarah closed her eyes. They weren't even at the pub yet and already the conversation was starting to veer off track. "I didn't mean it as an accusation," she replied lightly. "Just that I'm looking forward to it."

"Mmm."

She'd wait until they were at the pub, Sarah decided, seated at a table, starting to relax. Then they'd talk. She'd make sure of it.

Ten minutes later, that was exactly where they were— seated at a cozy table for two by the fire, just as Sarah had asked when she'd made the reservation. She'd ordered a glass of Pinot Grigio, Nathan a beer, and the lighting was low, the smell of good food and woodsmoke from the fire pleasant, and despite the tension still knotting her shoulder blades over the state of her marriage, Sarah was hopeful they could enjoy the evening.

"This is nice, isn't it?" she commented, gazing around the pub with its smoke-stained beams, wooden floor and fairy lights strung about. She turned back to Nathan, her heart sinking to see he was actually on his phone, scrolling with a sort of weary indifference. "*Nathan.*" Her voice came out sharply, and despite the irritation she saw flash on his face, she knew she was not going to back down. Maybe that had been part of the problem; Nathan had become used to this new, strangely submissive Sarah. Well, not right now. "We're out together for a meal. Why are you on your phone?"

"Sorry," he said, and with seeming reluctance he slid his phone back into his pocket. "What do you want to talk about?"

And now she felt completely tongue-tied. She'd wanted to be honest tonight, Sarah reminded herself, so maybe that was what she needed to be. No more tiptoeing around the truth, whatever it was. She'd just up and say it. The thought made her heart start to pound, and she reached for her wine, took a fortifying sip.

"What's really going on, Nathan?" she asked quietly as she put her glass back down on the table.

His eyes narrowed as he shifted in his seat. "What do you mean?"

Strangely, her heart had stopped its relentless pounding, and she felt wonderfully, quietly calm. Why on earth hadn't she said anything sooner? It was far better to know than not to know, surely? "Things have changed between us over the last few months. You come home late most evenings, you don't make time for the kids, you're closeted in your study on weekends, you seem irritated with all of us, or at least with me—"

"I told you, Sarah, things at work are *busy*." He sounded exasperated, and for a second, Sarah asked herself if she should stop pushing, if she could simply believe him and let it be. It only took that one second for her to realize she couldn't.

"I know things are busy," she told him quietly, "but it's more than that, isn't it? It feels like it's more, to me."

"And what is that supposed to mean?"

Sarah reached over to place her hand on top of his. The contact shocked her, in a way she hadn't expected; when, she wondered, was the last time they'd touched? It had certainly been a while. "Nathan, please. I'm not trying to cause an argument or accuse you of anything. I'm your wife, and I love you. I feel as if a distance has come between us, and I want to know what's going on. What you're thinking. Feeling." She wasn't normally this much of an emoter, but Sarah was glad she'd said as much as she had. You could only act like an ostrich for so long, she realized. A reckoning had come with the inn, and so it would come with her marriage.

For a second, no more, she thought Nathan would tell her. She saw a flicker of indecision, of sorrow, in his eyes and he opened his mouth. Her heart felt suspended in her chest.

He glanced down at their hands, hers still resting on top of his. "I..." he began, and Sarah's whole body tensed. Then he gave a little shake of his head. He started to pull his hand away; Sarah felt it slip from underneath hers but then he stopped. Sighed. "Nothing's going on," he told her wearily. "I've been pressured at work, and I suppose it's affected how I am at home." With his free hand, he scrubbed at his eyes. "I'm sorry. I'll... I'll try to do better. Get home early sometimes, take the kids out." He didn't look at her as he made these promises.

Sarah was silent, absorbing what he'd said, and, more importantly, what she felt he hadn't said. He'd been going to say something else and then changed his mind, she was sure of it.

"What's causing all this pressure?" she asked after a moment.

He shrugged, and this time he did pull his hand away. "We've lost a few big clients in the last couple of months, so there's certainly a pressure to find a few more, but the problem is, everyone's being so cautious these days. No one wants to move firms, risk any new investments, take a *chance*, so none of it is easy. I've been working on courting a new client, putting together a package. That's why I've been home so late most nights."

"Okay." She could accept that, she thought, even if it didn't necessarily account for the way he'd been acting with her. "And when are you making a pitch?"

His glance slid away from hers. "Soon."

Once upon a time, Nathan would have been happy to give her the details—the kind of client, the specifics of the pitch, the investments he was researching. He would have asked her opinion, her advice. No longer, it seemed, and she didn't want to have to press him. A sigh escaped her, long and low. She felt as if she'd reached the end of the road, conversation-wise, and she didn't know where to go from here. She also felt too tired to make more of an effort.

"A couple of weeks, maybe?" Nathan offered, and it sounded like an apology, an olive branch. Sarah felt she had no choice but to take it.

"That's not too bad, then," she replied, trying for a smile, just as one of the pub's staff came up to their table with a sunny smile.

"Are you ready to order?" the waitress asked, and with an apologetic smile and a sinking feeling in her chest, Sarah reached for her menu.

"Almost."

The evening had barely begun, and yet in some ways it felt as if it were already over. How many more times would she even have the energy to try to get to the bottom of what was going on?

CHAPTER 6

GWEN

Gwen stood in the doorway of the café in Monmouth where she'd agreed to meet John McCardell. It was one of those fancy new places, with chrome chairs and glossy tables, a thousand different drinks on the chalkboard menu over the till—oat milk, soy lattes, even drinks with pistachio or pumpkin. The clatter of cups and the chatter of customers was ringing in her ears.

She didn't know why she was so nervous. Yes, it had been about ten years since she'd seen John, but he *was* an old friend, and it would be nice to have a catch-up, once they got past that initial haven't-seen-you-in-years sort of awkwardness.

Gwen gazed around the crowded space, looking for his familiar face, although, in truth, it had been so long, she wasn't entirely sure she would recognize him, or that he would recognize her.

"Gwen!"

She heard his voice—low and deep, with that rich thread of humor running through it. She turned, blinking at the sight of the man striding confidently toward her, a warm smile lighting up his features.

He was exactly the same—and yet he wasn't. His hair had

turned entirely white, although it was still thick and wavy, and there were far more creases in his weather-lined face than before, although his eyes were as blue as ever.

"John!" she exclaimed, and took a lurching sort of step toward him before he enveloped her in a quick, easy hug, kissing her on the cheek.

"I've got a table in the back," he said as he released her. "Look at you! You haven't changed a day."

"Oh, I have," Gwen protested. "I know I have. But you haven't!"

Did all conversations with old friends go this way, she wondered, with both of them insisting they hadn't changed, when of course they had?

"Well, I've gone gray, that's for certain," John replied, running a rueful hand through his hair. "Or really, white. But as Izzy tells me, it's better than being bald." He gave a little, apologetic grimace. "Not that there's anything wrong with being bald, of course!"

David had certainly had a thinning spot before he'd died, Gwen acknowledged with a small smile. "No, indeed," she agreed. "But in any case, you look..." Somehow, she found she wasn't quite sure how to finish that sentence.

"Let me get you a coffee," John said, filling the silence with an easy gallantry. "What would you like? A latte? Americano? Mocha?"

"Just a tea, please," Gwen replied. She didn't think she could take any more caffeine; her nerves were already jangling.

"Tea, it is."

She headed back to the table he'd pointed out while he went to order her drink at the counter. Gwen was glad for a few moments to compose herself. She didn't know why she was feeling so nervous, but the plain fact of the matter was that she was. She took a deep breath and let it out, smoothing one hand over her neat gray bob. She hadn't lost her hair when she'd had her chemo, thankfully, but its texture had changed, and she wasn't entirely used to the thicker, coarser strands. She hadn't mentioned her battle with cancer in the email; it was the kind of thing she didn't really want to go into, but not going into it felt dishonest. Well, who knew what they'd actually end up talking about? Maybe they'd just keep it to pleasantries.

"Here you are." John set down a tray with a teapot, cup, and little milk jug, as well as an Americano for himself, before taking the seat opposite her.

"Thank you," Gwen murmured, taking the tea things, conscious of his speculative gaze upon her. It felt as if he was studying her, and she couldn't quite make herself meet his eye.

"I was trying to think how long it's been since we've seen each other," John remarked at last. "And I think it must have been Izzy's wedding—ten years ago now, and we were barely able to exchange hellos."

"Yes," Gwen murmured, "I think you may be right."

John shook his head slowly. "How did the time get away from us so badly? I'm ashamed that I haven't reached out more since David died. I should have."

"Life gets busy," Gwen replied with a small smile. "And with the B&B as well as trips to America to see Matthew and his family, I'm afraid I didn't have a lot of spare time to visit friends —or have friends to visit, for that matter. I think I've probably lost touch with a lot of people." Old university friends, or neighbors from when they lived out near Swansea, before buying the inn. In truth, she didn't have that many close friends anymore— a few women in the village, some neighbors, and her family, of course. She hadn't felt the need for more... at least she didn't think she had.

"Still." He pursed his lips. "We never even talked properly at Izzy's wedding. I have an awful feeling you were parked at a table with my cousins, and probably had a miserable time."

Gwen let out a little laugh, surprised and gratified that he'd remembered such a detail. "Well, it's always hard to go to those kinds of events on your own," she replied diplomatically, and John gave a little hoot of laughter.

"Especially when you're seated with my positively po-faced cousins. They don't have a shred of humor between them, I'm afraid. I should have swapped your place."

"It hardly matters now," Gwen said with a smile. "It was ages ago."

John's own smile faded. "Yes, it was."

It felt like the right time for her to say, "I really was so sorry to hear about Michelle."

John nodded somberly. "Thank you. I know you know what it's like. Like missing half of yourself, really. For the first few months afterwards, I kept expecting her to appear. Nonsensical, I know, and maybe because it happened so fast, I struggled more to cope, but I'd turn around to tell her something—something silly, like *pass the milk* or *do you know if we need to pick up the dry cleaning*—and then I'd realized that she wasn't there." He shook his head, his mouth twisting wryly, although his eyes were shadowed with deep sorrow. "The funny thing—well, the terrible thing, really—is that every time it came as a little shock, a proper jolt, even, like I had to remember all over again that she was gone. You'd think it would stop surprising me, and eventually it *did*, but you know what? That actually made me feel sadder. Daft, eh?"

"No," Gwen replied quietly. "Not daft at all." They certainly weren't keeping to pleasantries, and she realized she was glad, because she knew exactly what John meant about losing someone, and was grateful he'd articulated the sense of grief so clearly. "I remember I didn't want to wash the blanket we kept on the sofa because it smelled of David," she confessed. "And one day I realized it had lost that scent, and that felt like its own loss."

"Yes." John nodded, his face filled with sorrow but also

warmth. "I kept a container of pineapple juice in the fridge for months, because Michelle drank it. I didn't—never touched the stuff—but every time I looked in the fridge and saw it there, it made me feel better. Eventually, when Izzy came to visit, she threw it out, without telling me, and I was—well, I was furious." He let out a little laugh. "I tried not to show it, but I was absolutely raging that she'd thrown that rancid juice out. Now that *is* daft."

"Well, maybe a little," Gwen dared to tease, and John gave another little laugh, his smile wide and infectious. "But I understand it," she assured him. "You want to hold onto the past even as it slips away from you. When it finally slips away completely, and you know there is nothing you can do about it, it does feel like another loss, but in time it can come to be something of a relief. We aren't meant to hold onto these things, not that tightly, anyway."

"No," John agreed quietly. "You're right." He took a sip of his coffee and then put it down again, smiling at her as he shook his head.

She was a little surprised at how much she was enjoying his company; she hadn't known him as well as David had, and she'd been a bit worried that with only the two of them, the conversation would dry up. "I was nervous about coming here today," she admitted a bit recklessly, busying herself with pouring out her tea so she didn't have to see how he took that confession. "I know it's silly, and I don't even know why—"

"So was I," John replied. "It's been so long... and well, loss changes you, doesn't it? You're not sure if you're the same person that you used to be, or if people will notice."

"Yes," Gwen agreed feelingly. She'd been changed by David's death, but she'd also been changed by her cancer diagnosis. She realized she wanted to tell him about it now. "I've had cancer myself," she said, ducking her head a little. "Stage four breast cancer. I've been in remission officially for about six months."

"Gwen, I'm so sorry." To her surprise, John reached over and briefly touched her hand. "That must have been incredibly difficult."

"Well, it wasn't easy, but I'm grateful for coming through it. And Matthew and his wife Ellie were absolutely wonderful, and my daughter Sarah as well. Everyone rallied around, and in the end, I think it brought us all closer."

"Illness can do that, can't it?" John remarked. "It reminds you of what's precious in life, and to hold onto it—if you can."

"Yes." She'd certainly been reminded of the importance of family, and not letting the little things get in the way of loving those around you.

"So how is the Bluebell Inn?" John asked. "Or Family Bed and Breakfast, as it was called on your website, I think? Looked like a beautiful place, from the photos."

"It was all Ellie's idea, to make it more of a family destination," Gwen replied. "Game nights, helping in the garden, that sort of thing. And it's worked so far—everyone pitching in, enjoying themselves. They seem to, anyway, and we've had a few families come back for a second or even third time."

"Sounds like you've really made something extraordinary of it," John remarked warmly.

Gwen hesitated to reply as she suddenly recalled the financial trouble the inn was in.

"Well, sort of," she said after a moment. "The truth is, we're not actually making a profit. If we don't make some changes to how we do things, we might have to close our doors, which would be a shame, considering we've only been going for a little over a year."

"That would be a shame." John frowned. "I suppose it's a tough market these days, what with the cost-of-living crisis and inflation and all the rest."

"Yes... we're hoping to do a big splash at Christmas, to raise some interest. My daughter-in-law contacted a national newspaper, and they're going to come and take some photos, do a write-up." She gave a little grimace. "We have a lot of work to do, to get the place ready for Christmas by the end of October. They're coming in less than two weeks!"

"Well, if I can help in any way..." John offered hesitantly. "I'm just kicking around Monmouth for the next few weeks. Izzy's working right up until her due date, so I haven't got much to do. I'm not sure why I came so early, to be honest, but she insisted, and I did want to see her."

"Oh, well..." Gwen wasn't sure how seriously to take his offer. Was it just the kind of thing someone said to be nice, or did he really mean it?

"Of course, I'm sure you have it all in hand," John continued quickly, giving her an easy out—and yet why should she take it?

"Actually, we do need help," Gwen told him. "We're all running around like headless chickens at the moment, not sure where to begin." John, she recalled, had run his own landscaping business before he'd retired. Perhaps he could help in the garden? "We need to do something Christmassy with the outside space, and I don't know what to do, besides stringing up some fairy lights."

"You were always good in the garden," John protested, smiling. "I remember how you could identify every single plant and flower whenever we went on a hike, back when we did those caravan holidays."

"Do you?" Gwen was touched. She had a sudden, piercing memory of walking along the Pembrokeshire coast, pointing out different types of heather and fern to the children, John and David strolling behind, Michelle usually striding ahead, if not breaking into an outright jog, determined to get her steps in. They had been happy times, and yet they held a certain bittersweet poignancy, now that only she and John were left. "Well, if you wanted to give us some advice about doing up the garden for Christmas," she suggested, "it would be greatly appreciated."

"I'd *love* to," John replied with enthusiasm. "I could use a project, frankly. Just let me know when and where."

"All right." Gwen felt suddenly rather bold and reckless; it was a heady sensation, and one she wasn't used to feeling. "How about tomorrow?" she asked, and John looked so surprised by her suggestion that she rushed to add, "We haven't a moment to spare, really, but if you're busy, I'd completely understand. Izzy probably wants you around, even if she is at work." She let out an uncertain laugh, not feeling quite so reckless now; John still hadn't said a word. "Maybe you didn't expect me to take you up on your offer," she joked feebly, although she wasn't entirely sure she was joking.

"No, no," he finally said, leaning forward, his blue eyes alight. "I'm thrilled, honestly. You have no idea—I've been wanting to have something to do, and I'd love to see the B&B. I can't remember the last time I was there—didn't Michelle and I come with the kids, a year or so before David died?"

"I think so." Gwen had a hazy memory of a rushed weekend, trying to spend time with John and Michelle, while also catering for four other guests. Life really did get busy; it was a shame that relationships were often the casualty.

"I can certainly come then," John told her firmly. He touched her hand again, so briefly she barely felt it, and yet something awakened inside her at the warmth of him, an unfurling of a feeling, a yearning, she'd forgotten about, like a dormant seed finally reminding her of its existence, coming to life.

The realization was incredibly disquieting. In the twenty-two years since David had died, when she'd been only forty-seven, she'd never dated anyone. Had never even *thought* about it, because there had been the Bluebell Inn to manage, and Sarah and Matthew to shepherd through their young adulthood, and, frankly, there weren't too many options in little Llandrigg, not that she'd even looked. A few friends had half-joked about finding her someone, or getting her on one of those awful apps, but she'd always brushed such suggestions aside, never considering them seriously herself. She'd loved David so much, and after he'd gone she'd learned to be happy with her children and then her grandchildren, the Inn, good old Toby, her chickens, her baking, and some decent historical dramas on the telly, along with the occasional gripping novel.

It had all been more than enough, and yet now... Now she felt that little spark of interest, a tiny flare of excitement, right at the center of her, and she didn't know what to make of it at all, especially when it was with David's best friend. But maybe she was overreacting, she told herself, as she took a sip of her tea and refocused on their conversation. Perhaps she was just out of practice of socializing in this way.

After they'd finished their tea and coffee, John suggested a walk through Monmouth, and they strolled along the bustling high street, gazing into various shop windows and chatting about nothing important at all, and yet it was one of the most pleasant afternoons Gwen had had in recent memory. She told him about her grandchildren and showed him photos on her phone. He laughed in appreciation at some of Ava's funny remarks, and how Josh loved puzzles and Jess asked her opinion on various outfits even though, Gwen admitted with a laugh, "I have zero fashion sense. Give me a waterproof mac and a comfortable pair of shoes any day."

"You look pretty well turned out to me," John replied affably, scanning her simple skirt and sweater set with obvious appreciation, and she studied a tea service in the window of a charity shop, more discomfited by his easy remark—and his unapologetic admiration—than she cared to reveal. She knew he didn't mean anything by it, it had just been one of those offhand comments, but it had affected her more than she wanted to acknowledge to him, or even to herself.

They ended up on a footpath by the river Wye, strolling along its gently rolling current all the way to St. Peter's, a little whitewashed church perched right on the riverbank. They wandered through the church's cemetery, its headstones tumbled and mossy, their epitaphs barely legible.

"'Here lies Elspeth Jones,'" Gwen read out loud. "'Beloved wife of William for forty-eight years.'" She let out a small sigh as she considered the unknown couple. "I don't know whether it's easier or harder, to have so many years with someone before you lose them. On one hand, you have more memories to treasure, but on the other hand, you're less used to living life on your own."

"How long did you and David have?" John asked as he came to stand beside her.

"Twenty-six years," Gwen replied on another sigh. "We were going to go to Paris for our twenty-fifth wedding anniversary, see the Eiffel Tower and the Louvre like we'd always wanted to do, but we kept putting it off. We felt we couldn't leave the Bluebell, and it always seemed as if there would be a better time. After he died, I wished we'd gone when we'd had the chance." To Gwen's surprise, she felt tears starting in her eyes. She hadn't wept for David in many years; time was a healer, in that regard, but talking to John, remembering old days, somehow it made it all feel so fresh again. "What about you and Michelle?" she asked, managing to blink the tears back. She did not want to cry in front of John, not when they'd been having such a lovely afternoon.

"Forty-four years." He stared at the headstone in front of them, his face drawn into thoughtful lines. "It sounds like such a long time and yet it went by in a blink. And to answer your question—I don't know if it's harder or easier. Loss is loss, I suppose, and love is love. Not the most profound of statements, I know, but I don't think I was ever a particularly deep thinker."

"It sounds rather profound to me." She smiled at him, blinking back the last of her tears, and he smiled back. Although it was nearing the end of October, the sun was still warm, the sky a hazy blue as they stood in the forgotten, little cemetery, the only sound the twitter of birds in the trees above. It felt like a moment in time, a snapshot of memory she wanted to keep and to treasure. "Thank you," she said suddenly, "for reaching out. I'm so glad we've been able to meet up."

"So am I. And I'll be seeing you tomorrow," John reminded her, "and who knows, maybe even the day after that, and the day after that, depending on how much help your garden needs."

As John walked her to her car, parked behind the high street, the sun had already started to slip behind the trees, and there was a chilliness in the air that reminded Gwen how close it really was to winter. As she fussed in her handbag, looking for keys, he enveloped her in a quick, tight hug.

"Take care, Gwen, and I'll see you tomorrow."

"Tomorrow," she agreed, and as she got into her car, she found her cheek was warm and still tingling where John had pressed it, briefly, to his.

CHAPTER 7

ELLIE

"Mummy... *Mummy!*"

Ellie blinked the sleep out of her eyes, her mind a haze of confusion, as she felt an insistent tugging on her arm. The clock on her bedside table read 3 a.m., and Ava was standing about six inches from her face, Matthew sleeping on her other side, snoring gently.

"Ava!" Her youngest hadn't woken up in the middle of the night in years now. Ellie had got used to a good night's sleep; she felt completely disoriented at being woken up at such an hour. "What's wrong, sweetheart?"

"I'm wet."

"Wet?" Ellie's heart sank. She reached one hand to touch her daughter's nightgown and felt that it was sodden. "Oh, Ava..."

"And my bed's wet."

"Let me come and see." Half-stumbling in the dark, Ellie threw on her dressing gown, shivering in the cold night air, while Matthew slept on. The heating had switched off a few hours ago and the attic rooms where they all slept were freezing. In Ava and Jess's room, Ellie saw with dismay that the sheets were soaked right through to the mattress. "Ava, darling," she asked helplessly, "what happened?" She hadn't wet the bed since she was about three.

"I don't know." Ava began to cry, and Jess stirred groggily.

"What's going on?" Jess muttered as she drew her duvet up over her head. Two years on, she'd become mostly accepting of having to share a bedroom with her little sister, but at times like this, her fifteen-year-old daughter understandably resented it.

"Shh, shh, it's not a problem, Ava. Don't worry, darling. I'll sort it out for you." She gave her daughter a hug before remembering she was wet, and now Ellie was wet, as well. She really didn't need this kind of hassle in the middle of the night, especially when she'd been up past midnight herself, trying to find a cheap way to source red velvet ribbon for the Christmas decorations. Ten pounds a meter was extortionate, but it looked so lovely, and Ellie wanted the Bluebell Inn to be every bit as welcoming as the photo spreads she'd printed out and which had caught everyone's imagination. "Come on, sweetheart. You need a quick rinse off and then we'll sort out the bed."

While Ava was standing under the shower, Ellie stripped the bed as quietly as she could, and then laid a towel on top of the mattress to absorb what had soaked in before fetching a spare set of sheets from the linen cupboard. She'd have to do a proper disinfectant and clean in the morning.

She'd just finished making the bed when Ava shouted from the bathroom, "Mummy, I'm DONE!"

"*Argh,*" Jess groaned from where she was buried beneath her duvet. With typical teenaged drama, she turned over with several theatrical sighs, her back to Ellie.

She hurried to fetch Ava, wrapping her in a towel. It took another fifteen minutes to dry her off, comb her hair, and get her in a clean pair of pajamas, and then another fifteen minutes after that before her daughter finally dropped off to sleep and

Ellie staggered back to bed. As she crawled in next to Matthew, he let out a satisfied little snore.

Ellie sighed, rolling onto her side, closing her eyes, and willing sleep to come, which of course it didn't, because it was now four o'clock in the morning, she'd already been up for an hour, and she had far too much racing through her mind to drop off now. She gave herself another hour, tossing and turning and trying to sleep, before she finally slipped out of bed and went downstairs to make herself a cup of tea.

The kitchen was quiet, Daisy curled up in her bed, opening one eye to gaze dolefully at her mistress before she snuggled back down to sleep. Ellie made the tea and sat down at the kitchen table, shivering in the chilly air, as she pulled the to-do list she'd been working on toward her. They had three families booked in for half-term next week, which meant breakfasts and family dinners every day, plus crafts for the children in the afternoons, games in the evening, and the offer of a hike to Sugarloaf Mountain one day, and a trip to the Brecon Beacons the next. Plus, there would be the usual rigmarole of letting guests help out—supervising children as they collected eggs or helped to make scones or whatever else Ellie dreamed up for them to do. She'd offered a "harvest day" as well—picking pumpkins in Gwen's little patch, and making apple sauce. There would also be an evening of fun Halloween-themed games, including bobbing for apples and pinning the tail on the donkey, although, in this case, it would be pin the eyes on the ghost.

It would be busy enough, arranging all that, but on top of it all, Ellie had to think about Christmas. The journalist from the national newspaper would be here, photographer in tow, the day after the last guests left, and the Bluebell Inn was going to have to look like a Christmas fairy tale come to life. Ellie kept airily insisting to everyone that they could do it, but at five in the morning, when her eyes felt gritty with fatigue and her to-do list ran to two pages, she wondered, and even started to doubt, whether it would happen at all.

The trouble was, Ellie reflected as she took a sip of tea, Christmas had to be *super* special. It was a big decision for a family to go away for Christmas, to forgo the comforts of home for the unfamiliarity of a hotel, where your bed might not be comfortable, or the food to your liking, and where everything might seem just a bit strange.

"You're up early," Gwen remarked as she came into the kitchen, knotting the sash of her dressing gown firmly at her waist.

"So are you," Ellie replied with a tired smile. She knew Gwen was an early riser, but not this early.

"I couldn't sleep, so I thought I'd get a start on some scones for the afternoon teas next week. They freeze well."

"Good idea. The kettle's just boiled, if you'd like a cup of tea." She took a sip of her own tea. "Why couldn't you sleep?"

"Oh, you know." Ellie couldn't help but think Gwen sounded a bit evasive as she moved to the kettle to make herself a cup of tea. "Just lots to think about, I suppose."

"I forgot to ask, how was your catch-up with your old friend yesterday?" Ellie asked. In the usual chaos of a normal family evening, when dishes had to be washed, homework done, gym kit found, as well as her continued work on preparing for the Christmas week, she hadn't had time to chat with Gwen. "You said she's staying nearby?"

"*He*, actually, and yes, in Monmouth." Gwen turned around, raising her cup to her lips, her gaze lowered to its rim.

He? Why hadn't Ellie clocked that before? Not that it made any difference, except it almost looked as if Gwen was blushing. What kind of "he" was this?

"Oh, right. I suppose I assumed... but you did say it was an old friend of David's," Ellie recalled. She probably should have made the connection, and yet it simply hadn't occurred to her that Gwen was meeting a man.

"Yes, his name is John. We used to go on holidays and things together, when Matthew and Sarah were little. But it has been a long time."

"And he's doing well?"

"He's been widowed for the last few years, but yes, he is. In fact..." Gwen hesitated before she lifted her gaze to meet Ellie's rather resolutely. "He's coming over today. He was a landscape gardener before he retired, and I thought he could give us some Christmassy ideas for the garden."

"Oh!" Ellie tried to mask her surprise. Why shouldn't Gwen have a friend come over to help? She wasn't quite sure why she was so thrown, only that she was. "That's wonderful. The more the merrier, I say, especially if he's got some expertise."

"He certainly does," Gwen answered with a small smile. "And I think we need all the help we can get!" She cocked her head, her gaze sweeping over Ellie. "How come you couldn't sleep, Ellie? I hope this Christmas event isn't becoming too much..."

"No, it's not too much," Ellie replied, a bit too quickly. "Obviously, there's a lot to do, but I'm sure it will be fine." She reached once more for the to-do list. "I'm hoping to get on top of the Christmas decorations today."

"Oh?" Gwen's expression brightened. "I've got loads out in the shed. I'll bring them in, and you can have a look, if you want."

Ellie hesitated, unsure how to handle such a well-intended offer. She'd already had a look through the plastic bins of old decorations, and they were definitely on the homemade and looking rather worn side. As lovely as glittery pinecones made by Matthew and Sarah in primary school were on a family

Christmas tree, she wasn't sure they were really suitable for a commercial enterprise.

"Thank you," she said at last. "I'm sure there's some bits and pieces that will be really useful." If she'd meant to sound encouraging or at least tactful, she'd clearly failed, judging by the sudden fall in Gwen's expression. She'd thought they'd got beyond this pussyfooting around each other some time ago, but it seemed old habits died hard, if at all, especially around certain issues.

"Of course," Gwen murmured, glancing down at her cup of tea, "I'm sure some of it is a bit tatty and worn. You must do as you see fit."

And even though Ellie knew her mother-in-law was being sincere, the pinprick of hurt needling through her words was enough to have them both lapse into a rather morose silence.

Ellie glanced down at her list, wondering if she should have handled that moment better. There probably were some very nice things amidst all the homemade ornaments and twenty-year-old decorations. She should really have a proper look at it all. She opened her mouth to say something to that effect, in as encouraging a way as she could find, but Gwen had already gone to rinse her cup in the sink.

"I'll just go get dressed," she murmured and slipped out of the room.

Ellie let out a long, weary sigh. Too much was riding on the next few weeks to worry about hurt feelings on either side, and yet she felt mean for having such a thought. After their emergency family meeting, she'd really hoped everyone would pull together, and in many ways, they *had*, but no one seemed to feel the urgency, the anxiety, the way she did. Matthew continued to be cheerfully dismissive, while the children didn't seem as if they could get their heads around the idea of the inn having to close at all. The other day Ben had even suggested that it wouldn't be such a bad thing; he didn't always like having guests, especially ones with little kids, in his space. Jess loved doing the children's crafts with Mairi, but schoolwork and activities were taking up more of her time, especially as this was her GCSE year, and sometimes she could be irritable about having the house taken over. Josh too, Ellie realized, could sometimes chafe at the intrusion; during the summer, some little kids had taken apart the thousand-piece jigsaw he'd been working on when he'd had less than a hundred pieces left and thrown the pieces all over the room. He'd been disconsolate. Ava seemed to like the guests, at least, and what about Gwen? Her mother-in-law had been so enthusiastic about Ellie's vision to make it a family-friendly B&B, but lately she'd seemed less involved, less interested, happy to have Ellie and Matthew make all the decisions and be left to her own devices.

Really, Ellie reflected rather glumly, no one seemed to care as much as she did. Was it just because the changes to the inn had been her idea at the start, and so she was taking it more to heart? Its potential failure felt like *her* failure.

Well, she told herself, she'd just have to care enough for everyone.

Swallowing the last of her lukewarm tea, she stood up and headed upstairs to get ready for the day.

Two hours later, Ellie had seen Jess and Ben off on the bus for their school in Abergavenny, dropped Josh and Ava at the primary school in the village, and was back at the house, enlisting Matthew's help in dragging out the Christmas decorations from the shed. There were several rather dusty plastic crates as well as cardboard boxes that looked as if they might fall apart at any moment, overflowing with silver spangled tinsel, artificial greenery that was looking rather bedraggled, and tangles of colored fairy lights.

"I'm sure we can use some of this," Matthew said with far

more optimism than Ellie felt. She had created a mood board for both the dining room and living rooms, and they didn't include a plastic tablecloth decorated with cartoon Christmas trees or homemade ornaments with the year written rather shakily in globby, silver glitter glue.

"We need things to look... professional," she told him as she set aside a homemade angel ornament with glittery, plastic wings.

"*Professional?*" Matthew arched an eyebrow. "You think that's what families want at Christmastime?"

"They're coming here for an experience—"

"'A home away from home,'" Matthew interjected mildly. "Those were your words, when you first dreamed up the idea behind this place."

"Yes, but... a *nicer* home away from home. An aspirational one." She thought again of the photos of rooms she'd seen on Pinterest—everything color-coordinated, staged to look like a movie set, so warm and inviting.

Matthew arched a skeptical eyebrow. "Really?"

Ellie did her best not to answer defensively. "Yes, really. Why do you sound so... dubious?"

Matthew paused to open one of the boxes and sift through some of the decorations. "Mum loves this one," he said, holding up an embroidered doll of Henry VIII, the red stitching on his mouth coming off, making it look as if he were leering, which, Ellie supposed, was true to his character.

"Matthew...?" she prompted, wanting to get back to their discussion.

"We got it at Castle Howard, in Yorkshire, when we went on a holiday there," he reminisced. "I think I was about twelve. Dad had got his first digital camera and took about a thousand photos of the place—pictures of plants and dusty corners of the castle that we'd never want to look at again." He gave a soft laugh as he shook his head in remembrance. "There's an Anne

Boleyn one too, somewhere, and we always joked we couldn't hang them near each other."

Ellie smiled at the thought, even as she felt a twinge of exasperation. Why couldn't Matthew understand what she meant? They couldn't hang all these tatty ornaments about and expect guests to feel impressed or even touched. The guests wouldn't have the same memories Matthew did—of that trip to Castle Howard, or whatever he regarded with such sweet sentimentality now. They'd only see what Ellie saw—homemade tat. It felt far too mean a thing to say, though, and so she stayed silent, watching as Matthew unpacked a few more decorations—a miniature LED Christmas tree in garish, neon colors, and a felt Santa and Mrs. Claus that were decidedly worse for wear, Santa listing drunkenly to one side.

"What?" he said, when Ellie still hadn't spoken after he'd laid out a few such items. "They're fun, Ellie. They're *sweet*—"

"To you," she replied as gently as she could, "because you have all those memories, and they're meaningful to *you*. But our guests won't have those memories, and they won't be meaningful. They'll want something different."

Matthew frowned, his eyebrows pulling together. "And what," he asked, "is it that you think these mythical guests want?"

"I hope they're not mythical," she joked, but Matthew didn't even crack a smile. Ellie sighed, hardly able to believe they seemed poised on the precipice of an argument—and over what? Christmas decorations? Tatty ones? "Look," she said in as conciliatory a tone as she could manage. "I understand that these decorations are special to you. They mean something, I get that. I really do." She smiled in appeal, even though Matthew hadn't dropped his frown. If anything, it had deepened into a positive scowl. Ellie decided to try a different tack. "What is your vision for the inn at Christmas, Matt?" she asked. "What do you see working?"

"Are you asking that question seriously?" her husband asked, and Ellie let out a laughing huff of protest.

"Yes!"

"Because I feel like you've already got this vision, and you just want to prove to me how mine is wrong."

Ouch. Ellie blinked. Perhaps the hardest part about what Matthew had said was that it hadn't been in anger or even frustration. He'd spoken completely calmly and levelly, which meant he really believed what he said. Well, if he was going to be that honest, then so was she.

"I do have a vision," she told him. "I shared it during our family meeting. I see us creating something special, something high quality for families, but with a difference."

"How?"

"Well, with all the things I mentioned before—"

"I mean," Matthew cut her off, "how are we going to be any different from any upscale hotel or B&B that's offering the same thing, Ellie? I'll tell you how. We'll be worse."

Ellie blinked. "Matt—"

"Look, I get that you don't want to hang my stupid glittery pinecone on the Christmas tree. I really do. And I'm not mad about that or anything, far from it. You're right, the guests won't have the memories I do, and some of these decorations do look decidedly worse for wear. But, Ellie..." Matthew hesitated, and Ellie tensed. "I get the feeling that you want to create some sort of boutique experience," he continued after a moment, his tone turning gentle, "and we just don't have the resources for that. If we want to succeed, we need to do something different from all the other places, the hotels and inns that have more money, more staff, more space. That was your point from the start, when I was absurdly obsessing about infinity showers and fitness centers. *You* were the one who showed me how I'd got off track."

"I understand what you're saying, but I'm not talking about

infinity showers and fitness centers," Ellie stated after a second, when she'd absorbed Matthew's words, their implied criticism.

"I know you're not, but isn't that still the gist of the thing? The Bluebell Inn is never going to compete with all those highbrow establishments—not in decorations, or food, or anything we offer. We shouldn't even try."

Ellie tried not to let this hurt. She knew he was right, at least in part, but that didn't mean they had to resort to twenty-year-old Christmas decorations! Surely there was a happy medium somewhere. "So, what do you suggest instead?" she asked, and Matthew shrugged, smiling.

"I admit, I don't have a vision the way you do. You've always been so brilliant at pulling things together, making them work. I'm not trying to step on your toes here—I'm just trying to remind you of what your original vision for this place was, and to be true to it with this Christmas week, as well, whatever that means."

And a fat lot of help that was, Ellie thought ruefully, although she kept from saying it out loud. She'd *had* a vision already. She really didn't think she was trying to create something highbrow, just nice. But, right now, the last thing she needed was an argument, even a kindly meant one. She was already exhausted and feeling fragile, and she really didn't want to fight with her husband.

"Okay," she said, summoning a smile and slapping it on her face. "Let's see what we can salvage from all this."

"Salvage?" Matthew repeated, an eyebrow raised, and Ellie couldn't keep from letting out a groan.

"Come on, Matt! Give me a break. I am not putting a miniature LED Christmas tree that Gwen bought from Asda for five pounds twenty years ago up on the mantel! I'm willing to be reasonable, but you need to be, as well."

"Fine." He grinned, and Ellie felt the tension that had been knotting her shoulder blades start to loosen, just a little. So much was riding on this week, on its success, and yet being tense and cross about it all wouldn't help matters. She needed to adopt a little of her husband's easy insouciance, even if the pressure to succeed sometimes felt like a thousand-pound weight on her shoulders. Matthew picked up the garish tree, admiring its neon colors. "Tell you what? I'll put it in our bedroom instead."

Ellie managed a laugh. "Deal," she said, smiling at him, and he smiled back. She was glad they'd managed to avoid an argument, at least.

CHAPTER 8

SARAH

Sarah was doing her best to stay upbeat. It was the first Saturday of half-term, and Nathan had informed her last night that he couldn't take any time off the way he normally did. He'd said he was too busy, pulling together this big pitch. She accepted the news—which had been given more like a warning than an apology, although he had said sorry—with what she hoped passed as equanimity.

"We'll probably be over at the inn for most of the week, anyway," she'd told him. "Mairi is running crafts every afternoon and Owen is helping with the outdoor assault course. I'm going to try to help Ellie with this big Christmas push."

"What big Christmas push?" Nathan had asked, and Sarah had had to bite her tongue, because she'd told him all about it during their dinner out, but clearly he'd forgotten.

"A Christmas holiday week, don't you remember?" she'd explained. "It's a way to help the inn's fortunes, because it's been struggling financially."

She'd been able to tell from her husband's noncommittal response that he hadn't been interested in hearing about it the second time round, either.

Now she did her best to push the memory of that conversation and the worries it had caused to fester to the back of her mind. She'd taken the week off work for half-term, and she'd decided to pitch in as much as she could with Ellie's Christmas plans for the inn. If she couldn't save her marriage—and she really was starting to wonder if she could—then at least she could try to save the inn. Despite her earlier doubts, she wanted to give this Christmas week the best chance she could.

"What crafts have you planned for this week, Mairi?" she asked, with potentially more enthusiasm than she usually would have used for such a question.

Mairi shrugged as she gazed out the car window and twirled a strand of hair around one finger. "The usual. Finger painting. Leaf printing. Stuff like that."

Sarah glanced at her daughter, noticing her seemingly disconsolate expression. Mairi had always been a self-contained person, much like Sarah herself was, but lately her daughter seemed even more isolated, obsessed with—and so very anxious about—her exams. "Sounds fun," she offered, and Mairi simply shrugged.

Once, Sarah reflected, Mairi would have chattered on about the crafts, asked Sarah's opinion about whether she thought they would occupy the children, enthuse about the paints or the playdough. Not in the last year, though, Sarah acknowledged. Mairi had become more and more withdrawn, seeming stressed and distant and borderline angry a lot of the time. Was it just the usual teenaged angst or something more? How on earth could she tell?

When her children had been younger, she reflected, things had seemed so much simpler. She'd read all the pregnancy and parenting books and had felt fully confident in her choices—organic food, a strict sleep schedule, time-outs and redirecting for discipline, limited screen time, on and on and on. Now, however, when their moods were mercurial, when the most innocuously asked question could set them off into fury or despair, when life felt like a minefield, and you didn't know where or even what the mines *were*—well, it was a lot harder than she'd ever expected it to be, especially now that Nathan seemed happy to take a backseat in terms of parenting.

She'd picked up a book on parenting teens "for success" a few years ago, and had read it with avid determination, assiduously making notes and then doing her best to implement its can-do strategies. She'd carefully followed its directives about how to build motivation and have teens accept consequences, but the thought of implementing those strategies now, or even skimming through the book again, only wearied her. She didn't want to follow the steps for successful parenting, or, really, for anything anymore, and she wasn't even sure why. Was she having a personality change or was she just tired of slogging through life without feeling much purpose or joy?

"Hello!" Ellie's voice was bright and maybe slightly manic as she threw open the front door a few minutes later, as they all headed into the inn. "The guests are going to arrive in about an hour—we've got three families booked: one with a baby, so I don't think they'll be doing any crafts, another with a four- and six-year-old, and then another with a nine- and eleven-year-old. You think you can manage it?" she asked Mairi, sounding just a little too jovial.

Sarah glanced closely at her sister-in-law, and thought the color on her cheeks looked a little intense, her smile a bit forced.

As Mairi and Owen sloped off to join their cousins, Sarah followed Ellie into the kitchen.

"Ellie," she asked, "are you okay?"

Ellie turned around, eyebrows raised, hands on her hips. "Don't I seem okay?"

"Well..." Sarah hesitated, because while she and Ellie had come a long way in their relationship, she still wouldn't say they were best friends or anything like that. "No, actually," she said bluntly, and then wished she hadn't when Ellie flinched.

"I'm tired," she admitted after a moment. "Ava wet the bed last night, which meant getting up, changing sheets, all that."

Sarah frowned. "Oh dear—"

"It's not just that," Ellie continued with a burst of feeling. "It's *everything*. The stress of making this all work. The journalists and photographers are coming in a little over a week and I feel like we've done basically nothing to get ready for them."

Sarah glanced around the kitchen, which looked essentially the same, with its old Aga and Welsh dresser full of dusty Willowware—comfortable, shabby, but ultimately welcoming and lovable, always the vibe the inn had gone for. "What have you done so far?" she asked practically.

Ellie blew out a breath. "Well... I'm trying to source some decorations for the interiors, but that's ongoing. We've updated the website with details about the Christmas week, and your mom has planned a delicious menu... Mairi and Jess are working on some ideas for Christmas crafts, and Matthew has found a Christmas tree for the photo shoot, which we're hopefully going to decorate next weekend, as soon as the guests have gone." She paused, looking strangely hesitant, before adding, "And also your mom has a friend coming round today to help in the garden, make it more Christmassy. He's a retired landscaper."

"*He?*" Sarah couldn't keep the surprise from her voice. "Who is that?" In over twenty years of widowhood, her mother had never had a male *friend*, not as far as Sarah could remember. No one she'd mentioned or introduced to her children, anyway.

"I don't think she told me his name," Ellie replied, "but he'll be here shortly, so you'll find out soon enough. She said he was an old university pal of your dad's."

"He was? Huh." Sarah tried to think of who that could be.

Back when she and Matthew had been children, they'd visited several of her parents' friends, but it was all such a long time ago, and she'd more or less forgotten who they'd been. "Well, that's interesting," she said at last. "I look forward to meeting him—or seeing him again, if I've met him before. I don't know whether I have or not. Anyway," she finished, doing her best to bolster Ellie's seemingly flagging spirits, "it sounds like you've done a lot to prepare already. When is this shoot, exactly?"

"A week Monday, but in the meantime, we have this week's guests. I'm not sure what I was thinking, arranging a Christmas photo shoot the day after half-term ends! We're going to be run off our feet..."

"Let me help," Sarah offered. "That's why I'm here. I don't have to stick to just ledgers and numbers. What needs doing?"

"Oh..." Ellie looked quite touched. "Thank you, Sarah. I've been feeling a bit like a chicken with my head cut off, to be honest, running around in an absolute tizzy."

"Well, chickens with their heads cut off can only run around for so long! Let's have a cup of tea and then we'll tackle that to-do list there sensibly." She nodded toward the list she'd seen on the table; it was in Ellie's handwriting and had at least twenty items.

"You're a star," Ellie murmured, sinking into a chair at the kitchen table as Sarah went to fill the kettle. It felt good to be doing something proactive and practical, when she felt as if all she could do at home was mope or drift.

"So how are things with you?" Ellie asked brightly. "How's Nathan?"

"Oh, fine," Sarah replied, as a matter of habit, before she decided to be just a little more honest. "Nathan's a bit stressed about work, and Mairi's even more stressed about her GCSEs. She's always been something of a high achiever, but I am worried that she's putting too much pressure on herself." She crossed her arms a bit defensively as she waited for the kettle to boil; she wasn't used to admitting so much, to letting someone know that things weren't absolutely perfect and completely under her control.

"She's such a bright girl, isn't she? I'm sure she'll do wonderfully well, but it's hard when they put that kind of pressure on themselves," Ellie replied in her usual, warm way. Jess was doing GCSES as well, Sarah thought, but she didn't seem to suffer from the same kind of anxiety. "Can she take a bit of a break over half-term?"

Sarah gave a little shrug. "I've suggested it, but she's in full-blown panic mode now, with her mock exams next month, as I'm sure you know. Jess doesn't seem too worried...?"

"I think we have the opposite problem with Jess," Ellie acknowledged wryly. "I've been encouraging her to chip away at the revision, but she hates it when I nag. I've decided to more or less leave her to it, now. They're her exams, not mine, and her grades have been good so far. I suppose I haven't been too worried." She smiled guiltily, like she'd just confessed something she shouldn't have.

"You're lucky, then." Sarah sighed and reached for the kettle, which had started to boil. "To tell the truth, I was the same as Mairi, always striving to do better, to *be* better. I didn't want to be any other way, but..." She hesitated, unsure where she was going with that sentiment. She was still that kind of person, and she liked it. Being in control, unflappable, the one who knew what to do and kept her head in a crisis—like now, even, when Ellie was comparing herself to a headless chicken and here she was, calmly making tea. That was who she wanted to be, who she *needed* to be, except... she felt as if inside, she wasn't that at all. As if she didn't really know how to be that way, anymore. Somewhere along the road, she'd lost the ability.

"But?" Ellie prompted gently. She rose from her chair to fetch the milk, splashing a bit in both of their mugs.

"I don't know," Sarah replied with a tired laugh. Her

thoughts were too jumbled—as well as exposing—to explain to Ellie right now. She needed to sift through them herself a bit more first. "I'm just worried about Mairi, I suppose."

Ellie nodded in sympathy, although Sarah had the sense that she hadn't entirely convinced her sister-in-law that worry for Mairi was the only thing going on. At least Ellie hadn't pressed her any more about Nathan.

They spent the next twenty minutes tackling the to-do list over mugs of tea. Sarah studied the mood boards Ellie had mocked up for the interior decorating—blue and silver for the dining room, and crimson and gold for the sitting room. Loads of fresh evergreens and holly, wreaths on every door, personalized presents for each child.

"It does all look and sound amazing," Sarah murmured. "There's a wonderful garden shop on the way to Garway that does loads of lovely ornaments. We might even be able to get some wholesale. And the velvet ribbon for the table—you can buy that at the craft shop in Abergavenny quite cheaply, I think."

"Really?" Ellie brightened at the thought. "That's wonderful. Thank you, Sarah."

Sarah glanced down at the photos Ellie had printed out for inspiration. "It all looks fabulous. Really quite elegant."

Ellie's hopeful smile faltered a bit at the edges. "Not too elegant, I hope, though."

"*Too* elegant?" Sarah raised her eyebrows. "What do you mean?"

"Oh, I don't know." Ellie blew out a breath. "Matt said something to me the other day, about how I was trying too hard. How the inn wasn't meant to be super fancy, that kind of thing..."

"Well, I wouldn't say these are super fancy," Sarah remarked, glancing down at the photos again. "Just nice. But he's one to talk, when he was going on about those fancy ensuite bathrooms and such back at the beginning!"

"Yes, and he said as much. He thinks I'm falling into the same trap as he did."

"Hmm." Sarah glanced at Ellie's troubled expression, her forehead furrowed, and her mouth drawn into a worried frown, as she considered the matter. "Is that what you think?"

"I don't know what I think," Ellie admitted. "I just really want this to work. I don't want the inn to have to close."

"I don't think anyone wants the inn to close," Sarah replied mildly, and Ellie sighed as she reached for her tea.

"I know, but sometimes it feels like I'm more invested in keeping it open than anyone else." She glanced up, her cup halfway to her lips, a look of something almost like panic in her eyes. "I don't mean that as a criticism—"

"I know," Sarah replied, a bit bemused. Once, she probably would have taken it as such, bristled about how Ellie wasn't the only invested one here, but, right now, she simply didn't have the energy or emotion for such a sentiment.

"It's just... I don't know," Ellie continued quietly. "Your mum seems happy to potter around, and I can't blame her, after everything she's been through. She's past retirement age anyway, so she surely deserves her rest. And Matt has developed this attitude of... of insouciance, like it's all going to work out, even if we stand around twiddling our thumbs." She bit her lip. "Sorry, that's a bit unfair. He is working hard on the outdoor stuff. It's just... a feeling I get, I suppose."

"What about the children?" Sarah asked, and Ellie shrugged.

"I don't know. I'm trying not to scare them too much, you know, since they've already had so much change in their lives, moving to Wales in the first place. But the older ones don't seem that bothered, sometimes. I think Jess would like to have her own room, which could happen if the inn did shut."

"So why do you think you care so much?" Sarah probed, keeping her tone gentle. "Why has it become so important to you?"

"Because it's *mine*," Ellie burst out, then gave Sarah a guilty look. "Sorry, I know the inn isn't mine at all. But the original idea... that feels like it was. And if it fails, it feels personal. Like I've failed. Like I'm a failure."

She lapsed into silence while Sarah absorbed what she'd been saying. It was basically what she'd been feeling too—about her marriage. If it failed, then she failed.

"I think that's at the heart of what I'm afraid of," Ellie continued, "although, of course, there's also the uncertainty of what would happen if the inn had to close—Matthew would have to get a new job, and me too, probably." She gave a long, weary sigh. "Don't mind me. I'm just tired. It's been a long time since I've had such a broken night."

"Why do you think Ava wet the bed?" Sarah asked, determined to stay practical. "Was it a one-off? Do you limit her liquids in the evening?"

"No, but I think I might start, just in case." Ellie frowned. "I wonder if she's internalizing anxiety about the inn, actually... but maybe I'm just projecting, because I'm so anxious." She managed a rather feeble smile.

"It will get better," Sarah said, which was exactly the kind of bland platitude she hated and didn't believe in for her own life, yet she actually meant it. It *would* get better for Ellie. She had a loving husband, a great family, and she was determined to make the inn work. "Especially if we get cracking," she added, rising from the table just as the doorbell rang. "Early guests?" she guessed, and Ellie shook her head.

"No, no one's arriving before lunch. It's probably your mother's friend."

"Oh, right."

Curious, Sarah went to the door. The man standing on the

step as she opened it was familiar to her, but only in a vague way. He had a full head of white hair, bright blue eyes, and a quick, easy smile.

"*Sarah!*" he exclaimed, and she was jolted by his tone of familiarity, which he must have noticed because his smile turned a little sheepish. "You don't remember me, of course. I'm not surprised! It's been a long time." He stuck out a hand for her to shake, which she did, impressed with his sure, warm grip. "John McCardell. I went to university with your dad. We did some family holidays eons ago... I think the last one was when you were twelve or so? Izzy was seven, Michael nine. My kids are a bit younger than you and Matthew."

"Oh, right." She smiled and shook his hand. "I do remember you, sorry for the momentary lapse! It has been a long time." She realized she did recall those holidays, in a hazy sort of way. She stepped aside to let him enter. "Please, do come in."

"I've always loved this place," John remarked as he came into the hall, glancing around in warm appreciation. "It's such a beautiful home."

For a second, Sarah felt as if she could see it through his eyes—the worn, stone-flagged floor with its runner carpet in a faded Turkish pattern, the vase of dried sunflowers on the hall table, with the vintage gold-framed mirror above. The map of Monmouthshire, dating from the 1700s, on the opposite wall; the umbrella stand with its vintage umbrellas, the Chinese vase with its pattern of blue and white swirls, and a deep crack right through its middle from when Matthew had accidentally knocked it over when he'd been playing football in the hall. Everything about it was so familiar, she didn't really notice or even see it anymore, but as she looked around now, she could appreciate what a welcoming place it was, homely in the best possible way, and, like Ellie, she realized just how much she didn't want the inn to close.

"Yes, it is, isn't," she replied, turning back to John. "Mum and Dad have done marvels with the place, and so has Ellie, my sister-in-law." She glanced toward the kitchen doorway, where Ellie had come to stand, smiling uncertainly. "Ellie, this is John. John, Ellie."

John stepped forward with alacrity. "Lovely to meet you."

"And you," Ellie replied, taking his hand to shake. "I'm not sure where Gwen is..."

"I'm here." Gwen came in from the back, smiling at John in a way that seemed to Sarah both cautious and pleased. Again, she had that rather disorientating sensation of seeing something from someone else's eyes—in this case, her mother in John's eyes.

To her, her mum was simply her mum—familiar, loving, beloved. But now she saw a woman who, despite having only recently finished her cancer treatment, looked fit and trim and healthy for her sixty-nine years. Her hair was in a neat gray bob, and her deep blue eyes sparkled with humor. There was a faint flush to her cheeks, which Sarah suspected was from John's presence, and made her mother look even younger and more vibrant. As she took all these details in, she realized she didn't know how she felt about any of it.

"Gwen." John took a step toward her mother, hands outstretched as if to clasp hers, his smile deepening into dimples, and then, seeming to sense the familiarity—and even intimacy—of the gesture, dropped them with a little wry twist of his mouth. "How are you?"

"I'm well, thank you." Her mother tucked her hair behind her ears, glancing at both Ellie and Sarah, seeming a bit nervous. "Would you like a cup of tea or coffee before we head outside?"

John glanced briefly at Sarah and Ellie; Ellie seemed to be watching this little exchange with as much bemused interest as Sarah was. "No, why don't we just get going? We can come inside in a bit, to warm up. There's an autumnal nip in the air today!"

"All right." Gwen's smile turned shy. "I'll show you the way." She turned back to the door at the end of the hallway that ran the length of the house and led straight out into the back garden, and John followed her, giving Sarah and Ellie a jaunty salute before he disappeared out the door.

"Well." The word escaped Sarah in a gust of breath. "That was... interesting."

"He seems nice," Ellie ventured, and Sarah nodded slowly.

"Yes... very nice."

"Do you... do you think there might be more to it?" Ellie asked uncertainly as they headed back into the kitchen. "She only met him yesterday for coffee, and before that she hadn't seen him in years."

"I don't know." Sarah leaned against the kitchen counter, her forehead furrowed in thought. "Not at the moment, I suppose, but there definitely seemed to be some kind of spark there. Don't you think?"

Ellie nodded, a playful smile kicking up the corner of her mouth. "Yes, I do. Not that I'd say as much to your mother, mind!"

"No, nor would I." Sarah gave a rueful little grimace. It was strange even thinking about her being with someone.

"How would you feel about it," Ellie asked cautiously, "if it became something more?"

Sarah considered the question honestly. "A bit strange," she admitted. "I'm ashamed to say I've never even thought about my mum dating someone, never mind something more serious, and yet she was only forty-seven when Dad died. That seemed so old to me at the time, but it's only one year older than I am now!" She let out a short laugh as she shook her head slowly. "I hope Mum didn't not date because of Matthew and me. She never even talked about it with us."

"I think she would have, if it had been a serious option," Ellie offered. "Don't you?"

"Maybe. And maybe it isn't even a serious option now... we might be getting ahead of ourselves!"

From outside, they heard a sudden shout of male laughter, and they exchanged knowing, smiling glances.

"Or maybe not," Ellie returned, her smile widening.

CHAPTER 9

GWEN

"You really have a lovely place here, Gwen." John's smile was warm and full of admiration as they strolled through the garden. There certainly was a nip in the air, just as John had said; the balmy weather had given in to the more expected autumnal crispness, a few cottony clouds scudding across a pale blue sky.

"Thank you," Gwen replied, glancing around the garden with an affectionate smile. "I'm afraid you're not seeing it at its best, though, at this time of year." The leaves had started to fall from the trees, creating deep drifts on the ground, and the shrubs and flowers that filled the beds and planters in spring with joyous, riotous color, were now mostly brown and bare.

"Still, I can tell. It's got a lovely mix of landscape and wildness—very popular in today's gardening world, by the way. Everyone's talking about rewilding and how weeds are just resilient plants—"

"Well, I don't know about that!" Gwen exclaimed, sounding as censorious as a schoolteacher, and John let out a shout of laughter.

"You don't want to let the weeds run rampant?" he asked, eyebrows raised, a teasing grin lurking about his mouth.

She thought of the chickweed and milk thistle that were the bane of her garden, and shook her head firmly. "Definitely not. They certainly are resilient, though."

"Very true."

They continued to stroll along, John stopping every once in a while to examine a plant or tree. Gwen tried to see the garden through his eyes—it was a bit of a jumble, she knew, but she liked it that way. Chickens pecking where they liked, a den built under the low-hanging branches of a willow tree, the obstacle course Matthew had built running along the length of the bottom, and amidst all that, a profusion of flowers, bushes, and trees, of every shape, kind and color, at least in season. She'd never gone in for much landscaping, just picked what she'd liked and thrown it all together—lilac, roses, hyacinth, honeysuckle.

"This is your vegetable patch, then?" John surmised as they stood by a fenced rectangle of bare brown earth, save for two rows of parsnips that were ready to harvest, and a dozen lovely, large pumpkins.

"Yes, not much going on there now, though, I'm afraid, but we had plenty in the summer." She nodded towards a small stone building tucked away in one corner of the garden. "David built that root cellar twenty-five years ago," she told John. "And we've put it to good use over the years."

"Wonderful. He always was handy, wasn't he? Even in university. I remember when my car wouldn't start, I'd just ask him. I'm much better with living things, but David was always amazing with the mechanical side."

"Yes, he was." It was nice to talk about David in this way, easy and uncomplicated, and yet for some reason, it created a strange, shifting sensation in Gwen that she found disquieting, and she wasn't sure why. "I always relied on him, for any kind of DIY," she admitted. "I'm fairly hopeless with anything electrical or car-related, although I've learned to manage over the years."

"Like me with the cooking. It's hard, isn't it, when you realize your own deficiencies? How much you depended on the other person." His faint smile turned sad, and Gwen nodded, grateful at how he understood. She realized she hadn't been able to talk with anyone like this since David had died.

"Yes, it is hard," she agreed. "But I suppose it creates an opportunity."

"I like your optimism." He glanced around the garden. "So, what are you thinking, in terms of doing this up for Christmas? Just walking through, I already have some ideas, but I'd love to hear what you think." His eyes were warm, his expression alert and attentive, and Gwen found that every coherent and sensible thought immediately flew from her head.

"Well... I don't know," she admitted, even though she'd had some ideas, earlier. She just couldn't think of them now, for some reason. "That's why I asked you along, after all," she added with a small, teasing smile.

John gave a little laugh. "Fair enough. Well, let me tell you what I see so far. I'd like to keep the mix of wildness and landscaped features that you have—even in autumn, the garden has a sense of discovery, of secrets or treasure to be found—"

"Yes!" Gwen exclaimed, surprised and gratified by his perception. "That was exactly the sort of thing we were trying to go for. We wanted the children to be able to explore—and discover. To feel safe but adventurous in a wild landscape."

"Yes, I completely agree," John acquiesced warmly. "It's a place of adventure, like you say, which is just how it should be. And so, I'd expand on that theme with whatever you do for Christmas—create spaces and experiences for the children to discover."

"But how?"

"Well, off the top of my head—you could use fairy lights to

devise a discovery trail of some kind through the trees, that they would have to follow. You could create a simple nativity scene with movable wood pieces for them to play with, and bring in some cozy, sheltered benches for around the firepit. Maybe a treasure hunt, finding the different decorations—woodland creatures made of willow or wicker, maybe? And, of course, you'll need a Santa's grotto."

"Yes, Matthew suggested a grotto. He was thinking underneath one of the willow trees?" Gwen offered, and John beamed at her with his infectious smile.

"Perfect!"

"That all sounds amazing," she told him slowly, "but I wouldn't know where to begin. We're on something of a shoestring budget," she felt compelled to admit with a grimace. She hardly wanted to burden him with their financial woes.

"Aren't we all?" John replied with a smile. "Most of it could be done here. The nativity scene could be made of simple pieces, carved from wood you have lying around—"

"Made by whom?" Gwen interjected wryly. "I'm afraid we don't have a resident woodworker at the moment."

"Well... by me," John replied after a pause, with a slightly shaky laugh. "I have experience working with wood, as well as willow and wicker. I could do it... if you wanted me to."

He sounded so uncharacteristically uncertain that Gwen turned to him, both touched and concerned. "That's asking a lot of you," she remarked, "especially when you're here to visit your daughter, and you have a grandchild on the way."

"I don't mind," John assured her, although Gwen thought he still sounded uncertain. "I like having a project. Retirement hasn't really suited me, I'm afraid!" He let out a little laugh that sounded rather sad, and Gwen suddenly had a jolt of understanding—John was bored, and maybe lonely, in this life of retirement and widowerhood.

And she understood; she'd felt the same after David had

died, even after the worst of the grief had passed. She'd felt as if she were drifting through her days, as if she'd lost her anchor. She'd had to completely reorient herself, and in some ways, over twenty years later, she was still in that process. John had been widowed for only two years. He still had to be reeling.

"Of course," he continued, "I don't want to commit to a project and then find I can't finish it. But the things I'm talking about wouldn't take too long—and, in truth, I'm not sure how useful Izzy's going to find me, once the baby comes." He smiled crookedly. "What she really wants is her mum." He glanced down at his feet, the smile sliding off his face, and impulsively, unthinkingly, Gwen reached out and rested her hand on his arm.

"I'm so sorry, John. It must be hard, about to have your first grandchild without Michelle."

"Yes, well. It's been two years—"

"And that can feel like nothing," Gwen interjected quietly. "And, at the same time, like a lifetime."

"Yes.' He nodded, swallowing hard. "Yes, that's exactly how it is."

Feeling a bit self-conscious now, Gwen removed her hand from his arm. "Well, if you think you can do all these things, I wouldn't say no," she told him. "Your ideas sound marvelous, and I don't think anyone else could even begin to manage it. Matthew made the obstacle course, but I think that's the extent of his woodworking ability, and he's got a lot of other things to do, besides."

"I don't want to step on anyone's toes," John said quickly. "This seems like it's a wonderfully homegrown, family affair. I don't want to come between anyone, or seem like I'm trying to take over."

His thoughtfulness touched her, even as it gave her a second's pause. Would Matthew feel hurt if she asked for John's help? The garden had been her son's domain, and he was rightfully proud of all he'd accomplished—the firepit, the obstacle course, the climbing frame.

"You wouldn't be," she said at last. "And, really, it's all hands on deck now. We've got photographers coming next week to do an article on our Christmas week, and as you can see, it's not looking very Christmassy!"

"Well, then, I'd best get started," John replied cheerfully. "Shall we have a cup of tea while we talk it over?"

They headed back to the kitchen, which was quiet. Ellie was upstairs, giving the bedrooms a last check, and the children were in the games room, setting up the crafts for the children arriving later in the day. Gwen didn't know where Sarah or Matthew were, but she was grateful for the quiet, as well as the privacy, as she made them both cups of tea.

She'd been rather excruciatingly aware of both Ellie and Sarah's speculative looks when John had arrived, as well as that awkward moment when he'd stepped out, hands outstretched, almost as if he'd been about to embrace her. He hadn't been, of course, and Gwen suspected the only reason she'd felt as if he had, had been Sarah and Ellie's glances of obvious, avid curiosity. What did they think was going on? she wondered in exasperation, even as she knew she could easily guess.

But she'd only reconnected with John yesterday, even if today it seemed as if he was going to become a regular feature of her life, at least for a little while. That didn't mean they were anything but old friends, though. Absolutely not. John was still clearly grieving Michelle, and as for Gwen herself...

She let that thought trail away without finishing it, because the truth was, she wasn't sure how she felt about this new development in her life. She certainly didn't want to feel out of step with John. He was lonely and missing his wife, and he wanted to help. That was all.

"David has some woodworking tools in one of the garden sheds," she told him as she handed him a cup of tea and joined him at the table. "You're welcome to take a look and see if there's anything you can use, or even use the shed as a space to work. I'll have to give it a bit of a clean first, though!"

"Never mind about that." John looked at her seriously. "Are you all right with this, Gwen? I... I don't want to be a lonely old man inserting myself into your busy life." He ducked his head, embarrassed, as Gwen gazed at him in surprise.

"That's not how you see yourself, I hope," she replied after a moment.

John smiled sadly. "Sometimes it is. Truthfully, I think Izzy asked me to stay because she felt sorry for me. Her husband Sam's parents are coming a few weeks after the baby is born—they're the ones she really wants to stay, because they'll be more helpful than I am, I'm sure. Not that I'm averse to changing nappies or anything like that!" he added hastily, and with his usual rueful grin. "I look forward to it. But in situations like these, I think a new mum really wants a woman's touch."

"Well, yes, I can see that," Gwen allowed, "but that doesn't mean she isn't appreciative of your help and company, as well."

John just shrugged, and Gwen's heart ached for him. Beneath that cheerful bonhomie was clearly an ocean of loneliness and grief. How well she understood it! It made her like him all the more, and, strangely, it made him more approachable and easier to talk to. Yesterday she'd been a bit disconcerted by his cheerful confidence, so at odds with her own uncertainty, but today she felt as if she understood him completely, or certainly better than she had before.

With the same unthinking impulsivity as before, she reached over and covered his hand with her own. "It will get better, you know," she told him quietly, "and easier. It takes time—more time than you'd ever think or hope, really. But it does happen eventually, I promise."

When he smiled at her, his eyes looked damp, and he rested his other hand over hers, the feel of it comfortingly warm and solid. "Thank you," he said simply, and they smiled at each other.

They were still sitting like that, hands clasped, when Matthew walked into the kitchen and did a very obvious double take, which had them springing apart like guilty teenagers. "Hello," he said to John, sounding thunderstruck. "I don't believe I know you?"

John stood up, smiling easily enough, although Gwen could tell he was a bit discomfited by Matthew's obvious, and not entirely friendly, surprise. "Actually, you do, although I must admit, it has been quite a while. I'm John, John McCardell, a very old friend of your father's."

"Of my father's?" Matthew repeated, and Gwen had to bite the inside of her cheek to keep from making some stupid retort. If Matthew was trying to defend her honor, or something silly like that, he was going about it in a rather clumsy way.

"Yes, Matthew, I'm sure you remember?" she remarked, her tone a bit tart. "John met Dad at Swansea. We had some camping and caravan holidays together, when you were small. With Izzy and Michael?" She glanced at John. "What's Michael doing now, anyway?"

"Working in London and happily single." John smiled and then glanced at Matthew, who was not quite frowning, but not smiling, either.

Gwen suppressed the flicker of irritation at her son's lack of warmth.

As if he realized it as well, he came to himself with a rueful smile and held out his hand for John to shake. "Of course, I remember now! Those were the good old days, eh? I have a distinct memory of eating a Mr. Whippy in the rain because Mum wouldn't allow ice cream in the caravan."

"Well, it can get everywhere and it's so sticky," Gwen replied with a smile, and John shook Matthew's hand.

"I think I have the same memory," he told him. "Adults

weren't allowed ice cream indoors, either!" He glanced back at Gwen with a humorous smile that she saw her son noticed—and had his eyes narrowing.

For goodness' sake, Gwen thought with genuine irritation now. Was she not allowed to have friends?

Seeming to sense the slightly uneasy mood, John glanced between them both and said, "Maybe now would be a good time to have a look in the shed for those tools?"

"What tools are you looking for?" Matthew asked. "I'm only asking because I've done a bit of a reorg of all the outside sheds, so if you're looking for something in particular, I could tell you where to find it."

"One of your father's toolsheds," Gwen told Matthew, "where he kept some woodworking things. I don't think you've had a look through that, have you?"

"No, I don't think I have," he admitted, and Gwen gave him a pointed glance before turning to John.

"I'll show you where it is," she said, and left Matthew alone in the kitchen.

Outside in the garden, John let out a small, uneasy laugh. "Are you sure I won't be stepping on any toes by working on this?" he asked.

"No, you won't be," Gwen replied firmly. "It's true Matthew has been involved in the garden quite a bit, but the things you're offering to do are jobs that he can't."

"Even so—"

"I want them done, and I like your ideas," Gwen told him. "Don't worry about Matthew." She opened the door to the shed, breathing in the musty smell of earth and sawdust. "Goodness, I don't think anyone's been in here in years," she exclaimed, as she brushed cobwebs from the workbench. "David had another toolshed for more everyday things. I think Matthew has that one well in hand, but he clearly hasn't been in here."

John stepped into the shed behind her, and Gwen was

suddenly, rather overwhelmingly conscious of how small the space was, how close John was. "As long as you're sure," he said, his voice low and near her ear.

A shiver went through her that she did her best to suppress. It was absolutely no good having these kinds of feelings, she told herself. Really, it was rather ridiculous in a woman of her age, and especially when John was clearly still missing Michelle. Besides, she wasn't at all sure she could trust her own feelings; after so many years on her own, maybe she was just getting a bit carried away.

"I'm sure," she replied, slipping past him as quickly as she could. Out in the garden, she took a steadying breath of cool, clean air. "But I'll leave you to it for now, if you don't mind. You can do what you like with anything in there. And if you need anything else, let me know, and I'll see if I can find it."

"Thank you, Gwen," John told her sincerely. "You don't know what it means to me, to have a project."

"You don't know what it means to *me*," Gwen replied, "to have you doing this for us!"

With a cheery smile, she turned and walked quickly back into the kitchen, steeling herself for a confrontation she knew she wasn't going to like.

Sure enough, Matthew was still in the kitchen, looking a bit like a sulky schoolboy.

Gwen shook her head as she closed the door. "What," she asked him, "was all that about?"

"Was all *what* about?" Matthew returned in a tone of injured innocence.

"Matthew!" Gwen shook her head, her hands planted on her hips. "Don't pretend you don't know what I'm talking about! You weren't very friendly with John. In fact, I might say you were almost *rude*."

"I wasn't," Matthew replied, although under Gwen's steely stare, his expression turned abashed. "All right, maybe I was, at least a little bit, but only because I was so surprised, Mum. I didn't even know he was coming today, or that you'd been in touch with him."

"I didn't realize I had to inform you of all my business," Gwen replied. "Or whom I'm friends with! I'm a grown woman as well as your mother, Matthew Davies, I'll have you remember." She stared him down until he dropped his gaze.

"Sorry," he mumbled. "I admit, I acted like an idiot. I was just surprised." He paused before asking cautiously, "But what are you saying, Mum?" He looked up at her. "Is this guy important to you?"

Gwen's breath came out in a rush as her shoulders slumped a little. "Matthew, I met him again for the first time in ten years yesterday. He's a friend, that's all."

"When I came into the kitchen—"

"That's *all*," Gwen emphasized, her voice taking on an iron-like quality she hadn't used with him since he'd been small. "Now, maybe you could see if he needs any other tools? He's got some plans for the garden that I think you'll like."

"He's helping in the garden. But—"

"He doesn't want to step on any toes, and I really don't think he will be," she cut across him. "He's thinking of carving a nativity set, and that isn't something you've thought about doing. You have plenty to be getting on with anyway, so, if you can trust yourself to be the kind and friendly person I know you truly are, why don't you go and talk to him about it?"

Matthew stared at her for a moment, and then, with a sigh and a smile, he nodded. "Sorry. Yes, okay, I will."

As he left the room, Gwen let out a shaky breath as she sank onto one of the kitchen chairs. The fiery indignation that had lent her the courage to have that conversation left her in a rush, so now she only felt old and tired and very uncertain. At that moment, letting John McCardell into her life seemed like a disconcerting prospect, indeed.

CHAPTER 10

ELLIE

"Oh, Ellie, this looks fab."

Ellie smiled in gratitude at Emma, mum of Josh's best friend Zach, and one of her close friends. Emma ran her own freelance PR business, and she'd helped Ellie when they'd first planned to relaunch the inn almost two years ago. It made sense to ask for her help now, although Ellie knew Emma's business had taken off, and she was usually booked up months in advance. She'd invited her over during half-term to have a look at her ideas, and to ask—or even *beg*—if she could help with the publicity. It was halfway through the holiday week, and fortunately a quiet afternoon, since all the families, including Ellie's, had gone out. The guests, loaded up with maps and picnic baskets, had gone to the Brecon Beacons, and Matthew had taken the kids bowling.

Gwen had gone out, as well, although she hadn't said where. Ellie half-wondered if she was meeting John, but somehow, over the last few days, he had become something of a no-go area of conversation, as well as a slight source of tension, for both Matthew and Gwen. Ellie didn't really understand it, but she had enough to be getting on with, without deliberately stirring up a hornet's nest of emotions.

"Do you really think so?" Ellie asked her friend now. In addition to managing their guests this week, she'd bought quite a few of the decorations from the suppliers Sarah had recommended, and she'd done up the sitting room as best as she could, to give Emma an idea of what she was aiming for. Even without the Christmas tree or roaring log fire—both of which would be present when the photographers came—she thought the room looked nice, indeed—crimson ribbon twisted around pinecones, fresh evergreens on the mantelpiece, and tall, creamy candles standing sentry in crimson and gold holders on the deep windowsill. Looking around, she was starting to feel optimistic that they just might be able to pull all this off.

"Yes, I love the quaintness of everything," Emma enthused. "Too often, Christmas decorations look so glossy and sterile, everything relentlessly color coordinated. Having a few homemade touches really adds to it, I think." She nodded toward the bookshelf, where Ellie had, in a reluctant concession to Matthew, stuck that silly miniature LED Christmas tree, half behind a vase. "I love that," Emma said, and Ellie managed a weak laugh.

Really? Of all the special touches Ellie had worked so hard on, Emma had to point out that tatty old tree?

"Ellie?" Emma asked in concern, and to her horror, Ellie realized she was suddenly near tears.

"Sorry," she said on what she hoped passed for a laugh. "I'm so glad you like it all. As it happens, there is a story behind that little tree."

"A story?" Emma raised her eyebrows, looking intrigued. "I'd love to hear it."

"Well..." Ellie shook her head, glancing around at all her *relentlessly color coordinated* efforts—everything crimson and gold, including a few throw pillows for the sofa she'd splurged on, along with a crimson and gold blanket over the sofa's back and a crimson and gold bow affixed to the log basket. Was it all too matching, too *twee*? Maybe she'd got this really wrong. The thought was dispiriting.

"Did I put my foot in it?" Emma asked, laughing uncertainly. "I was just saying that I like how real you've made it, while still looking totally gorgeous. I love those throw pillows, by the way."

Ellie let out another tired laugh. It was almost as if Emma could read her thoughts.

"Thanks," she said. "As for the LED tree, well, it belonged —*belongs*—to Gwen. She wanted me to use some of her old decorations, and so I did."

"Ah." Emma nodded knowingly. "A compromise?"

"Of sorts. I admit, I was kind of reluctant. Some of them are quite... homemade."

"But homemade ones are the best!" Emma exclaimed, before subsiding with a ruefully guilty look. "Sorry. I mean, I get you. For a hotel, you want a slightly more polished look, I suppose."

"Exactly," Ellie said on a sigh. The truth was, she wasn't sure of anything anymore. If the one thing Emma had noticed was that silly tree, and not all the little touches and extras she'd worked so hard on... well, what did it say about any of it? About *her*?

"I think you've done a really good job here, Ellie, and on such short notice," Emma told her, her voice warm with sincerity. "Seriously. I only mentioned the tree because I had one as a kid, and it brought back memories. I thought they were the coolest thing, back in the day, with those lights."

"I suppose they were," Ellie agreed. Perhaps she could get a few more decorations from Gwen's boxes. They could be officially labeled as retro, vintage.

"Are you okay?" Emma asked in concern, touching her arm, and Ellie managed a bright smile.

"Yes. Just tired, I think. Guests all week and then the

photographers coming on Monday... I'm worried I might have bitten off more than I can chew here."

"But you're doing it," Emma pointed out as she gestured to the room. "This looks ready to be photographed!"

"Yes, once Matt brings the tree in. Anyway"—Ellie turned from the room—"let's have a cup of tea while I beg for your help with the publicity."

Emma laughed. "You don't need to beg, and it sounds as if you've managed plenty on your own, what with this newspaper coming. I'm not sure what you need me to do."

"Well, I'd love for you to design a brochure," Ellie told her as they went into the kitchen. Daisy, who had been snoozing by the stove, perked up her little head. "I thought I could distribute some locally, in shops and cafés."

"Great idea. I could do that, no problem."

"Are you sure you have time—"

"For you, Ellie?" Emma grinned. "Of course."

They spent a few more minutes talking through the brochure, and Emma opened her laptop and showed Ellie a couple of graphics she'd been thinking of. By the end of the conversation, she was feeling encouraged again, and grateful for her friend's support. This was really starting to come together. Now all they needed were the guests to book...

Emma left a short while later, promising to email Ellie a mock-up by that evening, since time was of the essence. The house was still quiet, with everyone out, although guests would start trickling back for afternoon tea soon. Ellie decided to take a few moments to stroll outside and collect—and bolster—her thoughts.

She *was* encouraged, she told herself as she wandered through the garden, some of its trees already bedecked by fairy lights, to the bench by the little pond that Ben and Owen were still hoping to somehow turn into an ice-skating rink. The area under the willow tree was currently a construction site;

Matthew and Ben were working on a platform for Santa to sit atop. There was a nip in the air, and the sun was breaking through billowy gray clouds; the world felt caught between all the seasons, a hint of each one in the air, like either a memory or a promise.

Ellie sank onto the bench with a gusty sigh as doubts began to trickle through her once more. It wasn't just about the little LED tree, she knew. She wasn't that ridiculous, but it represented something more elemental that Matthew had been trying to point out to her. She'd got too invested in making the inn a success, she realized, not for her family's sake, or even the inn's sake, but for her own. It had been her idea at the start, and so its possible failure had felt personal to her, *too* personal. In all her efforts, she'd been trying to prove something about herself, and the realization was both humbling and a little shaming. No wonder she'd cared more than anyone else, she thought, and yet was that *wrong*?

Of *course* she wanted the inn to succeed. Yes, maybe she'd become a bit carried away with the idea of it looking polished and professional, but that wasn't wrong either, was it? And she'd learned her lesson. She'd include a few more of the home-made decorations; like Emma had said, they could be lovely little touches.

But what, Ellie thought disconsolately, really, was it all for? If Gwen wasn't bothered by whether the inn succeeded or not... if her children weren't... if it had been a fun adventure for a brief period of time and nothing more... Why keep it going at all? She didn't want to put in all this effort for her own sake, her own pride, while having to drag everyone else along.

And yet maybe she was being unfair. Gwen had got John involved, after all, and he'd come back twice already to work on the nativity set, which looked amazing—the figures done in smooth, sweeping and simple lines so children could move them about. Matt was working hard on the garden, and he and Ben had gone to investigate eco-friendly options to turn the pond into a rink. Jess had made some nice craft ideas and samples, and Gwen had created a beautiful menu for Christmas Eve and Christmas Day...

Everyone was pulling their weight, Ellie acknowledged, even if they weren't as personally invested as she was. But would the guests even book? They hadn't had any Christmas bookings yet—a fact which Ellie was trying not to let alarm her because they'd only just started their publicity. But it was already the end of October; most people would have probably made their Christmas plans by now, something Sarah had pointed out during one of their discussions. Ellie had replied that plans could change, but now she wondered. Had her determination, her desperation, blinded her? What if this really was all for nothing?

"Are you hiding down here?"

She turned to see Matthew strolling over with a smile.

"Just thinking," she replied, and he raised his eyebrows.

"Good thoughts?"

"Sort of."

He sat down next to her and tilted his head up to the sky, squinting into the sun. "You've really been worrying about this," he observed. "And working so very hard. But there's not much we can do about it besides give it our best."

"I know. It's just... what if our best isn't good enough?"

He lowered his face, turning to her with a smiling shrug of his shoulders. "Then it isn't."

"I don't understand how you can be so philosophical about it, Matt," Ellie exclaimed, shaking her head. "We moved our entire family all the way from America to Wales to run this place. We've poured everything into it for the last two years—time, money, energy, emotion. Why are you not that bothered? Are you just that laidback, or is something else going on?"

She didn't realize until she'd asked the question—and felt

Matthew's hesitation in response—that the possibility had been lurking in the back of her mind. Her husband's equanimity had been just a bit too surprising, and so unlike when they'd first moved here, and he'd thrown himself into renovating the inn with the same kind of passion and fervor she had—and broken his arm in the process. That setback had discouraged him, and eventually made him reevaluate his priorities. But why did he seem so different now?

"Matt?" she prompted when he still hadn't spoken. "*Is* something else going on?"

"No," he said finally, but he sounded strangely hesitant. "At least... not... not yet."

"*What?*" A frisson of anxiety rippled down her spine. "What is that supposed to mean?"

"It's very early days of a... a *possibility* I've been investigating."

"What?" Ellie said again, this time blankly. He'd never made a *peep* about some "possibility" before now. She had no idea what it could be. "Why didn't you say anything before?" she asked. "And what sort of possibility are we talking about?" Her mind was already starting to race. Was it a job in Cardiff? Some crazy new venture or scheme, or just another office position? Why hadn't he *said*? On some subconscious level, she'd wondered if something was going on, but she still hadn't expected *this*.

"I didn't want to add to your worries, with so much going on," Matthew explained. "And it really is in the very vague, probably-won't-happen sort of stage, so it seemed prudent to wait until I had more to go on, before I got anyone worked up."

"*What* probably won't happen?" Ellie demanded. She was starting to feel exasperated, as well as seriously alarmed. She still couldn't believe Matthew hadn't breathed a word of this— whatever this was—before now.

"A job opportunity," he told her, sounding reluctant to part with even that much information. He held up one hand to forestall any further questions. "I'll give you all the details soon, when we can talk about it properly. But we've got guests coming back any minute, and the kids all kicking around, and afternoon tea to put on. I wasn't trying to hide anything from you, Ellie, I promise. I just didn't want to add to your anxiety—"

"Well, you're adding to my anxiety now," Ellie returned, trying not to sound annoyed. How did he think she was going to react, to having this kind of uncertainty sprung on her? And what did he mean exactly, a job opportunity? He worked for the inn, for their family business.

"Sorry, sweetheart." At least he looked genuinely repentant. "I put my foot in it, clearly. I shouldn't have said anything to you yet."

"Or you should have said *everything*," Ellie retorted, exasperated. "Matt, what am I supposed to do with this—"

"We'll talk soon," he promised. "I mean it. This evening, even. But, right now, we've got to put on a tea and then a supper and games tonight—"

Ellie knew he was right, even though she didn't particularly appreciate that fact at this moment. "All right," she agreed reluctantly. "But we are *definitely* talking tonight."

Inside the house, everyone was springing into action. Ben and Josh were getting games out. Jess was setting up crafts in the corner of the games room, and guests were wandering about, some heading upstairs to refresh themselves before tea and others relaxing in the sitting room. A few of the younger children were racing around excitedly, and Ellie had to dodge out of the way as she headed into the kitchen. Gwen was slicing scones and dolloping clotted cream into little crystal bowls.

"Can I help?" she asked, already reaching for a jar of Gwen's homemade strawberry jam and decanting it into bowls.

Gwen gave her a quick, harried smile. "Sorry, I got back late. I should have sorted all this out before."

"It's all right, they're only just getting back now, and no one seems in a rush for their tea. Where were you, anyway?" Ellie kept her voice casual, although, in truth, she was rather curious.

"I met up with John," Gwen admitted, her head bent so Ellie couldn't see the expression on her face—or whether she was blushing. "We walked up Sugarloaf Mountain."

"Oh, lovely." Ellie kept her tone warm and easy, even though part of her was reeling. Had that been an actual *date*? Or was she reading too much into it, thanks to Sarah's remarks the other day? This was something else she and Matthew hadn't talked about; he'd seemed a bit out of sorts about John's presence in the garden, carving the nativity scene, and Ellie hadn't wanted to go into it. Maybe it was something else they needed to discuss tonight, she thought with a sigh.

She loaded up a tray with scones, clotted cream and jam, and brought it into the sitting room before checking on the children in the games room. What had once been a library nook was now a cheerful space, with shelves of board games and puzzles, a craft table, and a cupboard full of art supplies. Josh and Ben were setting up Monopoly, while Jess was laying out glue sticks for a leaf printing craft, Ava doing her best to help.

"How's it all going?" she asked brightly, and Jess shrugged.

"Okay, I guess."

"Just okay?" Ellie asked lightly. Jess was usually cheerful about doing the crafts. "Where's Mairi?"

"She said she had to study today."

Ellie recalled Sarah saying how stressed Mairi was about her exams. "I guess GCSEs can be a real killer," she remarked.

Jess gave another shrug, her head bent. "Yeah, although I've been doing okay," she pointed out, to which Ellie could only agree. Jess had been pretty much a straight A student since she'd started at school; she really hadn't had to worry too much about her schoolwork.

"What about Sophie?" she asked. "Could she help out this week?"

"She's busy with her music," Jess replied.

"How busy?" she asked. Ellie knew Jess's best friend had joined the school band earlier this year, and it had taken up a lot of her time, but she hadn't realized quite how much it seemed to have affected her daughter.

Jess kept her head bent as she replied in a muffled voice, "Pretty busy. She's got all her band friends now."

Had Jess and Sophie fallen out? Ellie wondered with alarm. Sophie had been her daughter's first friend at school; they'd proudly performed in the talent show together, and had been practically joined at the hip all through their first year here. Admittedly, she'd seen a little less of Sophie now that Jess was in year eleven, but she hadn't remarked on it too much, because her daughter seemed happy to hang out more with Mairi. But if Mairi wasn't available...

There was always something going on, Ellie acknowledged ruefully, and meanwhile she still didn't know what on earth Matthew had been talking about earlier. She just hoped she found out tonight.

CHAPTER 11

SARAH

It was the day of the photo shoot, and Sarah had taken the day off work to help Ellie with everything. She'd been at the inn all day Saturday and Sunday, as well, helping with the decorations, cobbling together crafts to show the photographer, wrapping empty boxes with lavish paper and ribbon to put under the Christmas tree that Matthew would take out once the shoot was over. It all felt like a lot of effort, Sarah reflected, not unkindly, and she wasn't sure what for yet, since they still didn't have any bookings for this much-feted Christmas week. It was starting to feel rather desperate. Not that she was going to say as much to Ellie. Like her sister-in-law, she really hoped this plan worked.

Yesterday Ellie had been practically manic in her determination to get everything done, and yet also strangely distracted. More than once, Sarah had asked her a question only to have Ellie startle and blink, asking her to repeat what she'd just said. Everyone had been too busy, bustling around, for Sarah to get to the bottom of what was going on, and in any case, she had her own worries. Mairi was more stressed than ever, and had backed out of doing the crafts with Jess, as well as taking care of Mabel. Sarah had been seeing to the horse every day, wanting to give her daughter a little breathing room, but also knowing they needed to have another talk about responsibility and consequences.

When she'd tried to broach the topic with Nathan, he'd seemed more or less unbothered by the development.

"If Mairi isn't interested in her horse anymore, then I suppose we could sell it," he'd remarked as he'd yanked off his tie. He'd come home from work on time for once, not that it had made much difference, since he'd spent the evening closeted in his study.

"*Her*," Sarah had returned a bit sharply. "It's a her, Nathan, not an *it*. Mabel, remember?"

He'd turned to give her a look that had said as plainly as if he'd spoken aloud, *Really?*

Sarah had done her best to curb her temper.

"The point is, we need to talk to her," she'd persisted. "She's getting far too stressed about exams, and she needs some balance in her life—"

"She also gets to decide her own priorities," Nathan had interjected, "and she's always been a sensible girl. Frankly, doing well at her GCSEs seems like a good priority to me, even if she is a bit stressed about it." He'd sounded reasonable, but also somewhat disinterested, even about his own children. When had this attitude started? Sarah had wondered. It wasn't new, she'd realized that much. He'd been acting like this for a couple of months, if not quite as obviously as he was now.

"But she has other commitments she has to honor," Sarah had continued. "Like doing crafts with Jess for the inn—"

Nathan had given her another one of those looks, and this time he'd accompanied it with the predictable response. "*Really?* You think gluing some glitter onto a leaf is more important than studying for her exams?"

Sarah had supposed she should take heart that he'd at least

listened to that part, because that was indeed what Mairi and Jess were doing, but he was still missing the point entirely.

"She said she'd do it," she'd told him. "Don't you want her to be a woman of her word?"

"Well, yes, of course, but maybe she didn't realize how demanding her studies would be. Isn't Jess in the same year? Why isn't she studying?"

"Jess is doing fine. Besides, it's only October, and kids don't need to be studying all the time."

Nathan had let out a huff of something almost like laughter. "That doesn't sound like something you'd say, Sarah," he'd remarked.

She'd sat down on the bed, slumping a bit, because she'd known he was right. It *hadn't* sounded like something she would normally have said. Usually, she was the one checking the time, making lists, telling Mairi she could get a quick half-hour of revision in before supper... what had changed? Was it her? She kept thinking everyone else was acting differently, but what if *she* was?

"I want my children to lead healthy, balanced lives," she'd stated quietly, and Nathan had given her a look of eloquent disbelief.

"Really?" he'd said—again—as he'd tossed his work shirt near—not in—the laundry hamper. "Because I always thought you wanted them to succeed, Sarah. I thought we both did."

"At what?" Sarah had fired back. She'd been trying to have a discussion, but it seemed poised to become an argument.

Nathan had shrugged as he'd pulled on his T-shirt for bed. "At everything," he'd replied simply, and Sarah had fallen silent because what, really, had there been to say to that? She'd known he was right—up to a point—but she also knew she didn't want that anymore. Not exactly, anyway, even if she would have in the past. "I thought you'd be cracking the whip, telling her to study more," he'd remarked in a careless kind of way as he climbed into bed and then reached for his phone to check it, its screen angled away from her. "That's what you usually do."

Sarah hadn't been able to reply, because once again she'd known he was right... and yet she hadn't wanted him to be. She didn't, she realized now as she pulled up to the Bluebell Inn, want to be that sort of person anymore. What it said about who she'd been, or what kind of person she wanted to be now, she had no idea. It was hard enough realizing she'd changed, or at least, *wanted* to change. And maybe no one else in her family was coming along for the ride.

Feeling glum at the prospect, Sarah climbed out of the car and headed inside, bracing herself for Ellie's usual state of panicked frenzy.

"She's in the sitting room," her mum whispered as she came into the kitchen. "It looks absolutely beautiful, but Ellie keeps twitching pillows and moving ornaments around on the tree. The journalist is meant to be here at ten."

It was only a little after nine now, which meant nearly a whole hour of keeping Ellie calm and upbeat. Sarah took a deep breath and let it out slowly.

"Are you all right, darling?" her mum asked softly.

"Yes. Why?" she replied, hearing how defensive she sounded.

Her mother shrugged and spread her hands in a gesture of apology. "You've just seemed a bit... distracted lately, I suppose. Maybe even a little... down?" She spoke hesitantly, the words almost an apology, and Sarah knew that if her mother had said something like this to her a few months, or even weeks, ago, she would have received a very terse reply in return, assuring her that she was absolutely fine, of *course* she was.

Now, thinking of how Nathan had spoken about her last night, the things he'd said so carelessly, not even considering how they might hurt... something in Sarah finally snapped, or maybe released, like a pressure being eased, or a balloon floating up to the sky. She was *tired* of keeping this all in. She didn't want to do it anymore.

"I have been distracted," she admitted. "And, frankly, a bit down, Mum, yes."

"Oh, Sarah." Her mother's face was wreathed in kindly concern that made Sarah's throat thicken and she had to swallow to ease the ache. "I'm so sorry. What's going on?"

"Nothing, really," she replied after a moment, when she trusted herself to speak normally. "That is, nothing I can say definitively. But Nathan..." Her throat started to thicken again, and she found she had to blink rapidly to keep the sudden tears at bay. *Oh, help.* She really didn't like this. She didn't like feeling so needy, so vulnerable, not top of her life at *all*.

"Oh, Sarah..." her mum said again, and then she found herself enfolded in her mother's arms, her head drawn to her shoulder, even though her mother was a good six inches shorter than she was.

Sarah let out a laugh rather like a hiccup and gave her mother a hug before she eased away, wiping at her eyes.

"Sorry. That took me by surprise."

"The hugs or the tears?" her mum asked rather shrewdly, and Sarah let out another laugh as she sank into a chair at the kitchen table.

"Both, really." She shook her head slowly. "I'm scared, Mum," she said so quietly she wouldn't have been sure her mother had heard, save for the widening of her eyes.

"Sarah, what—"

"Nathan..." She paused, glancing down at the table as she traced the worn grain of the wood with one finger. How many happy meals had she had at this table? How many board or card games, conversations filled with laughter... Her sense of bitter-sweet nostalgia morphed into something shrewder and more realistic. How many times had she sat here and done her home-work, books spread out, face screwed up into a focused frown?

How many times had she, as an adult, bolted a cup of tea that her mother had pressed on her, discreetly—or not so discreetly—glancing at her watch, thinking about the next oh-so important thing on her to-do list? How many times had she turned away from this table, claiming she didn't even have time to sit down at it at all?

"Sarah?" her mum prompted gently as she sat down opposite her, reaching out to clasp her hand. "What about Nathan? Is he... is he ill?"

Of course her mum would draw that conclusion, considering her own recent battle with cancer, as well as her kindly nature. She'd never assume the worst about someone, the way Sarah was struggling not to.

"Not as far as I know," Sarah replied with a sigh. "He's working all the time. He says he's pressed at work, trying to get some new client, and I believe him—at least I think I do... but it feels like something more is going on. Something he doesn't want me to know about."

She swallowed hard and then glanced up to see her mum looking more flummoxed than afraid.

"Don't know about?" she repeated, sounding as confused as she did incredulous. "What sort of thing do you mean?"

Annoyance, which felt slightly better than fear, needled her. "I don't know, Mum," she replied with another sound like a hiccup. "What do you think?"

Her mother shook her head slowly. "Sarah... you can't mean... you can't think..."

"I don't know *what* to think. I only know that Nathan is spending more time at the office than at home, and sometimes it feels as if he... as if he barely tolerates my presence." The truth of her words thudded through her; she hadn't let herself think it before, not properly, never mind actually say it aloud to someone else. To her mother. "Everything I do or say seems to annoy him, and maybe that's because *I'm* different, but it still feels like... like we're almost strangers to one another now."

"You're different?" Her mother frowned, picking the one part of her tearful confession that Sarah hadn't meant to let slip out. "What do you mean by that, Sarah?"

"I don't know." There was only so much a body could confess in one go, Sarah thought wearily. She had a feeling her mother was going to try to reassure her that Nathan was simply busy with work, and maybe distracted by it, and right now she wasn't sure she wanted to go down that well-worn route. It was the line she'd been feeding herself for months; she didn't need her mum to join in, as well. "Never mind," she finished, standing up as a way to end the conversation. "I'm probably just paranoid and tired. Don't listen to me."

"Have you talked to him about it—" her mum pressed, and Sarah shook her head.

"I've tried, but he just says it's work."

"Maybe it is just work—"

Just as she'd thought. "Never mind, Mum. Really. I'm fine."

Her mum gazed at her unhappily. "I feel like I've let you down," she murmured. "I'm sorry, Sarah. If your gut is telling you something is going on, then maybe something is going on."

Now that was unexpected and, Sarah realized, was far more unpalatable a thing for her mother to say than the tried and tired platitude about how he was just busy. She didn't want something to be going on.

And yet maybe something was... and she knew she had to face it.

"Hey!" Ellie popped her head into the kitchen with a bright smile. "Are you ready? The journalist is going to be here in half an hour!"

"Yes, amazing," Sarah replied in the same bubbly-bordering-on-manic voice Ellie had used. "What needs to be done? Everything looks fantastic, by the way." She avoided her mother's far too compassionate gaze as she followed Ellie out of the kitchen, toward the sitting room, which was decorated to within an inch of its life—lots of red and gold, with the occasional quirky—and really rather odd—accessory. "Is that the old tree Matthew got as a Secret Santa present one year?" Sarah asked with a huff of surprised laughter. Somehow, she hadn't clocked it before, amidst all the bustling around.

Ellie rolled her eyes. "Yes, I think it is." She glanced anxiously around the room. "Is it all a bit... too *much?*"

"No," Sarah replied, because even if it was, she wasn't about to say so to Ellie right now, with the photographers and journalists practically on their doorstep. "It looks lovely," she told her, which was true. The room looked amazing.

"Well, we'll see what the journalist thinks. I know it's not a patch on some of the really classy hotels—"

"But you always knew we could never aspire to that," Sarah reminded her, with a kind smile. "Right?"

"Yes..." Ellie didn't sound convinced.

"The guests who come here are looking for something else," Sarah reassured her. "Like the families who left yesterday. They loved the laidback vibe, the familiarity, the casualness of it all. That's what you need to aim for."

"I guess," Ellie said without too much enthusiasm. Sarah was only reminding her of what Ellie herself had said back at the beginning—so why, Sarah wondered, was she doubting herself now?

"I'm sure it will be great," she told her, and Ellie nodded, not looking at all confident.

Matthew came in then, seeming far more cheerful than his wife. "Everything ready? I just saw a car coming down the lane."

"Already?" Ellie squeaked, and Matthew pulled her into a quick one-armed hug.

"Relax, Ellie. However this goes, it's going to be okay."

"Easy for you to say," Ellie muttered, shooting him a rather pointed look as she pulled away from his relaxed embrace.

Sarah's eyebrows rose of their own accord. What on earth was *that* about?

Matthew met her gaze with a wry smile. "Some other things are going on," he said in a low voice as Ellie hurried to the front door. Sarah had no time to ask what those were.

A few seconds later, she heard a flurry of voices, plummy London tones that sounded strange here in little Llandrigg, and as Sarah and Matthew started forward, they met Ellie with a female journalist, early thirties and elegant, dressed in flowing trousers, a relaxed cashmere jumper, and a scarf thrown over one shoulder. She was followed by a male photographer in a T-shirt and dirty jeans, hoisting a camera.

"Susannah Ellington," the journalist introduced herself, holding out a manicured hand. "And Danny, my photographer. Why, isn't this so very... quaint," she continued, without waiting for either Sarah or Matthew to introduce themselves. She looked around the sitting room, wrinkling her nose a little. "So very... homely."

As much as that was the vibe they'd been going for origi-nally, Sarah had a sinking sensation in her gut. Already she had a feeling this wasn't going to go according to plan.

"Well, that's the idea, really," Ellie replied bravely. She'd clearly clocked the journalist's tone, as well. "There are plenty of posh hotels around, and we wanted to do something differ-ent. Imagine a staycation, but one where someone else does the dishes, the cooking, and the entertainment and activities are organized for you. Everything with a lovely, homegrown feel but in a new yet comforting space... the best of both worlds."

A flicker of interest passed over Susannah Ellington's face, and Sarah felt a rush of admiration for Ellie. She was certainly rising to the occasion.

"And that's what our guests have loved," Matthew chimed

in smoothly. "As you can see from the comments in our guest book out in the hall. Visitors have absolutely adored being cared for in a way that is both friendly and personalized, with all the thoughtful touches that you'd expect from a five-star hotel, but in the comfort of a house that really does feel like a family home... in all senses of the word."

Susannah's eyebrows lifted as a smile quirked her mouth. She looked impressed, if somewhat reluctantly so. "Why don't you give me the full tour," she suggested, "and then we'll take some photos."

Ellie and Matthew exchanged quick, relieved smiles as Gwen came into the room as if on cue, bearing a tea tray, complete with antique teapot, sugar bowl and creamer, and a plate of homemade flapjacks.

"I thought you might enjoy some refreshments while Ellie and Matthew talked you through the inspiration behind the Bluebell Family Inn," she said with a warm smile. "And then I'd be happy to talk to you about how it all started. After that, we'd love to take you on a tour."

Susannah looked both discomfited and charmed. "Why, thank you," she said after a moment. "That'll be lovely."

And she sat down, while Gwen, smiling serenely, poured her a cup of tea.

CHAPTER 12

GWEN

"I think that went all right, don't you?" Ellie asked as she brought the tea things into the kitchen.

The photographer and journalist had just left, after several tense but hopeful hours, having taken dozens of photos of the sitting room, the dining room, the garden, and one of the bedrooms upstairs that Ellie had done up in Christmas style, complete with a miniature Christmas tree with several luxuriously wrapped gifts underneath, bespoke chocolates on the pillows, and hot chocolate and marshmallow mix added to the little tea caddy. She really had given thought to all the extra touches... Gwen just hoped it had the desired result. She'd been encouraged by the morning's activity, if rather exhausted by it all, but she smiled at her daughter-in-law, who was looking more than a little frazzled, as she took the tray from her.

"Yes, I think so. Ms. Ellington warmed to us, it seemed!"

"Yes, it did seem as if she wasn't all that impressed at the beginning," Ellie replied with a grimace. "We're probably not a patch on all the big spa hotels she usually covers. Thank goodness Matthew came in with all his comments about a five-star hotel in a house that feels like a home."

"What was that I just heard?" Matthew remarked as he came into the kitchen with an easy smile. He seemed quite relaxed and upbeat compared to Ellie, Gwen thought. "Were you actually *complimenting* me?"

"I do it on occasion, you know," Ellie replied. The words were meant to be teasing, Gwen suspected, but the tone held a bit of a sting. As she saw Ellie give Matthew a rather tart look, which he returned equably, she wondered what lay beneath the slightly barbed exchange. She'd sensed a bit of unspoken tension between her son and his wife these last few days, and she wasn't sure if they were both simply stressed about saving the inn—Ellie more so than Matthew, admittedly—or if something else was going on.

And what about Sarah? Recalling her daughter's tearful confession this morning made Gwen's stomach hollow out with anxiety and concern. Did Sarah really suspect that Nathan was... well, Gwen didn't even want to put that thought into words. Surely not! Not *Nathan*. She'd always thought he was a good match for Sarah, even if she'd sometimes found him a little intimidating herself—he'd always been focused on work, unapologetic about his ambition, and perhaps slightly disdainful of those who didn't share his opinion or drive. She remembered him taking part in the parents' race at Mairi's sports day in primary school—he'd brought a pair of proper trainers, and had been close to exultant when he'd won by at least ten meters.

But then, that was a bit how Sarah was—or at least how she'd used to be. Just as ambitious, certain in her own views, striding ahead of everyone else with assertive confidence. Gwen wasn't entirely sure where her daughter had got such confidence from—certainly not her, and David, although opinionated, had been a fairly unassuming person. But Sarah had been determined to make her mark from the word go—even as a baby, she'd pushed Gwen's hands away when she was feeding her, attempting to grab the baby spoon herself when she was barely six months old. It wasn't a bad way to be, Gwen thought, and, in truth, she admired Sarah's certainty about what she wanted out of life. But if Sarah had somehow changed, had Nathan, too?

"When will the article appear, do you think?" Matthew asked, drawing Gwen back into the present.

"She said in two weeks," Ellie answered. "They move fast, it seems. And hopefully that will give us some bookings! It had better, since by then it will be mid-November." Gwen saw a shadow of worry creep into Ellie's eyes.

"I'm sure it will," she replied robustly. "Think of all the publicity!"

"There's also the brochures Emma made," Ellie continued, clearly trying to rally. "They're lovely and colorful. I'm going to start taking them to cafés and shops and things, get the word out." She sighed before she managed a smile. "Sometimes it feels like no more than a drop in the bucket, but I don't know what else we can do. We don't have any bookings for all of November."

"November's always a downtime, though, isn't it?" Gwen replied, determined to stay positive. "Lots of places close for the whole winter." Privately, she was glad; she could use the break, especially after the busy half-term week and all the ensuing bustle planning this Christmas holiday. And she'd like to see a bit more of John...

A few days ago, they'd hiked up Sugarloaf Mountain— John's suggestion and something Gwen would never have even thought of doing on her own. He'd brought a thermos of tea and she'd contributed some homemade flapjacks, and after walking up, they'd sat at the top, gazing over the hills rolling out to the horizon, white with frost, sipping tea and munching flapjacks and feeling, Gwen thought, completely at peace with the world.

John had come to the inn a few times over the last week, to work on the nativity set for the garden. He was making the simple pieces out of an old oak tree that had fallen at the bottom of the garden years ago, their smooth, easy shape perfect to be handled by children. Matthew had cut up some of the tree for firewood, but John had asked if he could use the rest and Matthew had, although only somewhat graciously, agreed.

Gwen wasn't sure what exactly was bothering her son about John's presence, but clearly something was, even if he was trying to hide his unease. He hadn't talked to her directly about John, and Gwen wasn't about to broach the subject herself, especially as she didn't know how she felt.

She enjoyed John's company, liked having him as a friend, but was anything more going on between them? Was she a foolish old woman even to think like that, especially when she was pretty sure John wasn't thinking that way?

Well, she was trying not to worry too much about it, and in any case, there was certainly enough to be getting on with—the Christmas week, Sarah's worries, and now this seeming tension between Ellie and Matthew.

"We could still get some bookings for November," Gwen offered, although she didn't think it likely. "Sometimes parents like to do holidays in term as they're usually cheaper...?"

"Maybe..." Ellie replied.

Matthew gave her a rather significant look. "What will be will be," he said philosophically, and Ellie merely pressed her lips together and looked away.

What was going on there? Gwen wondered. Did she dare ask?

"Right, I'm going to take down the decorations for now," Ellie said. "Because if I don't, Ben or Ava or even Daisy will get into them and the last thing I need is all that velvet ribbon tangled into knots or something. It wasn't cheap."

With a tired smile, Ellie turned from the room, and with her exit, a little tension left, as well, the air seeming to expand. Matthew gave a small sigh and shake of his head.

"What about you?" Gwen asked him. "What have you got going on today?"

"I'm going to work in the garden for a bit," he told her. "Tidy up the flower beds and keep at the Santa's grotto." He paused. "And then I have a Zoom call later this afternoon."

"A Zoom call?" Gwen asked in curiosity, noting the way he'd hesitated before he'd mentioned it. "Something about the inn?"

"No." Her son sounded strangely cautious. "About a job, actually. I've been approached by a firm... but I haven't wanted to say anything just yet, because it's very early days."

"A *job*?" Gwen couldn't hide her surprise. "You mean... like you had before? In finance?"

Uncomfortably, Matthew shifted where he stood, hands jammed into the pockets of his trousers. "Yes, as a matter of fact. I was approached by a boutique company I really respect. Out of the blue, really, but... I felt like I had to consider it."

Gwen heard a note of pride in his voice, and understood it. After being made redundant at his old company nearly three years ago, it had to be a balm to be approached and maybe even pursued by another. Still, it was a possibility that hadn't even crossed Gwen's mind.

"And where is this job?" she asked. "Cardiff? Birmingham?" She heard the wavering note of hope in her voice and knew before Matthew had even answered that it wasn't in either of those cities. There was a reason, after all, why he hadn't mentioned this before.

Matthew ducked his head. "Like I said, it's early days, Mum."

"Where is this job?" she asked again, and now she could hear her voice sounded a bit flat.

"New York City," Matthew admitted.

"*New York...*" Gwen felt a little faint.

Even in her worst imaginings, she hadn't thought about

Matthew and his family moving back to America. They'd only been here for a little over two years! She'd thought London, perhaps, or at worst, Manchester or somewhere up north. But New York? *America*? When he and Ellie had moved to Wales, she'd simply assumed it would be for good, or at least for a very long while—the rest of her life, at least! But now, after just two years, he was thinking of moving back? She could scarcely believe what she was hearing.

"It's a really good opportunity," Matthew continued, his enthusiasm obvious. "I wouldn't be a middle manager anymore, but on the forefront, developing investments. It's exactly the kind of thing I wished I could do before. I wouldn't be considering it otherwise."

"No, I don't suppose you would." Gwen found she had to sit down, and she carefully lowered herself into a chair at the kitchen table, her mind still reeling. Daisy roused herself from in front of the Aga to come and sniff at her feet, and Gwen bent down to stroke the little dog, grateful for that small comfort.

"Mum, it might not come off," Matthew told her. "In fact, it probably won't. This company is a new one, small and bespoke, but with a really good reputation. I've been out of the game for a while. I've told Ellie as much—"

"*That's* why Ellie has been cross with you," Gwen said aloud, and Matthew flinched.

"Not *cross*—"

"No, no," Gwen agreed quickly, "but I still sensed something between you. Is she not pleased about the potential move?" It seemed ironic, considering how reluctant Ellie had been to move to Wales in the first place.

"She's... concerned," Matthew replied carefully. "Understandably so. We're settled here now, the children especially, and it's not really the done thing to keep crisscrossing the ocean on a whim." He smiled crookedly. "Her words."

"Ah." Gwen could hardly blame Ellie for that sort of sentiment. A transatlantic move was a very big deal, and they'd done it once already, leaving everything behind to start afresh. If she were Ellie, she'd probably feel the same. "But she'd be so much closer to her parents," she acknowledged, her mind racing through the implications. "Don't they live right outside of New York?"

"Yes, they do, and that's something she has considered. She hasn't said no to the idea, not flat out, anyway, but she was taken aback by it. Understandably. It's a bit out of the blue."

A *bit*?

"Yes, I can imagine she was." Gwen sighed and leaned back in her chair. She felt rather tired, all of a sudden, what with all the news that had been coming at her, and the photo shoot this morning.

Daisy, having finished sniffing her feet, jumped up in her lap and settled there comfortably. Gwen fondled the dog's silky ears. Would they take Daisy with them to New York? Probably. And what about the inn? Admittedly, she hadn't been as bothered as she might have expected to be, to think about it having to close its doors, but that had been when she'd still thought she'd have her family around her, the house full of laughter and love. She felt bereft suddenly, in so many ways.

"Mum, don't worry, please," Matthew said, coming to sit next to her. "Like I said, it might not happen."

"I'm not worried," Gwen told him. "Not exactly. I am a bit surprised, of course. But you have to do what's best for your family, Matthew. I know that." She smiled at him, or tried to. "I will miss you, though, if you do go." A lump formed in her throat just at the thought, and she managed a slightly watery smile.

"And we'll miss you," he assured her, reaching over to squeeze her hand briefly. "But you do know it's an easy flight from New York? And Llandrigg is only a little over two hours from Heathrow."

Closer to three hours, but Gwen wasn't about to belabor the point. "And what about the inn?" she asked. "I won't be able to run it without you, not the way it currently is, anyway."

"I know." Matthew hesitated. "Obviously, I don't want to leave you in the lurch. If this Christmas idea of Ellie's comes off, and the inn becomes a going concern again, then I'll turn down the job—if it's even offered—and stay here. No question."

Gazing at the warmth and sincerity in her son's hazel eyes, Gwen knew he meant it. But could she really tie him to this place, if he had such a seemingly stellar job offer, especially when she'd already been thinking of retirement herself? Of course she couldn't, and she wouldn't want to.

"Well, let's cross that bridge when we come to it," she said after a moment, her hands buried in Daisy's fur as the dog nestled in her lap. "So, what is this call this afternoon? Is it terribly important?"

"It's an interview panel with the company's VPs. I've already had two rounds of interviews, and this is the third. If they want to proceed, the next step is to fly me to New York."

"My goodness." Gwen was still struggling to absorb this unexpected development. "When would that be?"

Matthew shrugged. "Could be November, could be January. It depends how quickly they want to move forward."

And how quickly did *Matthew* want to move forward? Gwen wondered. Would he or his family even be here after Christmas? She could barely get her head around the thought of them moving at all, never mind that quickly.

"I don't suppose you've told the children?" she asked, and he shook his head firmly.

"No, we don't want to get them worked up. If they fly me out to New York, we might have that discussion then."

"That makes sense." Gwen paused, unsure how to phrase the question that was bubbling up to her lips. "But Matthew, isn't it... isn't it a bit difficult, to pursue two such different paths at once?" How could Matthew really invest in the inn, with this tantalizing possibility in front of him? Not that she wanted to say as much outright.

"It has its challenges," her son replied easily, "but like I told Ellie, what will be, will be. If the job doesn't work out, then something else will come along, or we can redouble our efforts with the inn. It's been a good run these last few years, hasn't it?"

He made it sound like they'd flipped the "closed" sign on the door already.

"Yes, it has," Gwen admitted. "The last two years have been wonderful, in their own way." Despite the strain of her cancer battle, and the uncertainty of starting the inn up again. She'd so enjoyed having her son and his family around her. "They really have," she said and, again, felt a lump in her throat. She found she had to take a steadying, and rather ragged, breath.

"Mum." Once more, Matthew reached for her hand. "I won't leave if you don't want me to."

"I'd be a poor mother indeed, if I forced you to stay," Gwen replied, managing to inject a little needed tartness into her voice. "Anyway, as you said, it isn't for definite yet. Let's see what happens, with both this interview and the inn, before we make any decisions—or any promises." She smiled at him and patted his hand, and with an answering nod, he rose.

"Right, then. I'll make a start outside."

"All right."

She watched him go before she set Daisy back on the floor, and then started tidying up, more out of habit than anything else. Her mind felt as if it were buzzing and yet strangely empty at the same time. She rinsed the teacups in the sink, thinking how optimistic she'd felt just a few short hours ago, when she'd brought the tea tray into the sitting room, and the rather sniffy Susannah Ellington had started to seem impressed! Already it felt like it had happened to someone else, in a different lifetime.

For Matthew and his family to move all the way back to

New York... well, she'd still have Sarah here, Gwen reminded herself, and what with her troubles with Nathan, it might be that her daughter needed her support more than ever now. And if the inn closed, well, she'd been thinking of retirement anyway, and life was full of endings as well as beginnings—one ending led to another beginning, after all, or so she could try to tell herself.

But, right now, even as Ellie tidied up and Matthew worked on the garden, as they all made plans to make the inn a success, it might, Gwen acknowledged, all be for nothing. No wonder Ellie had looked so stressed!

Her phone pinged with a text and Gwen picked it up, her heart skipping a beat as she saw it was from John.

Izzy in labour!! Can't believe I'm going to be a grandad. Might be busy for the next few days but hope to see you soon x

The "x", Gwen couldn't help but note, was a new addition to their admittedly infrequent text messages. Did it mean anything? It seemed comically absurd to be wondering such things at almost seventy years of age.

Before she could overthink it, she typed a text back.

Amazing news! Being a grandparent is wonderful. Keep me posted x

She let out a shaky breath as she put her phone back on the counter. She didn't know if their little exchange was at all significant or not, but it had felt so, at least in the moment.

Standing at the sink, Gwen glanced out the window at the back garden; the apple trees looked scraggly now, their branches bare, the brown leaves swept into deep drifts beneath. Only a few weeks ago, they'd been full of color, and the windfall apples beneath had still been good to gather—now the ones she hadn't managed to collect were nothing but a mulchy pulp. Life moved on, Gwen knew, and sometimes very quickly.

The question was, how was it going to move on—not just for Ellie and Matthew, but for Sarah and Nathan? And, she thought with a funny little lurch of her heart, for her and John?

CHAPTER 13

ELLIE

TWO WEEKS LATER

Ellie clicked refresh on the internet browser with the sort of grim determination that felt pathological.

No new messages.

Well, could she really be surprised? She'd hit refresh less than a minute before, and in any case, the spread in the Sunday supplement wasn't out until this weekend; she really was putting all her eggs in one potentially dubious basket.

A sigh escaped her as she pushed back from the desk in the little office off the kitchen—really more of a broom cupboard— that was the inn's operating HQ. Outside, the trees were now devoid of leaves, thanks to a ferocious, wintry wind that had been blowing the last few days, and the world looked bare and brown underneath an iron-gray sky. The riotous and colorful beauty of fall had faded into winter, reminding Ellie that Christmas was just six weeks away. She'd seen Christmas decorations in Abergavenny already, the streetlamps festooned with lights, and a massive Christmas tree set to be put up in the square.

Ellie had been working hard the last ten days, since Susannah Ellington had come to interview them, dropping off brochures everywhere she could think of, posting on social media relentlessly, planning more Christmas activities and decorations—although for whom, she really wasn't sure. They still didn't have a single booking for their Christmas week—a fact that in mid-November was immensely dispiriting.

Maybe this just wasn't meant to be.

She knew it was Matthew's voice echoing inside her head. They hadn't talked much more about the bombshell he'd dropped on her nearly two weeks ago now—a job in New York! Moving *again*? Ellie had barely known how to feel about any of it, except hurt and a little angry that he hadn't thought to tell her before then.

"You really didn't think this was something to mention to me?" she'd asked that evening, when they'd finally had a chance to discuss what he'd hinted at during half-term. They'd been standing on either side of the bed in what amounted to a face-off, keeping their voices low in case the children overheard. It was at times like this Ellie wished they had a proper house, rather than a couple of rooms in her mother-in-law's attic.

"I wasn't trying to be secretive," Matthew had replied in an irritatingly reasonable voice. "I just didn't want to cause anxiety or put pressure on you, when you've been working so hard to get this Christmas idea going."

"And yet that's *exactly* what you've done," Ellie had returned, unable to keep an edge of bitterness from sharpening her voice. "Matthew. *New York*?" She'd shaken her head, overcome with emotion.

"It would be close to your parents," he'd reminded her, his tone turning coaxing. "They're only half an hour outside the city."

At that thought, a sudden, bittersweet pang of longing and

nostalgia had assailed Ellie, taking her by surprise. To be close to her parents again, closer even than they had been before. They could stop by after school, or on weekends... She'd missed seeing them, since moving to Wales, and they weren't getting any younger. She loved the possibility of being able to see them more, and yet...

Move, all the way across the ocean? Leave everything they'd worked for here—not just with the inn, but friends and family, as well? And start over somewhere new, since they wouldn't be moving back to Connecticut, where they'd lived before coming to Wales. It felt like far too much to process.

"Do you really want to do this?" she'd asked, slumping onto the bed. "Start over, *again*? And with the kids, too? New schools, new friends..." How would any of their four take to that? She really hadn't known.

"I'm not sure," Matthew had admitted, sitting next to her on the bed. "I'm not gunning for it, if that's what you mean. Yes, the job is exciting, and I miss that kind of work more than I expected to. Working on the inn has been fun, and to be honest, I think I needed the break from the pressure—as well as the disappointment. You know how my redundancy hit me pretty hard." He'd grimaced, and Ellie had reached for his hand.

"Yes," she'd said quietly. "I know."

He'd held her hand in his, turning over her palm, gently stroking her fingers and reminding her that they were a team, not on opposite sides as she'd sometimes felt. If Matthew had a genuine desire to go for this job, she needed to hear him out... even if her initial instinct had been to clap her hands over her ears.

"Maybe I should have told you from the beginning," he'd said quietly. "And I'm sorry that I didn't, especially if you feel that I should have. I genuinely didn't want to stress you out. That was the only reason, I promise."

"I know." She couldn't blame him for not telling her, Ellie had acknowledged. Matthew knew how her mind worked—usually around a million miles per hour. If he had mentioned a job, she would have been imagining them already over there, and then fretted about the children and schools and whether she could make new friends a *third* time. As she'd already been doing, actually, since he'd told her.

"If this isn't something you can get on board with," Matthew had stated, "and maybe you need to think about it for a bit, I want you to know I'm willing to let it go." His gaze had turned both tender and earnest as he squeezed her hand. "I mean it, Ellie. I let my redundancy drive us apart for a little while, and that is a huge regret for me."

"Oh, Matthew—" She'd shaken her head, not wanting to revisit those bleak times, yet knowing he was right. It *had* driven them apart, briefly at least, but they'd found their way back to each other, and that was what was important.

"I mean it," he insisted, "I'm not about to make the same mistake twice. Yes, I'm excited about this job. I'll be honest and admit that. But it's not my everything. It doesn't need to be, and I don't want to up and move if it's not the right thing for you and the kids, as well as for me."

And yet, Ellie had thought, he'd spoken as if it *was* the right thing for him. As if he already knew that.

She'd sighed and risen from the bed, reaching for a stack of folded laundry, and putting it away simply because she'd needed something to do. She'd ached with tiredness, from working all hours on the inn's Christmas plans, and also because Ava had been wetting the bed more nights than not. Ellie hadn't known what was going on with her youngest child, but she'd planned on making an appointment with the GP just in case.

"I don't know whether it is or not," she'd told him as she'd moved around the room, opening and closing drawers as she put clothes away. "It's a lot to take in. But..." She'd turned to face him, her arms now empty. "Are you not happy here, Matt?"

"I *am* happy here," he'd protested, and then given a slight grimace. "But it doesn't always feel like... enough. When the inn's full it's great, there's lots to do, and I like being busy. And if we had more money for the kind of projects I'd envisioned—a swimming hole, an art studio in one of the barns—then maybe I'd feel a bit more... invigorated. But, as it is, it feels as if we're just scraping by, lurching from one day to the next, barely making ends meet."

"Yet you were the one who said most operations like this don't have much in the bank!" The words had burst out of her, almost of their own accord, like an accusation.

"That's true," Matthew had replied, back to using his reasonable voice. "And I don't mind keeping things close to the bone, if need be. I just want to see a future here."

"And you don't think there's a future for the inn?" She'd heard how despondent she'd sounded. She'd wondered if he was right.

"I don't know," Matthew had admitted quietly.

Ellie had taken a deep breath, let it out slowly. "Okay," she'd said, thinking through it as she formed the words. "Okay. I will seriously consider this job opportunity for you, but I want you to do the same for me."

"What—"

"I want you to put your *whole heart* into this Christmas week," Ellie had continued staunchly. "I know you've been working on it, Matthew, but you haven't put your heart into it, have you? Be honest about that."

He'd hesitated, looking as if he wanted to argue the point, but then with a small, apologetic smile, he'd nodded. "All right. That's fair, I suppose."

"So, we give this all we've got," Ellie had continued, "and see if we can make this Christmas week work, if it gives the inn the boost it needs. And if it doesn't... well, then, we go out with a bang and we look at what New York has to offer."

He'd smiled, rising from the bed, and walking over to enfold her in his arms.

"Deal," he'd said softly, and Ellie had hugged him back, grateful they'd worked it out, that they were still on the same side, after all.

Since then, Matthew had had another interview—on the same day as the photo shoot—and it had, according to him, gone well. He was still waiting to hear about whether he'd be asked to visit New York, and until he did, Ellie had resolved not to fret or even think about it. There was enough to be getting on with.

Unfortunately, her mind kept wandering to the what-ifs anyway.

With a frustrated sigh, she clicked on refresh again. This time there was a new email in the inn's business inbox—from Susannah Ellington. Ellie's breath caught in her throat as she clicked to open the message.

Dear Ellie,

Wanted to give you a sneak peek of the article! Hope it brings you lots of bookings.

–S

That sounded promising, Ellie thought, her stomach tightening with nerves as she waited for the PDF of the article to load.

Then it did, and her breath came out in a surprised—and pleased—rush. The photos looked really good, she acknowledged with a ripple of pleasure. The roaring fire, the Christmas tree, even her silly throw pillows! It created a homely vision of what Christmas could be. She could almost picture a guest relaxing on the sofa with a glass of mulled wine and a mince pie, Christmas carols playing, lights twinkling on the tree...

She started reading the accompanying text.

At first glance, the Bluebell Inn, in the tiny hamlet of Llandrigg, in South Wales, looks as if it has seen better days.

Ouch. Ellie winced, her stomach cramping. That was definitely not the opening she'd been hoping for.

She forced herself to keep reading.

Upon stepping over the threshold, however, I realized I'd come across something truly special. Warm, welcoming, and just a touch shabby, walking into the inn feels like coming home—except you don't have to cook, clean, or do any work. Inn owner and resident baker Gwen Davies puts you instantly at ease, and her scones are melt-in-the-mouth delicious. Meanwhile, her son Matthew and wife Ellie work hard to make guests feel welcome, and their Christmas week looks sure to be full of thoughtful touches as well as homely comforts.

Okay, that was better. A lot better. Ellie could have done without the shabby remark, but she supposed it was more or less fair, and overall, the tone of the article was positive, focusing on the warmth of the place, the homegrown comforts and the sense of welcome.

She continued reading, trying not to take the occasional slightly barbed comment to heart.

While the inn retains a slight datedness, there can be no doubt that it could be a wonderful place to spend your Christmas, free from the concerns and cares that often burden this holiday season, if you stay at home. While you won't be receiving five-

star hotel treatment, you just might be getting something better.

Well, it could be worse, Ellie told herself bracingly, and ultimately the article was recommending the inn. She could certainly take encouragement from that, and yet it wasn't—there could be no denying it, she knew—the glowing review she'd been hoping for. But maybe it had been foolish to hope for such a thing, just as it had been to try to turn the Bluebell Inn into some sort of luxury hotel experience when it so obviously wasn't, and never would be, just as Matthew had said. Just as she had said, once.

Ellie sighed and shook her head. Why did she have to keep learning the same thing, over and over again? And would anyone in the world book to stay here, based on that positive—yet less than effusive—review? It was hard not to feel dispirited, just as it was hard not to hope. She was caught between the two, unsure whether to jack it all in or keep on trying.

"Cup of tea?" Gwen asked, popping her head around the doorway. "I was just about to put the kettle on." Her gaze narrowed as she took in the computer screen, the photo of the sitting room on display. "Is that—"

"Yes, the article. Susannah sent it ahead of the weekend."

Gwen frowned. "You don't sound entirely pleased about it."

"I don't know what to be," Ellie admitted. She angled the screen toward Gwen, and then pushed back from the desk to give her room to read. "Have a look."

"Okay..." Gwen stepped closer, slipping on the spectacles she wore on a chain around her neck to read the text. Her forehead furrowed as she scanned the lines, muttering under her breath, which, despite everything, made Ellie smile. "Better days... shabby... datedness!" She glanced at Ellie, looking affronted. "I don't think the inn is dated. Not anymore."

"Well, we didn't change that much in the end, with the

renovations, did we?" Ellie replied, trying to be pragmatic. "Some new linens and another bathroom, but the carpet runner in the hall, for example, is still the same."

Gwen drew herself up. "Yes, and that's an antique! But antiques aren't *dated*."

Her mother-in-law looked so put out that, improbably, Ellie found her lips twitching and she gave a sudden, surprising guffaw of laughter.

Gwen's eyebrows rose, and for a second she looked as icily imperious as a queen, only to suddenly collapse into giggles, which made Ellie laugh again, even harder this time.

Soon, they were both laughing, tears streaming from their eyes, hands wrapped around their middles. Ellie wasn't even sure what they were laughing about, or if there was anything to laugh about in the first place. All she knew was it felt good to laugh, like a muscle that had needed to be stretched—it hurt, just a little, but it also brought relief.

"Goodness," Gwen said, wiping her eyes, when they finally started to subside. "I think I needed that."

"I think I did, too," Ellie admitted.

"Ultimately, it's positive," Gwen stated, sounding as if she were trying to convince herself. She glanced at Ellie. "Really."

Another bubble of laughter escaped her, and Ellie found herself again collapsing into giggles—or maybe hysteria—a distinct possibility. She pulled herself back from the brink just in time. "Yes, it is," she agreed. "And that's the important thing. Whether it brings in any more bookings..."

A sudden ping from her computer had them both turning back to the screen. Ellie clicked back on the inbox, a ripple of incredulous hope rippling through at the sight of a new email with the subject header *Booking Inquiry*.

"That was fast," she murmured dazedly, as she clicked on the link. "Maybe...?"

Gwen leaned forward. "What does it say?"

Ellie scanned the few lines, hardly able to believe it. "It says they're interested in booking for the Christmas week... a family of four! How...? The article hasn't even been published yet."

"Maybe from one of your brochures?" Gwen suggested, just as another email pinged into the inbox, this time with the subject header *Reservation Requested*.

"I don't believe this!" Ellie exclaimed. She clicked on the message. "It's a request for a family with a baby—for Christmas! At this rate, we'll be full in the next five minutes!" And she almost started laughing again.

"Look, they've said they've read the article." Gwen pointed to the last line of the email. "Did it go online early or something?"

"It must have done. Wow, even I wasn't hoping for results *that* fast."

"Especially since the inn is so shabby," Gwen returned, pursing her lips, and then they did both start laughing again.

This time, at least, Ellie thought, there was definitely something to laugh about. Two bookings in the space of a few minutes! It felt too good to be true, and yet it was. Her plan was actually, amazingly, *working*.

"I think this calls for a celebratory cup of tea," Gwen announced, heading back into the kitchen. "And a scone."

"With butter and jam!" Ellie called. She might even have two...!

She hit refresh on the inbox, just in case a third booking had come in, but there were no new messages. Well, still, two bookings, and the article hadn't even been published in the paper yet. That was a good start, indeed, better than she'd ever expected, even in her wildest hopes. Well, maybe not her wildest... In her flights of fancy, she'd envisioned guests storming down their doors, booking out the place for the next three years. But this really was very good.

"Tea's ready!" Gwen called, just as Ellie's mobile phone

rang. Half-wondering if it could be another booking, she answered it merrily, only to falter when she heard the serious tone of the school secretary.

"Mrs. Davies? This is Gwent Comprehensive calling. The headteacher would like you to come in as soon as possible to talk about Ben."

CHAPTER 14

SARAH

"No Mairi today?"

Sarah glanced up from Mabel's glossy flank, curry comb in hand, as she gave Trina a grimacing sort of smile. "Mock exams this week, I'm afraid. They're taking up all her time."

Trina cocked her head, her gaze sympathetic yet also shrewd. "I don't think I've seen her here for a few weeks at least?" she asked, not unkindly.

Sarah let out a sigh as she put down the comb, giving Mabel's flank one last stroke. She'd enjoyed these few minutes at the stables; a sense of calm always came over her here as she breathed in the smell of hay and horse, listened to Mabel's soft nickering. "No, you haven't," she agreed. "She's been very stressed about her exams... too stressed, really, I think." No matter how many times she tried to talk to Mairi about it, reassure her that she was going to do fine, it only seemed to wind her daughter up more.

"Oh, *right*!" Mairi had screeched at her last night, "as if you want me to get all *sixes* or something!"

"Sixes are decent marks—"

"No, they're *not!*" Mairi had stormed, flouncing out of the room. "Dad doesn't think so," she added as she ran up the stairs, slamming her bedroom door. Sarah had stood there, reeling both from Mairi's over-the-top reaction, as if she had said something completely objectionable and offensive, and the remark about Nathan that she'd flung at her. *Dad doesn't think so?* Had Nathan said as much?

She'd tried to talk to him about it—*again*—but he hadn't shared her concerns.

"All I was trying to say to Mairi, is that she can do much better than a six," he'd stated, as if her grade was actually the issue, and not the pressure she was putting on herself—and that Nathan, it seemed, was putting on her, as well. "She's predicted all nines, remember, Sarah. That's ten A stars. Why settle for a six?"

"I know what a nine is," Sarah had replied, for although the marking system had changed from letters to numbers fairly recently, it wasn't hard to figure it out. "It's not about her marks, Nathan, but her attitude. Her mental health."

"A little stress is a mental health issue?" he'd challenged, his eyebrows raised. "Then I should be signed off work for six months."

"Maybe you should," she'd replied, meaning it—sort of—but Nathan had just huffed and shaken his head, as if she'd made a joke, and a poor one, at that.

"Too stressed?" Trina prompted now, raising her eyebrows. "How so?"

"Just tetchy all the time, really."

Although Sarah feared it was more than that. Mairi was looking so pale and strained recently—dark circles under her eyes, nails bitten to the quick. And the other day, when she'd been putting her dishes in the sink, Sarah had thought she'd glimpsed a red mark on her inner forearm that had sent alarm bells pealing. But when she'd asked Mairi about it, her daughter had snapped at her.

Sarah had decided to leave it, at least then, but the memory of that brief glimpse had her stomach knotting with anxiety now. She didn't want her daughter to be this pale shadow of herself, worried half to death, anxious and unhappy. She just didn't know what to do about it.

And as for Nathan... well, she didn't even have the energy to *think* about Nathan right now. Work continued to be busy—or so he said—and Sarah was losing hope that it would ever calm down. Owen had stopped asking his dad if he'd kick a football around with him, and Nathan hadn't even seemed to notice his son's disappointment. Between worrying about Mairi's stress and Owen's grumpiness, Sarah couldn't summon the energy—or emotion—to consider the state of her marriage.

Her mum had tried to broach the subject again, but Sarah had shut her down swiftly, choosing to focus on the inn's burgeoning prospects instead. The article had come out in the Sunday supplement, and while it was definitely a mixed review as far as Sarah could tell, it still seemed to have done the trick. The Christmas week was already fully booked, and Ellie was ecstatic—as well as anxious. There was still a lot of work to do, to make the week a success, even by the article's so-called shabby standards. Sarah was glad to get involved and pitch in as much as she could. It kept her from having to mope around home, worrying about everything else, and she enjoyed seeing the inn come to Christmassy life.

The Santa grotto and nativity scene in the garden were taking shape, and her mother was baking around the clock, freezing masses of Christmas cookies—linzer stars and gingerbread, mint meringues and buttery cut-outs. Sarah and Ellie had tackled the reception rooms, sprucing things up and planning the decorations Ellie had bought, along with a few homemade ones "as accents." The other day, Sarah had put on some

Christmas carols, and they'd sung along as they'd worked, which had cheered them both up immeasurably. It was hard to stay anxious while singing "Rocking Around the Christmas Tree."

"Well, riding Mabel could be good for Mairi," Trina advised Sarah with a smile. "Great therapy, or so the Riding for the Disabled program tells me."

"How is all that going, anyway?" Sarah asked. "You said you were thinking about retiring a few weeks ago, weren't you?" She hoped Trina might have changed her mind.

"Yes." Trina paused and then admitted, "I've decided to put the stable yard up for sale, actually. I'm going to send an email out to all current clients, but I'm trying to tell as many as I can personally."

"Oh, Trina..." Sarah looked at her in dismay. She had really hoped it wouldn't come to this and she was sorry for her friend, because she knew how much this place meant to her, having taken it over from her mother.

Trina shrugged and smiled, doing her best to be philosophical. "It happens."

"If you sell it... will the new owners keep it going, do you think?"

She shook her head. "I'm afraid not. I took some financial advice and it's not worth it to sell it as a business, so I'm just offering the land. Who knows what someone will do with it... it's not that big, so they might make it private. But, like I said, you don't need to worry. There are a couple of farms around here that offer stabling."

"At this point, I don't know if we'll even keep Mabel," Sarah admitted with a sad sigh. "The way Mairi's lost interest recently..."

Trina's expression softened. "Maybe you should keep Mabel for yourself."

"Maybe," Sarah agreed, although she wasn't really sure she

could justify the expense. And yet she loved Mabel, and being with her was a sort of therapy. She felt calmer now than she had when she'd arrived, her scattered thoughts pinging around like they were in a pinball machine. A few minutes with Mabel had grounded her in a way nothing else did. "And what about the Riding for the Disabled program?" she asked Trina.

"They'll have to go to Chepstow, unfortunately."

"That's too bad," Sarah murmured, and Trina nodded her agreement.

"Sometimes," she said, "you don't have a choice in these matters."

Sarah was still thinking about Trina and the stables as she headed home later that afternoon, the evening already drawn in, the sky darkening. On a night like tonight, with the air so chilly and still, it was easy to believe Christmas was just a little more than a month away, especially now that the decorations had gone up in shops, festive lights strung out along the high street.

As she pulled into her drive, she simply sat in the driver's seat for a moment, steeling herself for the evening ahead—dealing with Mairi's anxiety and anger, helping her to study, while also prying Owen off his games console and trying to engage him in family life. Making dinner, doing laundry, tidying up as she went along, all the while waiting for Nathan to come home and most likely closet himself in the study for another evening of solitude and silence. The prospect made her feel defeated before she'd even begun.

I don't want my life to be like this, Sarah realized with a jolt. This wasn't just a wave in an otherwise untroubled sea; it was everything. She didn't want to live this way, trudging through life, cleaning up other people's messes, doing her best to seem in control. She didn't want to *be* this way. In the past, she wouldn't have stood for any of it. She would have told Mairi to get herself under control, made some study cards and bought some revision guides, considered the whole thing sorted. She would have confronted Nathan, snapped at him to make more of an effort, done and dusted. Neither of those would work now, she knew, and moreover, she didn't even want to attempt them.

Somehow, over the last few years, she'd changed—for better as well as for worse. She didn't want to be that overly ambitious and assertive woman who was secretly pleased people seemed intimidated by her anymore, and yet she still wanted to take control of her life.

How?

The front door opened and Owen stood there, looking gangly and uncertain as he peered out into the darkness.

"Mum?" he called. "Are you coming inside?" A pause, and then he added a bit plaintively, "I'm hungry."

With a sigh, Sarah opened the car door.

Everything in the house was just as she'd expected it to be—toast crumbs littering the kitchen worktops, along with an open jar of jam, a pack of butter, and two knives smeared with both. The milk had been left out by the kettle, and the lid of the sugar bowl was left off, with sticky grains of sugar scattered everywhere. It wasn't all that much, and she could clear it up in two minutes, but all the same it felt more dispiriting than, Sarah knew, was warranted.

"Owen, were you the one who had toast?" she asked, and he ducked his head.

"Yes—"

"Please clean up after yourself," Sarah told him crisply, before calling for Mairi. "You've left the milk out and the sugar all over the counter, Mairi," she said in a mild yet firm voice as her daughter slouched downstairs. "Please tidy it up, and then we'll think about tea."

"I have homework, you know," Mairi reminded her as she

brushed the sugar onto the floor—not exactly tidying up—and hurled the spoon into the sink.

"Revision does not preclude responsibility," Sarah replied. "Quite the opposite." She handed her daughter the broom and dustpan. "That's for the sugar that you just spilled onto the floor," she added pleasantly.

Mairi let out a howl of something almost like an anguish. "You're so *mean*—"

"I'm not," Sarah replied steadily. She was glad she was finally being firm. It felt good to get a little bit of herself back, if not the fundamentals. Those, she knew, had truly changed. "After you've tidied up," she suggested, "why don't we go out for dinner? Pizza Express has a midweek deal on. You can bring your revision and I'll test you while we wait for our pizzas."

Mairi looked surprised—Sarah had never been a proponent for this kind of extravagance—and Owen asked hopefully, "Is Dad coming?"

"I'll text him right now and ask him to meet us there," Sarah promised, slipping out her phone. She glanced at Mairi, smiling to soften her earlier sternness. "What do you say?"

"All right," Mairi said quietly, and then gave her mother a sheepish look. "Sorry, Mum."

Nathan didn't come to Pizza Express. He didn't even text Sarah back, which felt ominous. Still, she rallied for the sake of her children, and they all had a good time, with Mairi's mood brightening when she got all her German vocab right when Sarah tested her.

"You're going to be fine," Sarah assured her as they walked out to the car afterward. "But, more importantly, you're doing your best, and that's all you can do, whether that's a six or a nine or even a two or three. The number doesn't matter, Mairi."

Mairi shot her a funny, uncertain look. "This doesn't sound like you, Mum."

"Doesn't it?" Sarah knew it didn't. Like Nathan, she once would have been cheering Mairi on to get all nines, insisting that she was capable of it. *If you just put in a little effort, Mairi, you can get the grades you deserve.* "Well, I clearly don't need to put pressure on you, because you're doing that all by yourself, and I don't like to see it, sweetheart. You're sixteen, and life is short."

Mairi nodded, not looking at her, and as she reached for the handle of the car door, her coat sleeve slid up and Sarah spotted that livid red line again on her wrist. This time there could be no pretending she hadn't seen it, or that it might be something else. Gently, she took hold of her daughter's arm; Mairi froze for a second and then tried to pull away.

"Mairi," Sarah said, keeping her voice low. Owen was already in the car, but she wanted to make sure he couldn't overhear. "You've been harming yourself."

Mairi didn't bother to deny it. "It's no big deal," she said, yanking her arm away from Sarah's grasp. "Everybody does it. It's just a way to deal with stress. I won't do it again."

Was that what her daughter really thought? Sarah felt a wave of unbearable sadness sweep over her. *I don't want to live this way.* And she didn't want Mairi to live like this, either.

"We'll talk about it later," she said, hoping it sounded more like a promise than a threat. "I want to help you, Mairi."

Her daughter didn't reply as she threw herself into the car, closing the door behind her with a slam.

Back at the house, Mairi disappeared upstairs to revise, and Owen went to have a shower. Nathan still wasn't home, and Sarah busied herself mindlessly tidying up the family room before she decided what she really needed was a glass of wine.

She opened a bottle from the dusty wine rack in the pantry and rather recklessly poured herself a large glass. She wasn't much of a midweek drinker, but she found she needed a little Dutch courage for what came next.

She was halfway through her drink, sipping slowly, when Nathan opened the front door twenty minutes later. It was past eight o'clock, and he hadn't texted her about dinner—or anything else.

His footsteps sounded cautious, almost as if he were tiptoeing. She knew the exact moment when he paused by the study door in the hall, wondering, no doubt, if he could slip in there without her noticing. Mairi and Owen were still upstairs; the house was so quiet, Sarah fancied she could hear him breathing.

"I'm in the family room," she called out, her voice sounding strange to her own ears—friendly, yet also flat.

After another few seconds' pause, Nathan walked into the kitchen, standing at the island as he took in the sight of her sitting on the sofa, wineglass aloft.

"Hard day?" he asked, and Sarah turned to gaze at him.

There he was, her husband of twenty years, looking so familiar and yet also like a stranger. Rumpled hair, rumpled suit, bags under his eyes, lines of strain by his nose and mouth—was it really *just* work that was keeping him out so often, making him so distant? And, if it was, should she try to be more understanding?

And yet she'd been understanding for nearly a year, and things between them had only become worse.

"It's been as hard as most others," she replied, and took another sip of wine. "Because they've all been quite hard these last few months, Nathan—not that you've cared or even noticed."

Nathan let out a weary sigh as he raked a hand through his hair. "Do we have to do this now, Sarah—"

"Do what?" Sarah asked, genuinely curious. "What are we

doing, Nathan? Because I'd love it if you could tell me the truth, and not fob me off about how busy work is."

"Work is busy—"

"I know. I *know*." She straightened where she sat, putting her wineglass on the coffee table as she looked at him with a mixture of earnestness and despair. "But something else is going on, and I wish you'd just tell me what it is. You're home late nearly every night, you barely talk to me or the kids, you can't even rouse yourself to reply to a text—"

"Is this about Pizza Express? Because by the time I saw it, I'd figured you'd already gone and come back. There didn't seem to be any point."

"No point even in *replying*? In letting us know you're sorry you couldn't make it?" Sarah shook her head slowly. "It would have been good if you'd been there, you know. Owen was disappointed you didn't come, and Mairi—" Her voice caught. "Mairi's been cutting herself, Nathan."

His eyes widened. "Cutting—"

"Yes, you know, self-harm? Teenaged girls often do it—take a razor blade or something and slice their skin open." A shudder went through her. "And Mairi's doing it, because she's so stressed."

For the first time, she saw what looked like true remorse cross her husband's face. "I had no idea. I'm so sorry." He blew out a breath. "What can we do?"

It was the first *we* she'd heard in a long time.

"I think we should talk to her together. It could help a lot if you told her you didn't need her to get all nines, because she cares what you think. She told me so."

"I didn't mean for her to—"

"I know, but she did." Sarah softened her tone. "We need to rethink our priorities, Nathan."

His face hardened once more. "You mean I need to rethink mine."

"For the sake of our children?" If not her, being the unhappy implication. "Yes." He didn't reply and she continued, the words settling right into her bones, "Sometimes I feel like you don't think about us much at all. It isn't even that you don't care," she paused, as the truth reverberated through her. "It's that you don't even *think* about caring anymore. Why is that, Nathan? What's changed?"

He let out another sigh as he gazed around the darkened room, almost as if he were looking for someone else to help him out, but there was no one there, no one but the two of them—and the truth. Whatever it was, Sarah knew she was ready for the truth at last. She needed to hear it, even if it hurt.

"Please just tell me!" she implored in a low voice. "Whatever it is. I'd rather know than not know, at this point."

Nathan stood there for a moment, not saying anything, and then, with slow, deliberate steps, he walked over to the big armchair in the corner of the room and sank into it, his head falling into his hands.

Sarah gazed at him—the slump of his shoulders, his lowered head—and felt her stomach knot with anxiety. She'd told him she wanted to know, but now she wasn't sure she actually did.

"Nathan..." she said softly, and he lifted his head, looked at her wearily.

"I'm not having an affair, if that's what you think," he told her. "Because I can see in your face that that's what you were afraid of."

Something in Sarah eased, just a little, at the same time something else tightened up. The tone he'd used wasn't a reassuring one. It was one that said there was something else—but what?

"Okay," she replied after a moment, when he hadn't said anything else.

"I'm just *tired*," Nathan told her, and the throb of emotion in his voice took her by surprise. He almost sounded as if he were near tears. "Tired of everything."

"Everything...?" Sarah repeated cautiously.

"Work. Life." He paused and then stated with a certain deliberateness, "Us."

Sarah went completely still, but she felt as if she'd been knocked back, was staggering around. Us. It was a simple yet scathing indictment.

"So, what are you saying?" she asked quietly, when she trusted herself to speak. She felt empty inside, or maybe just numb. "About... about us?"

"I don't know." He scrubbed his hands over his face, and then ran them through his hair. "I think... I think I need a break."

A break? Sarah felt as if she'd been handling the home front pretty much singlehandedly, and now Nathan needed a break— from what? Her? His family?

She swallowed down the angry words that were bubbling up and kept her voice measured as she asked, "What kind of a break?"

"I think I need to move out for a bit."

The way he said it, in a tone of resolve, of acceptance, made Sarah feel as if he'd been thinking about it for some time. This wasn't a new idea—not to him, at least. It certainly was to her.

"But what about Mairi and Owen?" she asked, her voice rising. "We were just talking about tackling Mairi's issues together. Are you going to bail on that? On being a father?"

"No." He looked up at her, his eyes wide, his expression turning anguished. "I don't... I don't want to, Sarah, but I feel like I can't go on as I am. I'm not sleeping, I have panic attacks, sometimes I feel as if I can't breathe—"

"Why didn't you tell me any of this before?" she demanded. She wanted to feel sympathetic, but Nathan had been treating her as if she was to blame for his issues, rather than someone who could help him with them. "Nathan?" she pressed.

He dropped his gaze, shaking his head. "I don't know. I've felt like... like you're part of the problem."

Sarah recoiled, absorbing the awfulness of his statement.

"I don't mean that unkindly," he added, and she let out a hard huff of laughter. How could he possibly *not* mean that unkindly? "I'm sorry," he said. "I really am. I just... I can't do this anymore."

"Do what?" she made herself ask. "Marriage? Family life?"

He closed his eyes. "I know how it sounds. And how you're making me feel—"

"So it's *my* fault?" She was practically screeching.

"No, I don't mean that." He blew out a breath, his head dropping into his hands. "It's really my fault. I'm the one who is feeling this way. I just... I just need some time to get my head around... around everything."

She didn't like the sound of that at all. "What's changed, Nathan?" she asked quietly. "For you? Why has everything got so much?"

"I don't know. Maybe I'm having a midlife crisis." He smiled grimly, although Sarah didn't think he was far off. What else could this be? "I just wake up in the morning and think about going to work, and then going home again, over and over, and I feel like I just... can't."

Sarah felt a flicker of sympathy, no more. "Everybody feels that way sometimes, Nathan."

"I've felt that way every day for nearly a year, Sarah. I'm sorry, but I really do need a break." He was back to being intractable, defiant.

A break? What on earth was that supposed to mean? What kind of break, and how long for? "So, what are you saying?" She made herself ask the question as if what he'd said was reasonable, when, in truth, she felt like screaming, swearing, flying at him. He was allowed to have a midlife crisis and she wasn't? Basically, he could be as selfish as he liked and she'd have to be the one to hold their family together, *still*.

"I'm saying," Nathan replied, and now he sounded completely final and firm, "I'm going to move out. I'll explain to Mairi and Owen later, and we can talk to Mairi about her exams, but I think I should leave tonight."

CHAPTER 15

GWEN

TWO WEEKS LATER

"John, they're simply beautiful."

Gwen gazed admiringly at the finished nativity pieces, shaking her head in wonder. It was heading into late November, and things with the inn were really starting to shape up in an exciting way, ahead of a Christmas week that was now fully booked. The garden was decorated as a winter wonderland, with fairy lights adorning every evergreen, a Santa's grotto was in place under the willow tree, with its own platform and carved chair for their Santa—that was, Matthew with a white beard and a hat and coat of red felt—and now these nativity pieces were arranged on their own makeshift stage that Matthew had gamely built—Mary, Joseph, baby Jesus in his manger, a shepherd, a sheep, and a wise man, all made of smooth, burnished oak and suitable for little hands to move around and play with as they liked.

"I've really enjoyed making them," John told her. "Gave this old man something to do."

"You're not that old," Gwen teased, smiling at him as she

felt her heart give a now familiar little skip, and he smiled back. They'd seen a good deal of each other over the last few weeks—often sharing lunch or a cup of tea after John had worked in David's old workshop, and going out on occasion, as well. They'd had dinner at a pub outside Abergavenny, and gone to Hay-on-Wye to browse its many bookshops and art galleries. And just yesterday they'd driven all the way to Cowbridge to wander through its Christmas market, admiring the stalls of hand-painted ornaments and jams and chutneys. Gwen had bought a few things for the inn.

John's gorgeous little grandson, Oliver, had been born two weeks ago and Gwen had oohed and aahed over the photos, feeling quite nostalgic for when her own grandchildren had been that small. John had naturally been bursting with both joy and pride.

In all these exchanges and excursions, Gwen felt as if they'd shared something, and it filled her with a burgeoning excitement as well as a quiet, private joy. Surely John felt the same, or at least *something* of the same.

"Well, sometimes it feels like I am a bit creaky," he replied now, "especially with my various aches and pains! But I'm glad the pieces are all right. Should be fun for some little ones to play with, as long as they don't bash each other over the head with them, that is."

"They're more than all right," Gwen assured him. "They're absolutely *perfect*." She gazed at the figures on their stage with a smile, a lightness in her heart despite the anxieties of the last month.

Sarah hadn't told her anything more about what was going on between her and Nathan, and she'd also shut down Gwen's attempts at conversation, but there could be no denying her daughter was looking strained and dispirited. Matthew was still waiting on news from his Zoom interview—it had been several weeks since he'd had the online meeting, but apparently the board of directors had had to have some sort of consultation before they made a decision, and he might not know if he'd be flown out to America for a while yet. Even so, it seemed to Gwen he was taking out his phone every two minutes to check if he'd missed a call or an email, and then smiling shamefacedly when he realized what he was doing.

And then there was poor little Ava, who was still wetting the bed most nights, and looking quite pale and tired as a result. And Ellie had had some sort of distressing call from school recently, about Ben. What exactly had happened, neither Ellie nor Matthew had told her, but they'd had to go into school to meet with the headteacher, and came home afterwards looking rather grim. Gwen had got the sense that she wasn't meant to ask anything, but Ben was clearly in some sort of trouble, because he'd been suspended from school for a day, his phone had been taken away and he'd been banned from his games console—a punishment that was as difficult for the adults as for Ben, since it meant he often slouched around the house complaining he was bored.

And yet... despite all that, there was John. John smiling at her with that warmth in his eyes, that easy affection in his voice. John making her heart skip a beat and her mind start to daydream as they wandered through the Christmas market in Cowbridge, or chatted about the paintings in an art gallery in Hay, or talked in quiet voices in a candlelit pub. It was all completely innocent, of course, and John had given her no real reason to think there was anything between them but old, abiding friendship, and yet... Gwen herself felt there was more. She felt it in her own heart, and she couldn't keep it from giving way to hope.

She'd told herself a thousand times there was no fool like an old fool, and not to read too much into John's friendliness, and yet it was so very hard not to. She hadn't realized how much she'd missed this kind of easy companionship until she'd had a taste of it again.

"Cup of tea?" she asked, and John nodded.

"Yes, that sounds wonderful. And actually... there's something I wanted to talk to you about."

"Oh?" Now Gwen's heart was skipping *double* beats. "Sounds serious," she remarked lightly, and John's smile deepened, although she thought she detected a shadow of worry in his normally bright blue eyes. What could he possibly be worried about? Should she feel nervous—or hopeful?

Gwen, I've so enjoyed these last few weeks and I was wondering if you'd ever think about making it something more...

"No, not too serious," he replied, but he *sounded* serious, and Gwen didn't reply as they headed back to the house.

"So, what is this not-too-serious thing?" she asked once she'd made tea and cut two thick slices of Battenburg cake, sliding them onto plates and then putting one in front of John. She took a seat opposite him, keeping her tone and expression playful. "You're getting me a bit worried now!"

"No, nothing to be worried about," John replied after a pause. "It's just... well, Izzy's mother-in-law is coming to help out next week. It's better, really, because she needs a woman's touch, and while I'm happy to say I've changed my fair share of nappies, I don't really know what I'm doing when it comes to mothers and babies and that sort of thing. I can't advise her on sleep schedules... or, you know, breastfeeding, or anything like that." He ducked his head, seemingly embarrassed, while Gwen absorbed the import of his words.

"No, I don't suppose you could," she agreed after a pause. "Although I'm sure Izzy has appreciated having you here." *As have I*, she thought but decided not to say.

"So," John said, glancing down at his plate of untouched cake, "with Sam's mother coming soon, I'm going to be heading back home this weekend. Seems best all around, and I'd like to be back in my own bed again, pottering around my own garden, that sort of thing. I'm sure I'll come and visit again, maybe even for Christmas, or perhaps Izzy and Sam will come to me. But, really, it's time to get back to normal, for everyone. I'm sure you'll be glad you have me out of your hair at last!" He let out a huff of laughter. "I've spent so much time here—too much time, I'm sure—in part because I felt like Izzy and Sam needed their space. It's been good to have somewhere to go while they settle into being new parents, so I have to thank you for that."

Gwen blinked, doing her best not to feel stung, or at least not to show it. *That* was why he'd spent so much time with her? Simply to give Izzy and her husband some *space*?

"I... see," she said finally, although she feared she didn't see it all, or maybe it was that she saw too well. She saw all too clearly how she'd been building castles in the air out of nothing... absolutely nothing! She'd known that on one level, or at least suspected it, but to hear it stated so plainly still hurt.

All their outings and conversations, had they really just been an... an *entertainment* for him, no more than a way to pass the time? Was she even surprised, considering how he'd admitted more than once that he was still missing Michelle? *She'd* been the one who had felt the loneliness she hadn't even realized was inside her being so wonderfully assuaged, who had allowed silly, schoolgirl sorts of hopes to buoy her confidence, her mood. She was the one—the only one—who had dared to think something more might be going on between them, or at least might one day.

There's no fool like an old fool.

The truth of it felt like a slap in the face, waking her up to this harsh reality.

"I'll miss you," John continued with an awkward, grimacing sort of smile, in the tone of someone saying a final farewell. "You've been such a lifesaver, Gwen, these last few weeks. Helping out here, spending time with you... it's been..." He paused, swallowing. "Well, it's certainly kept me busy. I've really enjoyed it, I can't even tell you how much."

Gwen forced an answering smile. Once her heart might have sung at his words, but his tone seemed to be more *it was nice, but...* She didn't have it in her to respond.

"I hope we can keep in touch," John continued rather stiltedly. "Maybe by email? Let's not just keep it to Christmas cards anymore, hey?" He smiled at her, shaggy eyebrows lifted in hesitant expectation.

Email? As if that wasn't the final nail in the coffin of her fledgling hopes. He hadn't even suggested meeting up, and he only lived an hour and a half away. It would have been the simplest thing to say he'd like to see her again, maybe meet somewhere convenient in the middle for a coffee or lunch, but no, that wasn't even to be considered, it seemed.

"Yes, let's email. That's a good idea." Gwen managed to say in a voice that she thought almost sounded normal.

"Good." John nodded, a few too many times. "Good," he said again, and then he picked up his slice of cake and took a bite, and Gwen did the same, even though she now had absolutely no appetite. The cake was as dry as dust in her mouth as she forced down a mouthful and John reached for his cup of tea. Things which had always seemed so wonderfully easy and relaxed between them before now felt terribly strained and awkward.

Was it all her fault? Had John sensed that her affections were becoming engaged, and decided he needed to gently put her in her place? The thought was mortifying. She was sixty-nine years old, for heaven's sake! This sort of does-he-does-he-not dithering was surely beneath her.

And yet it seemed it wasn't, because the truth was, Gwen felt horribly disappointed, and even hurt, by John's gentle yet firm goodbye. It showed her just how differently they'd viewed the last few weeks.

"I suppose I should get a move on," John said after a few moments of tense and, at least for Gwen, unhappy silence. He gave her an apologetic sort of smile. "I want to spend some more time with little Oliver before I head back home."

"Yes, I suppose you do."

"Yes, I'm leaving on Friday," he explained. "So... I suppose this is goodbye for a while."

It was only Tuesday, Gwen thought, but thankfully managed not to say out loud. She hadn't realized John had been practically *itching* to leave her company! At least, that was how it felt right now, as he rose from the table, reached for his coat.

"Yes, I suppose it is," she replied in a voice that sounded overbright. "You've been absolutely brilliant, John, with the nativity set. Thank you for chipping in so wonderfully. We all appreciate it."

For a second, John's face fell, as if she'd said something hurtful, and maybe she had. She'd put a little emphasis on the *we* for her own sake, Gwen knew. She felt too bruised not to attempt to claw back some of her dignity, after John had so completely and unthinkingly—or not—dismantled her frail hopes.

"Of course," he murmured, and they stood there in the kitchen, facing each other, giving awkward sorts of smiles and no hugs. Then John buttoned his coat, nodding as he did it. "Well, then," he said. "This is goodbye, I guess."

"Yes, goodbye," Gwen replied, and then, because she was surely too old to stand on stupid pride, she stepped forward and, rather clumsily, put her arms around him. "I'll miss you, John," she said, and to her horror, her voice choked just a little. Well, never mind. "It's been so very lovely to see you."

John's arms closed around her as he drew her to him in a way that felt both painful and sweet. She'd wanted so much more than this. At last, Gwen could admit the hard truth to her own heart. She'd been halfway to falling in love with this man, she knew, and he hadn't felt the same. Well, she told herself as she stepped back from the embrace, that was all right. She'd learned something about herself, at least, and in the meantime, she'd enjoyed his company. She'd take what blessings she could find.

"Bye, then," John murmured, with a funny little smile, and then he was opening the door and heading down the walk to the drive, and Gwen watched him go, waving as he got in his car and drove away.

She stood there for another moment, the cold November wind blowing over her, before she slowly closed the front door.

Back in the kitchen, she tidied up the remnants of their tea —John had barely touched his cake, and neither had she—and then she simply stood there for a second, feeling rather lost. Ellie and Matthew were both out, the house was quiet, their guests due in just under a month. The emptiness reverberated all around Gwen, until she gave herself a little shake, told herself to stop acting so maudlin.

Still feeling restless, she reached for her coat and shrugged it on before heading out to the back garden. The garden looked as lovely as it could do at this time of year—the bright red berries on the holly bush, the lights strung about the trees, the winter honeysuckle and hellebore—or Christmas rose—as well as the yellow, buttercup-like aconites and purple pop of winter heather giving the normally bare patch a touch of wintry color.

Gwen wandered down to the bottom of the garden, past John's nativity set, the Santa's grotto, the pond that hadn't quite managed to be turned into an ice-skating rink, to the wrought-iron bench David had given her for their twenty-fifth wedding anniversary. She sank onto it with a sigh, tilting her head up to the pale blue sky. *Oh, David, I miss you.*

She hadn't expected to feel that old grief and longing, right on the heels of saying goodbye to John, but she did. She missed David sitting in his favorite armchair, doing the crossword, the way he'd glance at her over the top of his newspaper, eyebrows raised. She missed him bringing her a cup of tea in the morning, strong and with just a splash of milk, the way she liked it, made perfectly every time. She missed having someone in her life who knew how to make her tea, and who even knew when he'd got it just the tiniest bit wrong—*sorry! An extra splash of milk! Is it utterly undrinkable?*—and who laughed with her before she'd even started laughing, because they'd thought of the same joke at the exact same time. She missed someone being there, *knowing* her so absolutely, in a way she'd taken for granted because you did, you had to, until you didn't have that person in your life anymore.

She wouldn't wish grief or loss on anyone, but sometimes she looked at Ellie and Matthew or Sarah and Nathan with their petty problems that seemed so enormous to them at the time, and she wanted to give them all a good shake. *You don't know how lucky you are! Hang onto what you have, because one day it might be taken from you, and there will be nothing you can do about it. Nothing at all.*

Gwen leaned her head back against the bench and closed her eyes. It had been twenty-two years since David had died. In a few years, she would have been widowed longer than she'd been married. It was a strange thought, because even after all this time, David felt as much a part of her as her own sinew and bone.

How silly of her, she realized, to think that after a mere two years, John would be ready to think of romance. How completely ridiculous! She saw, plainly now, that her own aspirations in that area had not been matched by John's, and no wonder. He was in an entirely different place than she was—still adrift and anchorless, looking for a way to moor himself, to ease the loneliness that Gwen knew from experience could feel so overwhelming and even confusing, as if in losing someone, you'd somehow also lost yourself. He wasn't looking for a *partner*, or anything close to it.

Gwen let out a soft laugh, shaking her head. She'd been a fool, yes, but she felt more grounded now, almost relieved, in realizing it. She could be John's friend—by email or otherwise—without feeling disappointed. At least, not *too* disappointed.

Because, yes, she was still lonely—now that she'd let that genie out of its bottle, she doubted it would find its way back in. She might be sixty-nine years old, but she was fit and active and she was ready for something more in life. At least, in her friendship with John, she'd come to understand and accept that about herself.

Gently, she traced the intricate scrollwork on the bench, her fingers finding the familiar lines. She wasn't usually one for sentimentality, but she felt close to David on this bench, almost —*almost*—as if he were sitting right beside her.

"Is it all right, my darling?" she asked softly, feeling slightly silly for speaking the words aloud. "Is it all right if I move on, a little, in that way? I'll always love you, you know."

In the peaceful silence of a winter's afternoon, she thought she heard his reply.

And I will always love you. But yes, Gwen. Of course it's all right.

CHAPTER 16

ELLIE

ONE WEEK LATER

Ellie sat in the waiting room, jiggling her foot and glancing at her watch as Ava kicked her legs next to her. They'd been waiting in the doctor's surgery for over half an hour, and it was now nearing mid-morning.

"Mummy, I'm thirsty."

"Have some water, sweetheart." Ellie fished a water bottle out of her bag and watched, bemused, as her daughter guzzled half of it. At this rate, Ava would need the toilet again; she'd already gone once since they'd got there.

Ellie had made the appointment after another week of broken nights, although she still suspected Ava was wetting her bed because of stress. She'd seemed pretty peaky, but perhaps that could be from the missed sleep. Whatever the cause, it was best to get it checked out, and she was conscious she'd let things slide in that regard, thanks to the busyness of getting the Bluebell Inn ready for Christmas.

She'd let too many things slide, Ellie acknowledged with a

pang of maternal guilt and anxiety. Mairi's unhappiness at losing Sophie's friendship, Ben's troubles...

Ben. Briefly, Ellie closed her eyes as she recalled the phone call from the headteacher several weeks ago, requesting that she and Matthew come into school that very day. Ellie had been alarmed; they'd never been called in like this before, and although Ben was boisterous, he'd never been in serious trouble.

But this time he was.

"Ben has been accused of bullying by several boys in his year," the headteacher had begun without preamble, once they'd been seated in her office, with Ben next to them, hanging his head, unwilling to look anyone in the eye. Ellie hadn't been able to tell if he was ashamed or just irritated.

"Bullying?" she'd repeated faintly, shocked by the assertion. She'd turned to her son. "Ben?"

He'd shrugged, not replying.

"Two boys have accused him and some others of pushing and shoving them at breaks, and then today..." The headteacher had paused, ominously. "They demanded these boys give them their pocket money. This kind of behavior is absolutely unacceptable, as I'm sure you appreciate."

Pushing, shoving, *stealing*? Ellie had felt her body go cold, her mind numb. *Her* child had done these things? She couldn't believe it, and yet Ben wasn't denying it. He wasn't saying a word.

"Ben?" Matthew had barked, his tone stern. "Can you explain what happened?"

Their son had simply shrugged again.

"You do know how serious this is, I hope, Ben?" the headteacher had stated, leaning over her desk, her tone even sterner than Matt's. "I'm afraid this is going to result in a twenty-four-hour suspension from school."

Suspension. Ellie had gone even colder. How could this be

happening? "Ben, say something," she'd demanded, and her son had looked up, sulky and sullen.

"What do you want me to say?"

Back at home, they'd tried to get more information from him, but he'd been just as close-lipped, and with a frustration that had bordered on fury, Ellie and Matthew, in agreement, had sent him to his room with no screens allowed until further notice.

"Who are these other boys who did this with him?" Matthew had asked. "Maybe we should talk to their parents."

"I don't know." Ellie had felt that curdling of mother guilt. Why didn't she know her son's friends? She knew Owen, of course, but she seriously doubted he was one of the bullying boys. Ben had never been forthcoming about his friendships, tending to meet up on the village green to play football, or, in the last few months, getting the bus into Abergavenny—a privilege that Ellie was now semi-regretting. How had she not realized what her son got up to?

Over the next few weeks, she'd tried to engage more with him, encouraging him when she saw him being kind, reminding him to use an indoor voice or not to roughhouse too much with Josh, who was not always up for his brother's wrestling matches. She'd tried, gently, to get to the bottom of what had happened with the bullying, but Ben had lost his temper, rounding on her in an exasperated fury.

"It was just a *joke*, all right? We didn't mean anything by it. It didn't have to be such a big deal."

"Did you steal their money?" Ellie had asked steadily, her heart thumping.

Ben had rolled his eyes. "Like, a *pound*. We gave it back later."

He made it sound so innocuous, but Ellie feared it wasn't. Who were these boys Ben was getting involved with? Who was the ringleader? She hoped it wasn't her son.

"Ava Davies?"

Ellie looked up to see a nurse standing in the doorway, a wreath of glittery green tinsel hanging above its frame. With a smile for her daughter, doing her best to banish her worries about Ben, she rose from her seat and followed the nurse into the GP's office.

"How can I help?" the doctor, a young woman with a friendly, freckled face and sandy hair pulled back in a ponytail, asked pleasantly as they sat down in the office.

"We've had some issues with bedwetting in the last month or so," Ellie began with an apologetic smile.

"Oh?" The doctor raised her eyebrows. "And is this unusual?" She turned to Ava. "How old are you, sweetheart?"

"Six," Ava declared proudly.

"My, my!" The doctor turned back to Ellie. "How many times has she wet the bed?"

"Three or four times a week, but before last month, she'd been dry at night for years." Ellie gave Ava a small, encouraging smile. Fortunately, her daughter did not seem embarrassed by her bedwetting; she was smiling and kicking her legs against the rungs of her chair, looking around the office with interest.

The GP asked a few more questions which Ellie did her best to answer, although she wasn't entirely sure. Had Ava lost her appetite? Had she seemed tired or lethargic? Had she lost weight?

"I... I don't think so," Ellie replied helplessly. "Not that I've noticed." Which made her sound—and feel—like a bad mother. "She's tired, yes, but I'd expect her to be, with the broken nights."

"Has she been unusually thirsty?" the doctor asked.

"No, I don't think so," Ellie replied, only to remember how Ava had guzzled from her water bottle in the waiting room. And, now that she thought of it, Ava had been asking for a second glass of milk at dinner, which Ellie had been reluctant to give her, and her water bottle that she took to school had been empty in the afternoons, when before it had usually been half-full. Ellie had been trying to limit her daughter's liquid intake, but Ava had seemed thirstier than usual. "Yes, actually," Ellie admitted. "I think she has been."

"Well, it's worth doing a random blood sugar test, just to rule out diabetes," the doctor said with a smile. "Probably it's just a phase—this happens sometimes at Ava's age—but we want to make sure."

Diabetes? Such a possibility hadn't even crossed Ellie's mind. At the worst, she'd been thinking a virus, maybe a bladder infection. Guilt swamped her, that she might have missed some obvious signs and symptoms.

"All right," she replied a bit shakily, and the doctor filled out a form for Ellie to take to the nurse's office.

"Fortunately, there's time now, so we can get it down right away, and you'll have your results within seventy-two hours."

"Thank you," Ellie murmured, still reeling. Surely Ava couldn't have diabetes?

The nurse was as friendly as the doctor, and was able to take the blood sample while chatting to Ava the whole time, so her daughter barely noticed the needle going in, and was thrilled with her princess sticker.

Ellie had promised her a sticky bun from the Angel Bakery, and so it was nearly lunchtime before she'd dropped her back at school and headed back to the inn, her mind buzzing with her never-ending to-do list as well as this new anxiety about Ava. It was now just under three weeks till their first guests arrived, and Ellie still felt as if she had so much work to do—spruce up the bedrooms, order the food, organize gifts for the guests as well as her own children...

It didn't help that looming over all this was the mind-boggling possibility of moving to New York. Matthew still hadn't heard back about his Zoom interview several weeks ago, and Ellie didn't know if that was a good or bad sign. She didn't know which one she *wanted* it to be. She didn't have the head-space to think about it all while, at the same time, trying to get the inn ready for Christmas. It was as if she was operating on two separate planes, and she could only manage one. Thinking about New York would have to wait until *after* Christmas.

As Ellie came into the house, she heard a small sound, muffled, but almost like a sob, coming from the kitchen. She hesitated, wondering what was going on. Gwen...? She knew John had left to return home a few days ago, but her mother-in-law had seemed surprisingly philosophical about it, to Matthew's relief.

"I liked the guy," he'd told Ellie, "but it still felt weird. I know I need to get over that—"

"Yes," Ellie had interrupted him. "You do."

Matthew had let out an embarrassed laugh as he'd given her a shamefaced smile. "All right, all right. I get it. My mum is allowed to date. I know she is."

But Gwen *wasn't* dating John, as far as Ellie knew. Was she sad about it—sadder than she'd let on?

Cautiously, Ellie came into the kitchen, only to stop in surprise when she saw who was seated at the table, her head in her hands.

"Sarah...!" The name escaped her in something close to a gasp as her sister-in-law raised her head from her hands, blinking back tears.

"Sorry..." Sarah mumbled, wiping her eyes, and Ellie sprang into action.

"No, no. I was just surprised to see you here. Your car's not in the drive—"

"I walked from the stables."

"The stables?" Ellie stared at her in surprise and concern. "Where Mairi keeps her horse? But that's miles away."

"About three," Sarah agreed on a sniff. "I just needed a walk to clear my head."

"I think this requires a cup of tea," Ellie declared. "Or maybe even two." She'd never, ever seen her sister-in-law looking so distraught.

"The ultimate panacea," Sarah noted with an attempt at dryness. "Although this time I'm afraid a cup of tea isn't going to make me feel much better, Ellie, but you're welcome to make one."

"Well, maybe talking will," Ellie suggested hesitantly. She filled the kettle at the sink and switched it on. "That can often help, I find." Although she wasn't entirely sure it would help in Sarah's case. While she certainly got along far better with her sister-in-law than she had when she'd first moved to Llandrigg, there was a restraint and remoteness to Sarah that still intimidated Ellie, and put her off sharing confidences, but right now, she acknowledged, Sarah didn't seem restrained or remote at all. She just seemed sad. "What's going on?" Ellie asked gently, and Sarah let out a long, raggedy sigh.

"In a nutshell?" She gazed at the ceiling as if looking for answers there, or maybe just to keep from crying. "Nathan's moved out."

"Oh..." Ellie's breath came out in a rush. This she had not expected. Yes, she'd been aware that Nathan had not been as present as he used to be, and she'd even wondered if there was some tension between Sarah and her husband, but... *moved out*? That sounded terribly serious. "I'm so sorry," she said, a bit belatedly, and Sarah twitched her shoulders in the semblance of a shrug. "Did he..." She felt her way through the words, not wanting to be insensitive with her questions. "Did he give you a reason?"

"Not really. Not one I care to accept, anyway."

The kettle switched off, and Ellie busied herself making tea, wondering how to handle this news. Sarah didn't seem particularly forthcoming, but she'd been in tears, and she'd come to the inn, so maybe Ellie needed to press a little harder.

"Here you go," she said, putting a cup of tea in front of Sarah. "And a little chocolate wouldn't go amiss either, I think." She reached for the big, battered cake tin that Gwen kept all her creations in, and was rewarded with the sight of a pile of fudgy brownies. She took two out and put them on plates, giving one to Sarah before she sat down opposite her with her own tea and brownie. "Do you want to talk about it?" she asked.

Sarah crumbled a bit of brownie between her fingers, her head bent so Ellie couldn't see her expression.

"He said he was tired," she admitted after a moment, her voice low. "Tired of work, of life, and of... of me." A sigh escaped her. "And do you know what? I'm not sure I entirely blame him. Lately, I've been tired of me."

Ellie blinked, absorbing this. "Tired of you... how so?" she asked cautiously.

"Oh, just who I am." Sarah shrugged restively and then popped a big chunk of brownie into her mouth. She looked at Ellie directly, a surprising blaze of feeling firing her blue eyes. She swallowed and then asked, "Don't you ever get tired of yourself, of who you are, how you act, the way you come across to other people? Don't you ever just want to... I don't know, give yourself a good shake, or even a slap?"

"Er..." Ellie had no idea how to answer this.

"I don't actually mean you," Sarah continued impatiently, sounding more like her usual, assertive self. "I'm talking about me. I'm tired. I'm annoyed with myself, how I've been, and I don't want to be that way any longer. Maybe Nathan felt the same way."

"What has annoyed you?" Ellie asked after a second. She didn't know whether to ask about Nathan or not. "About yourself, I mean?"

"Everything." Sarah shook her head and then took another

bite of brownie. "Well, not everything," she conceded. "I'm not that much of a sad sack, I hope. But just how... pushy I've been. An insufferable know-it-all, more or less—and don't pretend you haven't thought the same!" She gave Ellie a pointed look and she smiled weakly in return.

"Well..."

"I know you have. Everyone has. It's not a secret, Ellie. At least not much of one." Sarah propped her head in her hand. "It's not just that, though, or maybe it's *more* than that. It's what I thought was important, what I valued. What I told and taught my children to value." Her voice choked a little before she evened it out. "That's what I'm starting to question."

"Okay." That, perhaps, was no bad thing—not that Ellie intended to say as much just now. "And Nathan...?" she asked cautiously.

"Well, Nathan, it seems, is tired of me in a completely *different* way." Sarah let out a rather hard laugh. "He's not having the same epiphanies, let's put it that way, or at least none that he's shared with me. This whole thing started—well, no, not started, but came to a head, I suppose, because Mairi has been so stressed about her exams that she started cutting herself."

"Cutting...!" Ellie stared at Sarah in dismay. "Oh, no..."

"We're working through it," Sarah confirmed grimly. "Nathan and I talked to her together—he managed that, at least —and she's agreed to see a counselor. I'm limiting the time she is allowed to spend studying each day." She let out a small, sad laugh. "Something I never thought I'd say, never mind do. But part of Mairi's stress came from the pressure she felt Nathan and I were putting on her... not overtly—at least I don't think so —but the kind of throwaway comments you don't even think about... or I didn't, not until recently. I tried to explain that to Nathan, and I think he's finally started to understand, although... this isn't just about Mairi. He's been working around the clock, and I know he has had some pressure there, but..."

She let out a sigh. "I don't think I know who he is anymore, and he doesn't seem to know who I am."

"Oh, Sarah." Ellie reached over and touched her hand. "I'm so sorry."

"So am I. I don't want to get divorced," she stated bluntly. "I don't want to give up on my marriage. But what do you do when your husband decides he does?"

"Has Nathan decided that? To give up and divorce?" Ellie had never come to know Nathan all that well; he worked long hours and although he'd been enthusiastic about the inn, it had been as a business proposition rather than a family enterprise. He was the sort of person who bounced on his heels and always seemed full of restless energy; you couldn't pin him down for an extended conversation—not, Ellie acknowledged, that she'd ever really tried all that hard.

"Nathan was the one who decided to move out, certainly," Sarah replied, "without much of a discussion. He's taken a short-term let in Cardiff, which, of course, means he won't see the children very often." She pursed her lips, looking more sad than angry. "He's seen them just once since he moved out, although he keeps saying he'll make plans to come round, take them out. He hasn't, so far."

"Oh, Sarah." Ellie shook her head, feeling sad not just for her sister-in-law, but also her niece and nephew. "How are they taking it?"

"Not great. Mairi is angry and has decided it's easier to blame me, which I actually understand, and Owen is even more monosyllabic than usual. Plus, he got into trouble at school... for bullying of all things." She shook her head despairingly.

"He did?" Ellie couldn't keep the surprise from her voice. "So did Ben. I'd assumed Owen wasn't one of the other boys—"

"And I'd assumed Ben wasn't." Sarah raised her eyebrows and gave a rather grim smile. "I didn't want to say anything about it, because... oh, well, I'm still the same inside, really, and

I hate admitting that I can't cope. That I feel like a failure—as a mother, as a wife." She put her hands up to hide her face as an unruly sob escaped her.

"Oh, Sarah, so do I!" Ellie exclaimed. "I was mortified that Ben was suspended for bullying. I think I would have preferred he'd been disciplined for cheating or something like that. But bullying..."

"I know what you mean," Sarah said through her fingers. "Although I wouldn't have been thrilled by the cheating, either."

Ellie gave a small laugh, then clapped her hand over her mouth, horrified that she could be so thoughtless as to laugh in the face of Sarah's obvious and overwhelming troubles. But then Sarah laughed too, a rusty sound, and she lowered her hands so they could smile at each other, a little shamefaced and battle-weary.

"I don't know where to go from here," Sarah admitted. "What do I do? I feel like I need a complete reset, but I don't know how to accomplish it in a way that works for Mairi and Owen, and also for my marriage..." She shook her head. "I don't want to give up on it. I made vows, and I take those seriously. But how do I convince Nathan, when he seems determined to have a midlife crisis of some kind? Does he just need time? I don't even know." A sigh escaped her, and she reached for her tea, which was now undoubtedly lukewarm. "I don't even know where to begin, or if I have the energy to. It feels easier to just keep trudging along, and yet I can't stand that thought. Not anymore."

Trudging along. It was, Ellie reflected, an apt description of how she sometimes felt. As buoyed as she'd been by the inn's Christmas bookings, she still felt soul-weary in a way she hadn't expected. Ben's issues, as well as Ava and Jess's... Josh was the only child of hers who seemed to be on an even keel, but she knew he was anxious about moving up to secondary school.

And now this possibility of moving to New York... she hadn't told Sarah about that, and now definitely didn't seem like the time, but she could relate to Sarah's sentiments. Sometimes life felt like nothing more than trudging drudgery. Was that just part and parcel of daily existence?

"Has Nathan been willing to have a conversation with you?" she asked. "To talk about the future?"

Sarah shrugged. "He hasn't been willing or unwilling, as far as I can tell. I haven't talked to him since he moved out. He stopped by to get a few things and took the kids out for dinner. He told me he'd be in touch soon, but he made me feel like a business acquaintance. I have no idea what's going through his mind." Sarah gazed down into her cup. "Maybe I should have twigged this a lot sooner. He's been distant for months, but I kept trying to convince myself it was just work. Then I was worried it was an affair—" She made a face. "It's what goes through your mind, isn't it? But he's insisted that there's no one else. It really is just *me*, it seems." For a second, she looked as if she might cry again, but then she pressed her lips together and gave a little nod. "So, that's my sob story."

"I'm so sorry," Ellie said again, uselessly. She had no other words, nothing to offer, except her sympathy. "I can't imagine how difficult it is for you—for all of you."

"In some ways, it's almost a relief," Sarah replied, her forehead furrowing in thought. "In a way I didn't expect. It was as if this pressure was building inside me, and when he said he was going to move out, it let out a little. But it has left me a bit deflated, so..." She let out a wry laugh and shook her head. "Anyway, enough about all that. I came over here because I wanted to throw myself into something, not moan about my problems. What needs doing? You still have your long list of projects, I assume?"

"Well..." Ellie was cautious, not wanting to overburden her sister-in-law, but Sarah looked determined. "There are always things to do. I wanted to go through the bedrooms, figure out a way to spruce them up a bit. I know we bought new linens and curtains and things two years ago, but I feel like they could use a few extra touches. Nothing too expensive, obviously."

"All right, then." Sarah stood up, slapping her hands on the table. "Let's get to it."

"If you're sure—"

"Ellie, I'm very sure," Sarah replied. "I do not want to dissect my marriage for another millisecond. Figuring out what throw pillows will make a bedroom pop is *exactly* what I need right now."

Laughing at this, Ellie stood up too. "All right, then," she said. "Let me lead the way."

As they walked through the downstairs, Sarah paused by the doorway to the dining room. "You've really done a splendid job," she told Ellie. "I love all the blue and silver—those baubles in the crystal bowl are gorgeous!"

"I bought them at the craft shop you told me about, in Abergavenny," Ellie told her shyly. "Thanks for the suggestion."

"You've worked so hard, and you've made a success of this," Sarah told her frankly. "I shouldn't have been such a wet blanket about it all. You've certainly proved me wrong!"

"That's not what I meant to do—" Ellie protested, alarmed that Sarah might think she'd been on some sort of vendetta.

"No, no, I'm glad of it," Sarah assured her. "Truly. It's good to see one thing going right, to be honest." She crossed the hallway to peek in the living room. "With a roaring fire and a glass of mulled wine... guests will love relaxing here. You've really done something special."

"Thank you," Ellie replied, as she found herself tearing up a bit. It was strange to get such sincere praise from Sarah, who gave it so rarely. "I couldn't have done it without everyone's help, including yours."

"Well, that was the point of this place, wasn't it? To all work together—a family effort."

"Yes... and you're part of that, too, Sarah." Tentatively, Ellie laid a hand on her sister-in-law's arm; this was new territory for both of them. "Whatever we can do to help you and Mairi and Owen through this... we do want to help. I can't imagine how hard it must be."

"Thank you." Sarah cleared her throat as she discreetly wiped her eyes and Ellie removed her hand from her arm. "Right, well, that's enough of that," she said, making Ellie smile. "Now, let's go deal with these bedrooms!"

CHAPTER 17

SARAH

A WEEK LATER

    Can we talk?

Sarah stood alone in the kitchen, staring at the text for a few seconds before she slowly, letter by letter, deleted it. She wasn't sure what she wanted from Nathan right now, but it was more than what those three words offered. She also, she knew, didn't want her request to be rebuffed. She could already imagine Nathan's reply: *Now's not a good time* or *If you really want to.* No thanks to either of those.

    And yet... they *needed* to talk. It had been over two weeks now since he'd moved out, and basically ghosted her, his wife of twenty years. She could hardly believe it, and would have felt hurt if she wasn't so numb. But numb was good; when she wasn't numb, she felt completely despairing, like a week ago, when she'd left her car at the stables and walked all the way to the inn in something close to a fugue state. She hadn't been able to think about what she was doing or why; she'd just concentrated on putting one foot in front of another, because that had been all she'd been capable of.

Still, when Ellie had stumbled upon her in the kitchen, basically having a mini breakdown, Sarah had actually been sort of glad. It had felt a relief to confess what was going on, what a shambles she'd made of her life, of *herself*. She hadn't been brave enough to say as much to her mother—not yet, anyway—but Ellie had provided a kind, listening ear, and she'd appreciated her sister-in-law's thoughtful concern. Maybe this was a new page for both of them.

They'd spent the rest of the afternoon going through the bedrooms, making a list of little embellishments that wouldn't cost too much, and finding a few things in other parts of the house—a vase, a picture—that helped make the rooms look a little more put together. Sarah had enjoyed the distraction, and she'd enjoyed the time with Ellie, too. She'd learned to get along with her sister-in-law over the years, but she'd assumed they were too different to truly be friends—that afternoon she'd started to believe otherwise. Maybe they weren't as different as she'd once thought they were. Not anymore.

Sarah glanced down at her phone again. She and Nathan really did need to talk, if just to figure out how to manage their children. Mairi was still teetering on the edge of a meltdown; seeing a counselor was helping, Sarah hoped, but Nathan's abrupt removal from her life had certainly added to her anxiety. And as for Owen... he was so silent, so surly. He'd never been the most talkative lad, it was true, but he'd had an easygoing and friendly nature, and now Sarah felt as if she barely recognized him. She couldn't blame Nathan for that, not entirely, but his distance didn't help matters.

Sarah closed her eyes briefly, then snapped them open and started composing another text.

*It would be good to talk through some things, figure a way
forward. When are you free?*

She studied the text; it was fairly innocuous, but also, she
hoped, pointed. They couldn't exist in this stasis for much
longer; at least *she* couldn't. Nathan seemed to be okay with it,
as far as she could tell.

She pressed send.

Sarah had just put her phone down and pulled out a packet
of pasta when Mairi flung open the front door, throwing down
her backpack and giving Sarah a malevolent look before she
stomped upstairs.

"Are you hungry?" Sarah called after her, doing her best to
keep her voice pleasant. "Tea will be in about half an hour."

The only sound was the slam of Mairi's bedroom door.
Sarah suppressed a much-needed sigh. She'd read online all
about marriage problems and divorce and how they affected
children, and Mairi blaming her was pretty much textbook. It
didn't make it any easier to live with in the day to day, but it did
give Sarah a modicum of patience she knew she needed.

Owen came into the kitchen after his sister, throwing down
his bag too as he went to the fridge in search of snacks.

"Tea's in half an hour," Sarah said again. "How was your day?"

He shrugged, his back to her. "Okay."

That, Sarah knew, was as much as she would get. What
happened with teenagers? she wondered. She'd once had these
lovely, adorable cuddly children who threw themselves into her
arms and promised her they'd love her forever, and then somehow, just a few years later, they'd turned into angry, monosyllabic *beasts*. The old her would have assumed she'd navigate the
trials of teenagerhood with ease and aplomb. The new one
recognized just how hard that was.

"How's Ben doing?" she asked her son. "I didn't realize

until I spoke to Aunt Ellie that he'd been involved in that bullying incident, too."

Owen made a grunting sort of noise, and Sarah took a deep breath, let it out slowly.

"Owen, please turn around and face me while we're talking."

"*I* wasn't talking," he replied, but at least he did turn around.

"So, it was you and Ben and one other boy," she continued steadily. The school had refused to give names, and so had Owen. "Who was the other boy?"

He fidgeted restlessly for a minute before admitting with a shrug, "Luke."

"Luke who?"

"Luke Jones."

Sarah didn't know the name, but that wasn't all that surprising. There were over two hundred children in Owen's year. "Is he new?" she asked, and he half-shrugged, half-nodded. She took it as assent. "Is he a friend?"

"I dunno..."

"You don't know?"

Another shrug.

Sarah decided to press; this was the most forthcoming Owen had been about the bullying incident since it had happened. "Whose idea was it, Owen, to push these boys around and take their money?"

He ducked his head. "I dunno..." he mumbled again.

It was the easy choice, Sarah knew, as a parent, to decide it was this Luke's. He was the unknown element, the potential scapegoat. But what if it *hadn't* been his idea? Maybe it had been Owen's, or Ben's, or both. She didn't want to be the kind of mother who refused to believe the unpalatable truth about her child, as much as she loved him.

"Owen?" she prompted. "If it was you, I won't be angry, but I'd like to know. I'd like to understand what happened."

"Why do you care now?" Owen burst out. "It's, like, ancient history."

Two weeks was not ancient history, but Sarah knew he had a point. "I've been a bit distracted these last few weeks," she admitted, "but I'm asking you now." She finally felt strong enough to grasp this particular nettle.

"Are you and Dad getting divorced?" Owen asked abruptly.

Sarah took an even breath. "Your dad and I haven't discussed it."

"Yes, but are you?"

"I don't know," she admitted, deciding she needed to be as honest with her son as she wanted him to be with her. "Like I said, we haven't discussed it, but... I hope we're not. But we are going through something of a rough patch, and we need to sort things out." If they could. "Now." She levelled him with an encouraging but firm look. "Tell me what happened with the bullying."

"It wasn't bullying." His voice was low, insistent.

"Okay, then, tell me what it was. What would you call it?"

He shrugged, hunching his shoulders, suddenly looking impossibly young. He'd had a growth spurt recently, and his school blazer no longer covered his wrists. His arms and legs looked too long for his body; he still had to grow into himself, both physically and emotionally. In that moment, Sarah's heart ached for her son, for the confusion he had to feel on so many fronts.

"It was just messing around," he mumbled. "We didn't... we didn't mean anything by it."

"I can appreciate that," Sarah answered carefully, "but at some point, you must have realized the other boys weren't viewing it in the same way."

Owen shrugged, looking down as he scuffed his feet.

Was there any real point in rehashing this episode? Sarah wondered. She was pretty sure her son knew it had been wrong. And yet... he hadn't said as much.

"Owen," she told him gently, "once upon a time, I feel like *you* would have been one of those boys, the boys you took the money from. Do you remember in year seven, how you felt a little out of place, at the start? You were having trouble making friends—"

He looked up, his expression turning mutinous. "Wow, thanks a lot, Mum!"

"*I've* had trouble making friends," she told him quietly. "And so has Mairi, and Jess, and Ellie. Loads of people do. I don't actually think it's a bad thing. It can make you more... empathetic." Not that that was an adjective she'd use to describe her thirteen-year-old son right now. "I'm just reminding you because I'm a little surprised you're on the other side of that equation."

He blinked at her for a few seconds, and then he said, in a mumble so low she strained to hear it, "It was my idea."

Sarah absorbed this, doing her best to keep her expression neutral and not condemning. "It was?"

He nodded, and a look of something almost like relief passed across his face. It felt good, Sarah knew from experience, to admit to things. "Yeah. We were just goofing around, and Luke was saying how these guys were, like, total weirdoes, and so I... I just... I don't know, I just pushed one of them, sort of like a joke, but then he got angry, and I don't know what happened, but it just kind of... got out of control." He stared at her unhappily. "I didn't mean to take their money. I know that sounds stupid, but they were holding it, just a couple of pound coins, and I dunno, I just grabbed it, sort of like a joke, but then it became this *thing* and they said I'd stolen it, but I gave it back to them after school." He looked miserable, and almost near tears. "I'm not a bully!"

"Oh, Owen..." There were no words, Sarah thought, to make it better, and so she simply wrapped him in a hug, grateful when he put his arms around her, his head burrowing into her shoulder.

"I'm sorry," he whispered.

"I know you are." She hugged him for a few seconds, longing to imbue him with her love, her acceptance, because she knew that was what he needed right now. "But those boys need to hear that, too," she told him, and he tensed, drawing away from her to look at her in abject horror. "You need to apologize to them."

"Mum, I *can't*—"

"I'm not saying it's easy," Sarah cut across him. "Far from it. But it's necessary, and I think you know that."

Owen shook his head frantically. "Please—"

Sarah well knew the awkwardness of such an encounter would be near unbearable for him, just as she knew it had to be done.

"Ask Ben to go with you," she suggested, keeping her voice firm. "That will make it easier, and it's my understanding that he needs to apologize as well. He went along with all this?"

"Yeah." Owen scuffed one shoe along the floor. "Pretty much."

"Well, then." She gave a brisk nod. "The two of you will apologize to the other boys, and maybe think twice about hanging around Luke Jones, if he's calling people 'total weirdoes.'"

"*Mum...*"

She held up a hand to forestall his protests. "I'm just saying. It's something to think about."

Owen let out a groan of protest, but Sarah thought he'd do it. At least, she hoped he would. And she felt she'd handled that better than she might have once done, all things considered.

Owen had just slouched up to his room with a bag of crisps

—Sarah had let him take them without comment—when her phone pinged with a text.

It was from Nathan.

I think you're right. Shall we meet tonight? Maybe at the pub, so we can have some privacy from the kids?

What did *that* mean? she wondered, her stomach hollowing out with anxiety even as her heart lurched with hope. Was this a good sign—or a *really* bad one? She'd meant what she'd said to Ellie; she took her vows seriously, and she was willing to fight for her marriage.

But the question remained... was Nathan?

The pub where they'd agreed to meet was on the outskirts of their village, just a five-minute walk from the house. Sarah had told Mairi and Owen only that she was going for a walk, not wanting to face the barrage of questions they'd ask her if they knew she was meeting their dad. It felt like a small but necessary deception, and they'd seemed to buy it, even if going for a walk at eight o'clock on a dark, wintry evening wasn't really like her.

She walked along slowly, half-dreading what was to come, but also half-hoping. As she walked down the street, she saw Christmas trees twinkling in neighbors' houses, lights strung outside, wreaths on the doors, once even an inflatable reindeer in the garden. They were all festive signs of welcoming homes, happy families. Not like hers.

Nathan was already in the pub, seated in a booth, when Sarah arrived. Another good sign—or a bad one? She had no idea. She felt as if she didn't know anything anymore, and the realization of her own ignorance was jarring.

"Hey." She shed her coat as she slipped into the booth.

Nathan was nursing a pint, but he stood up as she sat down. "What can I get you to drink?"

"A glass of red would be nice, thank you." She had a feeling she might need the fortification.

Nathan went to the bar for her drink while Sarah attempted to steady her jangling nerves. It felt as if a lot was riding on this conversation, and she didn't know how to approach it. But maybe she shouldn't try to find an angle, frame things a certain way. Maybe she just needed to be as honest—and as vulnerable—as she could be.

The thought was fairly terrifying.

She glanced around the pub, which was quiet on a weekday evening, a pleasant smell of woodsmoke from the fireplace hanging in the air, a few fairy lights twinkling along the smoke-stained beams. *I'm Dreaming of a White Christmas* was playing, at low volume on the speakers.

Nathan returned with her drink, putting it in front of her before sliding into the booth opposite with a wry grimace. "How are you?" he asked.

"Well." Sarah took a sip of wine. Here went honesty. "I've been better, to tell you the truth."

"Hmm." He looked away, and she had a feeling he hadn't wanted that answer. Not a good start.

She took another sip of wine.

"What about you?" she asked, trying to pitch her tone a bit friendlier.

"Well, I don't particularly like living in a soulless corporate flat," he replied. "But it is what it is."

Was it? He'd made the choice to move out, after all.

"It doesn't have to be this way, Nathan," Sarah said quietly. "I don't want it to be this way."

He didn't reply, merely looked away, which again didn't feel great.

"What happened?" Sarah asked. "To us, I mean? How did

we drift so far apart?" The question felt painful, exposing, and yet she knew she wanted an answer. She *needed* an answer.

"I suppose you have your answer in the fact that you asked that question," he said, turning back to look at her. "We drifted. In different directions."

"All right." She wanted this to be a discussion, not an argument, but it was hard not to feel defensive. "What direction did you drift in?"

He hunched a shoulder as he gazed into his pint. "I don't know. I don't feel like I went anywhere, really. More like I just stayed still and let life pass me by."

Sarah absorbed this for a few seconds. "So, you feel like you've been missing out?" she asked, even as she wondered *missing out on what?*

"I suppose." He sighed and leaned back in his seat. "I don't know if I can do a whole dissection of what happened right now, Sarah, because I still feel like I'm in the middle of it. I just need some time to sort myself out, figure out what I want."

"And am I just supposed to wait while you do that?" she asked, hearing the edge in her voice and wishing she could take the question back.

"You can do what you want," Nathan replied coolly. "If you don't want to wait, don't."

Ouch.

"And what about Mairi and Owen?" Sarah asked, when she trusted her voice to be level. "Are they supposed to wait around, too?"

Nathan shook his head. "I want to see them. Be with them. I just..." He blew out a gusty breath. "I'm sorry. I don't want to be a bad father. I'm not trying to be selfish or difficult, Sarah, it's just... hard."

It's hard for me, too. She bit her lips to keep from saying the words out loud. Whatever Nathan was going through, it was real to him and she knew being angry about it wouldn't help either of them, or their marriage.

"Nathan..." Sarah drew a deep breath and then continued painfully, "Whatever you're going through... whatever you have to sort out... I want to come back from this. I want our marriage to work, and I'm willing to do whatever is needed to make that happen. Counseling, couples therapy, whatever you think we need. You're right, we did drift. *I* drifted, in part because I was focused on other things. I think I just took everything for granted—you, the children, our life together. I was so determined to be a success at everything, to seem like a success—"

"I don't begrudge you any of that, Sarah," Nathan replied gruffly. "You're focused. You always have been. That's a good thing."

"Maybe," she allowed, "but... I'm trying to be different. More laidback and accepting—of the kids, of myself." She paused. "Of you." She leaned across the table, wanting him to understand and believe her. "I don't blame you, Nathan. We should have talked before, yes, but that's as much my fault as yours. If your job is giving you stress, let's think outside the box about how to handle it. You could quit, try something new—"

"*Quit?*" He looked at her in surprise, recoiling a little bit at the suggestion. "I don't want to quit!"

Sarah frowned. "You said you were tired of it—"

"I didn't mean it like that."

Something about his tone gave Sarah pause, and realization started filtering in slowly, like puzzles pieces falling into place, creating a whole picture that she didn't want to make sense of. "What did you mean, then?" she asked after a moment.

Nathan didn't reply.

She asked abruptly, "Will you go to counseling with me?"

"Sarah..."

The puzzle of her husband was almost completed, every damning piece lined up, except this last one. Sarah forced the question through lips that felt cold and numb. "Do you want to stay married to me, Nathan?"

He looked down at his drink. Several seconds ticked by, each one feeling agonizingly endless. In the fireplace, the logs settled in the grate with a scattering of embers and ash. Sarah waited, her hands flat on the table, her heart beating hard.

"I don't know," he said at last, and even though she'd been bracing for it, it still sent her reeling back as if he'd punched her.

"You don't?"

"I'm sorry, but I just need some time on my own. Right now, I feel like I *don't* want to be married, full stop." His expression was already morphing from one of genuine regret to something stubborn and defiant. "Maybe that will change with time, but I'm forty-six, Sarah, and I feel like I've let the last twenty years just slide by—"

"Twenty years? You mean, the entire length of our marriage?" she retorted in disbelief. "The years we had our *children*? Those years just *slid by* for you?"

He shook his head. "I knew you wouldn't understand."

"No, I don't understand." Her voice rose in anger, but she felt too wound up, too devastated, to moderate her tone. "You made *vows*. You have *responsibilities*. Never mind me, you have *children* who love you, who are hurt and confused by you simply walking out of their lives. Doesn't that mean *anything* to you?"

"I told you, I'll still see the children—"

"When? How? It's been two weeks and you've only seen them once."

His eyes flashed with both anger and guilt. "I know, and like I said, I needed some space."

"You don't have that luxury, Nathan!" The words came out in something close to a shout and Nathan scowled.

"Sarah, you're making a scene—"

"I'm making a scene? *I* am?" She rose from the table, her

whole body shaking with anger. "Forget about me," she told him. "Forget about our marriage, the vows we made in a church, for better or worse, for richer or poorer. All that. But think of your *children*. They don't deserve this, Nathan. They need you. They need a father. Walk out on me if you must, even if you do without so much as firing a warning shot, but don't walk out on them."

For a second, his expression softened, collapsing into lines of regret and sorrow. "I'm sorry," he said in a low voice. "You must think I'm a complete—"

"Yes, I do," she cut him off, her voice breaking. "But I still want to save our marriage. If you don't, then there's nothing much I can do about it, I suppose. But even if you become single again, you're still a dad. Don't forget that. Please."

And then, not trusting herself to say anything more without breaking down completely, she turned and headed out of the pub.

Sarah walked on autopilot, just as she had the other day to the inn, one foot in front of another, her mind blank because she couldn't manage anything more. She couldn't bear to think about any of this.

She'd got halfway home when a sob escaped her, and she fell to her knees, right there on the pavement, her arms wrapped around her middle. *Nathan...* How could this have happened to her? To them? Was he really going to opt out of their marriage like it was a business deal he could walk away from?

"Miss, miss... Are you all right?"

Sarah blinked up to see a kindly looking man walking his little terrier gazing down at her.

"Yes." She gulped back the tears she wasn't ready to let fall. "Yes. Sorry. Just..." There was no explanation to be kneeling on a cold, wet pavement, and so she lurched up, gave him a quick, apologetic smile, and kept walking. She couldn't go home and face the children by herself, not without breaking down all over again.

Resolutely, Sarah picked up her phone, dialed.

"Mum?" she said when her mother answered. "Can you come and get me? I need you…"

CHAPTER 18

GWEN

Gwen had learned to be good in a crisis. She'd had to, after David died, because she hadn't had him to lean on. When she'd been younger, she'd been a bit of a panicker; David would tease her about getting into a flap. Now, when Sarah called her, sounding so broken, Gwen felt as if she knew exactly what to do.

"I'm coming right now," she stated calmly. "Where are you?"

"I don't know." Sarah let out a hiccuppy sob which tore at Gwen's heart. "Somewhere between home and the Deverill Arms... um, Ash Grove?"

"I'll be there in five minutes."

Gwen felt surprisingly, almost eerily, calm as she slipped out of the house—Matthew and Ellie were in the sitting room, watching something on the telly—and into the car. She wasn't used to driving at night, and it took her a moment to orient herself in the dark, driving slowly down the lane with a crunch of gravel. Whatever Sarah was going through, whatever happened, she was glad to be able to help her daughter now, and grateful that Sarah had finally reached out to her.

Five minutes later, Gwen was slowly driving down Ash Grove in the neighboring village of Llanfarth, peering through the darkness that was relieved only by the occasional twinkle of Christmas lights from various houses. After a few minutes of crawling along the street, she saw Sarah huddled under a lamppost, looking miserable. *Oh, Sarah...*

Gwen pulled carefully over to the curb and Sarah opened the door on the passenger side and climbed in.

"Sorry," she said. "I had a major wobble. I'm a little better now." She wiped at her damp cheeks.

"I'm glad you rang me, Sarah. So glad." Gwen hesitated. "Do you want to talk about it? Or do you need to get right home?"

Sarah leaned her head back against the seat. "Nathan's left me," she stated flatly, her eyes closed. "He moved out two weeks ago. I'm sorry, I know I should have told you."

Gwen shook her head, pushing her own shock to one side to focus on her daughter. "Don't worry about that—"

"We met tonight, and I was hoping we would talk about how we could work this out. Instead, he told me he wasn't sure that he wanted to be married to me anymore. Or married, full stop. I wasn't actually surprised, come to think of it." A sigh gusted out of her, seeming to come from the depths of her being. "But at the same I was completely shocked, if that makes any sense."

"It does," Gwen replied quietly, placing her hand on her daughter's. "Darling, I'm so very sorry."

"It's Mairi and Owen I'm really worried about," Sarah told her, her voice hitching. "I mean, I am devastated, no question, but I know I'll recover. Eventually. But the children... Nathan seems like he's not all that concerned about seeing them. He says he will make more of an effort, so maybe that will change..." She shook her head slowly. "Is he having a midlife crisis? I don't know. It's like he woke up one morning and decided he didn't want our life anymore. Who does that?"

"I don't know," Gwen said after a moment, wishing there was something helpful she could say. "He might reconsider, Sarah—"

Sarah shook her head. "Right now, I don't think so. I'm not saying that just to be pessimistic, but... the truth is, he *didn't* wake up one morning and decide that—or if he did, it was well over six months ago, not today or yesterday or when have you. This has been going on a long time, longer than I even realized, I think, because I was so focused on other things. I do hope he reconsiders when it comes to the children, but as for me..." She glanced down at her lap.

"What do you want to do?" Gwen asked after a moment. "Are Mairi and Owen back at home?"

"Yes." Sarah gave something close to a shudder. "I just couldn't face going back to them, their questions. That house... I used to love that house, everything so modern and sleek, just as I liked it. Now I think I hate it and everything it represents—this picture-perfect life I never actually had." A sob escaped her, and she pressed her hand to her mouth. "I don't know what to do," she whispered through her fingers, an abject confession, one Sarah—the old Sarah—*never* made.

Once again, Gwen felt that sense of calm, of decision, come over her. "I know what you should do," she stated firmly. "I'll drive you back home and you'll tell Mairi and Owen to get their things. Then we'll head back to Bluebell and have a sleepover. Tomorrow's Friday—why don't they miss a day of school? Take a personal day. Everyone's allowed at least one, surely."

"Mairi would go ballistic, to miss a day of school right now—"

"But maybe," Gwen suggested gently, "that's exactly what she needs."

Sarah turned to gaze at her with damp eyes. "Maybe you're

right," she admitted shakily. "Maybe we all need a bit of a break —from life. Just not like Nathan's having!" She let out a wobbly laugh and Gwen smiled in sympathy at her daughter.

"All right, then," she said, and started the car. "Let's go."

Just a minute later, they were back at the house, and Gwen walked in with Sarah, who seemed to have gone very quiet and dazed.

"*Granny?*" Mairi came downstairs, looking surprised, and then suspicious. "Why are you here? And what's wrong with Mum?" She glanced at Sarah, who tried to smile and didn't quite manage it.

"Nothing's wrong with your mum," Gwen replied, "except that she's having a bit of a hard time right now, and we're all going to pull together. How does a sleepover at the inn tonight sound?"

"But it's a school night—" Mairi protested, sounding both scandalized and confused.

"How about a day off tomorrow?" Gwen suggested. "Revise at home if you need to, but only after pancakes for breakfast, with ice cream and whipped cream." She smiled at her grand-daughter. "I think you've been working rather hard, Mairi, and sometimes you need to hit the reset button. Take some time out to refresh."

"But—"

"For *everyone's* sake," Gwen finished quietly, raising her eyebrows meaningfully, and, thankfully, Mairi stopped protesting.

"All right," she said, glancing uncertainly at Sarah, who hadn't said a word. "I'll get my things. Mum...?"

"Sorry, darling," Sarah said, coming to herself with a weak smile. "I just think it would be nice to be around family right now."

"Dad..." Mairi's voice wobbled, making Gwen's heart ache for her.

"He's fine," Sarah told her. "He's going to see you very soon. We can talk about all that later." With what had to have been superhuman strength, she gave Mairi a reassuring smile. Gwen gently squeezed her daughter's arm in quiet support.

Five minutes later, they were all piled in Gwen's car, heading back to the inn, Mairi still apprehensive, Owen excited for a day off school. As they entered the house, Ellie came out of the sitting room, doing a double take at seeing Sarah, Mairi, and Owen all filing in behind Gwen.

"What... Is everything okay?" she asked, shooting Sarah a probing glance that made Gwen realize, in an instant, that Sarah must have already told Ellie something about what had happened with Nathan. It was understandable that Sarah would find it easier to talk to Ellie than her mother about certain things; she was glad Sarah had had someone to confide in.

"Everything's fine," she assured Ellie. "Just having a sleepover."

"I don't even know why we're here," Owen mumbled, sounding more scared than annoyed.

Again, Gwen's heart ached for her two grandchildren. Even if Sarah hadn't yet told them what had happened with Nathan tonight, they must have guessed the gist of what was going on.

"That's great," Ellie replied, injecting an enthusiasm into her voice that Gwen was thankful for. "Jess will be thrilled! And Ben, too. Why don't you both head upstairs?"

"I think I will, too," Sarah said. She was gray-faced with exhaustion. "I'll have to sleep in one of the guest rooms... sorry about that, Ellie." She practically swayed on her feet. "I'll try not to mess anything up."

"That's totally fine," Ellie assured her. "The guests aren't coming for weeks, anyway. You can be our guinea pig! Let me know how the experience is, whether the room needs any more finishing touches." She paused before adding a bit apologetically, "That is, if you want to. No pressure, of course."

"Thanks," Sarah replied briefly. She glanced at Owen and Mairi. "Shall we go up, guys?"

As the three of them headed upstairs, Ellie glanced questioningly at Gwen. "Did Nathan..." she began, only to trail off uncertainly.

"You might know more than I do," Gwen replied. "Where's Matthew?"

"He got a call from New York ten minutes ago," Ellie replied, trying to sound matter-of-fact, but with a bit of a wobble in her voice. "He's taking it upstairs."

Gwen's breath caught. So much was happening all at once! "Oh, Ellie..."

"I don't know what to think about any of it," Ellie confessed on a sigh. "And so, I haven't been thinking about it all. Not the most sensible option, I know."

"Maybe the *most* sensible," Gwen returned. "A body—and a brain—can only take so much. Sometimes it's better not to try to tackle everything emotional all at once." She thought, briefly, of the disappointment she'd felt about John. He hadn't emailed since he'd returned home, which was over a week ago now. The worst part was, she wasn't even that surprised. It was something she'd been trying not to think about, what with everything else going on.

"Poor Sarah," Ellie said quietly. "She told me Nathan had moved out a couple of weeks ago, but then didn't seem to want to talk about it after that."

"No, she hadn't said a word of any of it to me, really, until tonight."

Should she have pushed Sarah to share more? Gwen wondered. She'd felt pretty pushy, already.

No, she decided, Sarah had to handle this in her own way, in her own time. What was important was that her family was there for her when she needed them to be... and they would be.

. . .

Gwen woke early the next morning, her mind already buzzing before she'd so much as climbed out of bed. She'd gone to bed before she'd heard about Matthew's call with New York, and when she'd checked on Sarah before she'd turned in herself, her daughter had already fallen asleep. She'd looked completely drained, curled up on her side under the cover, her hands palm up by her face. Gwen had crept in and tucked the duvet a bit more closely around her shoulder. You never stopped being a mother.

Now she was determined to make a fry-up to end all fry-ups, plus the American accoutrements—pancakes, maple syrup, even ice cream, as she'd said to Mairi. As she came into the kitchen, Daisy clambered up from her bed by the Aga and went to sniff her slippers.

"Well, hello there," Gwen said, reaching down to stroke the puppy, only to stiffen in surprise when she heard her daughter reply.

"Good morning."

"Sarah!" Gwen pressed her hand to her heart. "I didn't see you there."

"Sorry to startle you." Sarah was sitting at the kitchen table, huddled in a fleece and pajamas, a cup of coffee in front of her.

"You couldn't sleep?" Gwen surmised gently, and Sarah nodded.

"My mind keeps going around in circles." She glanced at her mother, her face full of confusion, possessing a vulnerability Gwen hadn't seen her daughter reveal in a very long while, if ever. "Mum, I don't know what to do."

Slowly, Gwen lowered herself into a chair opposite Sarah's. "Well, you don't need to decide everything today," she said reasonably. Her heart ached for her daughter, but she was determined to be practical... as Sarah so often was. "In fact, you don't need to decide *anything* today. We're having a day off, aren't we? No school, no stress."

"I'm meant to go into work..."

"You never take sick days," Gwen reminded her. "Maybe take one today."

"Maybe," Sarah agreed with a small smile, before her face crumpled. She put her hands up to hide her expression, her shoulders shaking for a moment before she took a steadying breath. "It's not even a surprise," she told Gwen when she'd recovered herself a bit. "Which is awful, really. I've been dreading something like this happening for months."

"I'm so sorry, darling."

"Weirdly, though," Sarah continued, picking up her coffee cup and cradling it between her hands, "it's also something of a relief. I'm not even sure why. Maybe because I hated being in this limbo of not knowing. At least now I know."

"He might change his mind," Gwen felt compelled to point out.

"He might," Sarah agreed, "although, right now, I'm seriously doubting that." She didn't want to entirely give up on her marriage, but right now she felt too dispirited about the state of it to offer any further optimism. "And, in any case," she finished, "I can't live my life waiting for him to come back. I need to *do* something."

Gwen had a mental image of Sarah cutting up Nathan's suits, or throwing all his belongings out the window. Her daughter had to be furious as well as deeply hurt, but she was acting as level-headed as usual. Almost.

"What are you thinking you'd like to do?" she asked.

"I don't know." Sarah let out a sigh. "Nathan aside, I haven't been very happy for a while now. Not because of him, but because of me. And I want to change that." She pursed her lips before admitting, "I'm thinking about quitting my job."

Gwen managed to mask her surprised alarm at this news. Quitting your job when you might be about to get divorced did not seem like the smartest move, and definitely very unlike

Sarah, but maybe that was the point. "All right," she agreed equably. "What would you do instead?"

"I have no idea." Sarah slid her a glance that was almost amused. "This doesn't sound like me at all, does it?"

"No," Gwen replied with an answering smile, "but based on what you've been saying, that's not necessarily a bad thing..." She raised her eyebrows in query and Sarah nodded slowly as she took a sip of her coffee.

"No," she agreed as she set the cup down, resolve hardening her voice even as her expression lightened. "It's not."

CHAPTER 19

ELLIE

The sharp, clean scent of fir tree filled the house as Matthew and Ben staggered through the back door, the Christmas tree held between them. Needles were dropping everywhere, but Ellie could clean those up easily enough. Daisy pranced around them, barking excitedly at all the commotion.

"Careful... easy does it... watch that vase!" Ellie called as they maneuvered the tree through the hall and into the sitting room. The tree for the photo shoot hadn't lasted, of course, and this one was fresh and new, smelling wonderful and ready for the guests that were coming in just a few days, one week before Christmas.

Ellie could hardly believe how the time had flown by. It had felt as if someone had pushed the fast-forward button—on every aspect of life. The biggest news, of course, was Matthew's job, or at least the possibility of it.

The night Sarah had come over with Mairi and Owen, he'd been on the phone for over an hour; Ellie had assumed that was a good sign—for him—but she wasn't completely sure, just as she couldn't decide how she felt about it all, especially when there was so much to do.

Finally, when everyone else had gone to bed, and Ellie was curled up in the sitting room, watching the last embers of the fire flicker to ash, Matthew had come downstairs. His expression had been composed, a bit guarded, and Ellie hadn't been able to tell a thing from it.

"Well?" she'd finally asked, when it had seemed as if he wasn't actually going to say anything.

"They want to fly me over for a final interview, but it's looking positive. Very positive." His voice had been filled with quiet pride. "They want to fly you over, too."

"Me?" Ellie had straightened up, shocked. "Why me?"

"Because they want to make sure this move works for both of us, and for the whole family." His expression had turned earnest, hopeful. "This is a small, bespoke company, Ellie, but a good one, and they have a great personal touch. They care about their employees." Unlike the last behemoth of an organization he'd worked for, who hadn't seemed to care about them at all.

Ellie had been more than half-expecting the news that they'd want him to come, but she still felt overwhelmed by the reality of it, its seeming suddenness, even though they'd been waiting for news for weeks. "When?" she'd finally asked, because she hadn't known what else to say.

"I said I couldn't do before Christmas, because of the inn. So, first week of January, ideally."

"You said that?" She'd been touched, that he would put the inn first, over something clearly so very important to him. She'd also been glad he had, because she absolutely had not been able to imagine dropping everything to jet over to New York.

"Yes, they were fine with it. They're really..." He'd blown out a breath, smiled. "They're really great that way."

Ellie had felt a lurch of tangled emotion—affection for Matthew, pleasure and pride that he'd been given this opportunity, one he deserved, but also fear. Terror, really, because New

York? Their family? Moving *again*? Leaving Gwen, Sarah, the inn, their whole life here?

"So, will that work?" Matthew had asked. "First week of January? Mum will probably be able to watch the kids."

Ellie had gazed at the dying fire, taken a deep breath. This was important to Matthew, she'd reminded herself, and she needed to be as considerate of him, with this job, as he'd been with her and the inn. "Yes," she'd said, turning to smile up at him. "That will work."

Now, as Matthew and Ben wrestled the tree into its stand, she was trying not to think about the trip to New York in just a few weeks. They hadn't even told the children about it yet; somehow there hadn't been the time, even though, really, Ellie knew they should have made it. It was important, important enough that they needed a quiet space, without the normal chaos of a big family, so they could explain, listen, reassure. But, right now, they had a tree to decorate, and the Christmas season to enjoy.

Ellie had loved this time of year since moving to Wales—the cold, crisp days, the lights decorating the village and the massive Christmas tree on the green. She loved browsing the shops in Abergavenny or Monmouth while Christmas carols played and she picked out presents. The inn had been full of wonderful, Christmassy smells—cinnamon, nutmeg, ginger. Gwen always seemed to have a tray of something delicious in the oven. And now the most important bit—the tree!

"Right, Ava," Ellie said to her youngest daughter, who was dancing around on her tiptoes, desperate to start decorating their Christmas tree. "I think we're almost ready to hang the ornaments."

Ava had had three blood tests in the last few weeks; after the random blood sugar test had come back "borderline," she'd been scheduled for a glycated hemoglobin test as well as a fasting blood sugar test. They were still waiting on the results of those, but Ellie had begun reading up on Type 1 diabetes, as it was seeming more and more likely that Ava might indeed have diabetes. What she read had concerned her, not just for the obvious medical reasons, but also because it seemed to require so much attention and supervision, especially for a child as young as Ava. If Ava did have diabetes, it would, in some ways, involve the whole family, and it would be a major lifestyle change—always needing to check her levels, dealing with highs or lows, administering insulin, monitoring her diet and physical activity. Ellie wanted to be prepared, or at least as prepared as she could be for such an event.

Ben's bullying episode, at least, seemed to have been resolved. Both Owen and Ben had apologized to the boys whom they'd pushed around; it had been a necessary and difficult conversation—one neither Ben nor Owen had wanted to have at all, but both boys had seemed a little lighter afterward, and Ellie was hopeful that the whole thing had provided some teachable moments.

Josh seemed a little less anxious about secondary school after attending an open house but Jess was still in a funk about Sophie, who seemed to be hanging around a lot of other kids. *Life*, Ellie thought with both a sigh and a smile. *It never stops.*

"Can I hang one, Mummy?" Ava asked, holding up a glittery, gold ornament that had come from Gwen's box of treasures. "Can I, please?"

"Yes, you may." Ellie glanced at the ornaments she'd bought for the interior design look she'd been hoping for—little gold bows, scarlet-capped Santas, a selection of tasteful baubles in matching colors. Now all of it was mixed in with the kind of homemade decorations that, she told herself, made every tree unique. She'd come around to the idea of homemade decorations, even the well-worn ones. After all, the vision they'd sold the newspaper was of a family-friendly, homegrown type of place, and that was indeed what the Bluebell Inn was. It was,

Ellie hoped, what the guests wanted—glittery pinecones and LED Christmas trees included.

"I made this in year three, I think," Matthew remarked as he fished out a styrofoam snowman covered in silver glitter. "I can't believe Mum kept it!"

"I kept them all," Gwen replied as she came into the room. "What a marvelous tree! Isn't the smell gorgeous?" She smiled around at everyone before helping Ava to hang another old-fashioned ornament. "You've done such a fabulous job, Ellie."

"Well, I didn't do it by myself," Ellie replied. "Everyone has been amazing, chipping in and helping out. And John's nativity pieces look wonderful in the garden."

"Yes, he did do a good job with those, didn't he?" Gwen agreed.

Ellie hadn't really talked to her mother-in-law about John, or whether she'd see him again now that he'd returned home. Gwen hadn't seemed particularly sad about his departure, though, so perhaps she and Sarah had been reading too much into that relationship. In any case, she was glad Gwen seemed content, regardless of the future of the inn, and the nativity pieces were lovely, the oak smoothed to a silky softness, possessing a fluid, sinuous quality, easy for children to handle.

Even as they now got ready for their guests, as Christmas loomed promisingly on the horizon, the ultimate new beginning, Ellie couldn't help but think this was starting to feel more like an ending. A last hurrah rather than the kickstart she'd envisioned. It wasn't a bad way to bow out, she told herself as she looked around the cozy room, from the tree now bedecked with ornaments and tinsel, to the comforting, crackling fire, to the antique nutcracker standing sentry over a bowl of glossy walnuts, with a full house and a very merry Christmas.

"You look rather serious," Matthew remarked as the children continued to decorate the tree. Gwen had put on some Christmas carols, and the choir of York Minster was belting out

"O Come All Ye Faithful." He slid his arm around her waist, and she leaned her head on his shoulder.

"I was just thinking," Ellie replied before adding, "we need to talk to the kids about New York."

"I know." Matthew pulled her a little closer. "How do you think they're going to respond?"

"I honestly don't know. But the sooner we tell them, the better, really. Give them as much time as possible to adjust to the idea." Time she still needed.

He gave a little nod of assent. "Well, there's no time like the present, is there?"

"I suppose not." Ellie glanced back at their beloved brood with mingled affection and worry; Ava was on her tiptoes, trying to hang a glass-blown angel from a bough that was just a little out of her reach. Josh was searching through the box of decorations, looking for his favorites, and Ben and Jess were arguing, good-naturedly at least, over who was going to put the star on the top of the tree. They did this every year, each one insisting the other had done it the year before, and no one could actually remember. How would they all respond to the news that they were contemplating not just leaving little Llandrigg, but moving from a small Welsh village to one of the biggest cities in the world?

They'd been so good about the move here, Ellie thought with a rush of love and gratitude. They'd had their bumps at the start, it was true, but it had been a big adjustment and they'd made it. Was it really fair to ask them to make another one?

And yet that was exactly what they were going to do.

"Hey, guys," she said lightly. "When we've finished the tree, we need to have a family powwow round the kitchen table. I'll make hot chocolate." Ellie caught Gwen's eye, who gave a little nod of understanding.

"What?" Jess's eyes narrowed suspiciously. Clearly, her light tone hadn't fooled her oldest daughter—or any of her children, for that matter. All of them were now looking at her with varying degrees of suspicion and alarm. "What kind of *powwow*? When do you even use that word?" Jess demanded, her hands now planted on her hips. "What's going on?"

"We have an idea to put to you," Matthew said in his familiar, easy way. "And we want to know what you think about it. That's all. Opinions warmly welcomed."

"What idea?" Ben asked. He sounded interested, rather than suspicious, and Josh and Ava were both looking alert, even excited, which Ellie hoped was a good sign.

"Yes, what idea?" Jess asked. "What's going on? Is it about the inn? What do you have to tell us that's so important?"

"I'll make the hot chocolate," Ellie said, as she turned from the room. Clearly, the conversation needed to happen right now.

Ten minutes later, they were all settled around the kitchen table with mugs of hot chocolate with lashings of whipped cream—a special treat for what might be a difficult conversation. Gwen had quietly made herself scarce, which Ellie appreciated. Daisy was under the table, sniffing around excitedly, no doubt on the lookout for a splash of hot chocolate or dollop of cream.

"So, what's going on?" Jess asked as she wiped cream from her upper lip. "Why are you guys acting so weird and so serious?"

Ellie glanced at Matthew, willing for him to take the lead, which, thankfully, he did.

"I've had a job possibility come up," he told them. "The kind of office job I had before, working in investments. It's not for definite yet, but I've had a couple of interviews, and we're moving onto the next step, and I wanted to know what you all thought about it."

He was met, rather predictably, with four blank looks. None of their children had twigged yet that this meant a move.

"Okay," Jess finally said, sounding nonplussed. "Whatever."

"Does this mean you won't be around at the inn?" Josh asked, a note of anxiety creeping into his voice. "Because you'll be at an office?"

"There aren't any offices around here, Daddy," Ava told him, rather kindly. "I think you'll have to drive in your car."

Which provided the perfect, if rather poignant, opening.

"You're right, Ava," Matthew said with a crooked smile. "There aren't many offices in little Llandrigg. But the job I'm talking about is a little farther away than I could get to in my car." Matthew paused and Ellie saw Jess's eyes narrow as understanding began to dawn. "It's in New York City."

"*New York!*" The words exploded out of Jess, and Ben frowned.

"Would you fly there?" he asked. "And come back on weekends or something?"

Matthew let out a soft huff of laughter. "That would be rather a long way to go, don't you think?"

"So, what are you saying?" Jess demanded.

"We could all move back to the US, to New York," Matthew stated, his tone turning gentle. "The company I'd be working for would offer a very generous package. We could live in the city proper, rather than the suburbs, maybe right by Central Park! It would be pretty different from Llandrigg, I know, but it could be kind of an adventure, don't you think? How many kids get to say they've lived in a little village in Wales as well as the Big Apple?"

"About four, I'd say," Jess replied in such a dry voice that Ellie couldn't help but let out a laugh.

"Yes," she agreed, entering into the conversation for the first time. "You might be right there, Jess. Certainly not that many, if any—other than you."

"We're going to move..." Josh stated slowly, his forehead screwed up into a frown, "to New York?"

"Yes, Josh." Matthew smiled at his youngest son. "That's the idea."

"But... what about Granny?" Ava asked. She sounded more practical than worried. "Would she come with us?"

"Well, no, I don't think so." Matthew exchanged a worried glance with Ellie; they hadn't really discussed this aspect of their move yet. "I think she'd stay here in Llandrigg. But we could visit her, and she could visit us, the way she used to, more than before, even. And we'd see Grandma and Grandpa in America a lot more, the way we did before." He paused, glancing around at them all, with their varying expressions of confusion, worry, thoughtfulness, and alarm. It was, Ellie knew, a lot to take in. "What do you guys think?" Matthew said after a few moments when no one had spoken. "I know you need to think about it for a while, but... initial thoughts?"

"I want to go," Jess stated baldly, surprising Ellie completely.

"You... do?" she asked, a bit stupidly, as she stared at her daughter.

"Yes, New York is, like, *so* cool. And I've liked living here, and I love Granny, but..." Jess bit her lip. "I miss America. And I miss Grandma and Grandpa. And the whole inn thing has been fun, but... it's a lot, Mom, having guests around, especially little kids. One of the kids snuck up into my room during half-term and got into all my makeup. To be honest, I'm kind of tired of stuff like that."

"I'm sorry, Jess. I didn't know." Her daughter had, Ellie thought with bemusement, slipped into calling her *Mom* rather than *Mum* without even realizing it.

"I'm glad you're excited, Jess." Matthew looked thrilled by the fact; Ellie suspected he'd been expecting a lot more resistance. "What about the rest of you?"

Ben shrugged. "I dunno. I like it here. Could I play football —I mean soccer—in New York?"

"I'm sure you could," Matthew assured him. "There's a soccer club that meets at the 92nd Street Y... maybe we could try to live near there."

He'd clearly been doing some research, Ellie thought. She was grateful Matthew was thinking about the children's needs, but... it still felt overwhelming.

"What about you, Josh?" Matthew asked. "How do you feel about it?"

Josh shrugged. "I don't know." His voice sounded small. "I was moving schools anyway, but... I don't like things changing."

And he never had, Ellie acknowledged with a rush of love. When Josh had been three, he'd grown out of his winter coat, a red one with yellow lightning bolts on the sleeves, and he'd been absolutely disconsolate at having to wear a new one. Moving to Llandrigg had been challenging, too, but he'd adapted so well. It made her heart ache to think of him having to do it again.

"Change can be hard," Matthew agreed. "But it can be exciting, too. And, like I said, this isn't for definite. Your mum and I will be heading to New York in January, to have a look around. We'll know more then."

"You're going to New York already?" Jess looked startled. "Can we go, too? This involves us, as well, you know."

"I know it does. I... I suppose you could. We'd have to pay for your airline tickets ourselves, but you could visit Grandma and Grandpa... it might be worth it?" Matthew glanced questioningly at Ellie.

How was she supposed to answer that?

"Yes, we can think about it," she said a bit faintly. This still felt as if it were happening so very fast. Their guests were arriving in a few days, and yet their minds were full of January in New York. It felt nearly impossible to span the two.

"If we move to New York," Ava asked in her sweet, piping voice, "what will happen to the inn?"

Matthew gave Ellie a guilty look. They hadn't addressed the inn at all in their conversation, and they really should have. "I don't know," he admitted. "Maybe it will close. Or maybe it will stay open—"

"Aunt Sarah could help run it," Jess suggested suddenly. "She was talking about leaving her job and doing something else."

"Was she?" This was news to Ellie, although, of course, she knew Sarah was going through somewhat of a reinvention. "Did she tell you that?"

"Yeah, when we came over the other day. She said she'd like to do something really different, but she had no idea what it would be."

"Well, that's interesting..." Matthew mused, and Ellie could tell from the gleam in his eyes that he saw a very neat solution in the making.

Ellie just wasn't sure whether she felt the same way.

"That went well," Matthew told her later, when the kids were in bed and they were in the sitting room, having a glass of wine by the fire, the lights of the Christmas tree twinkling merrily. Gwen had gone to bed too, and the evening was quiet and peaceful, the air outside cold and still. They'd been predicted a dusting of snow, which would be perfect for Christmas. "Don't you think it did?" he prompted.

"You mean with the kids? Yes, better than I thought," Ellie admitted. As she had settled onto the sofa, she'd gazed around the room with a rush of satisfaction at how cozy and welcoming it looked, but now she felt the familiar churn of anxiety as she thought about the future. "Although you know how changeable they can be, at their age. Tomorrow they might be saying something completely different."

"Yes, they might be," Matthew agreed. "We'll just have to take it day by day, but it felt like a good beginning."

"Yes, it did." If a good beginning was their kids being excited about moving to New York.

"What about you?" Matthew asked seriously. "Are you coming round to the idea?"

She sighed. "That's what it feels like," she told him. "Like something I have to *come round* to."

Matthew winced. "Sorry, I didn't mean that in a pejorative way—"

"I know. It's just... it's still hard for me. I'm scared to start over, to make new friends, to leave behind what is familiar. I was scared before, when we left Connecticut, and I'm scared now."

"But if you've done it once so successfully, you know you can do it again," Matthew told her with a smile.

"Yes, but there's no Bluebell Inn to rescue and organize my life around in Manhattan," Ellie replied wryly. What would she do without the inn?

"No, but there are plenty of literacy charities you could work for," Matthew answered. "That was something you were passionate about. I know you've made the inn your own, Ellie, truly, and I'm so grateful you did, but it was more my project than yours, at the start. Maybe it's time for you to have your own career aspirations back."

Ellie narrowed her eyes playfully at him—at least *mostly* playfully. "Are you just saying that to make moving sound more appealing?"

"Well, maybe," Matthew admitted with a laugh. "But I mean it, too. Ava's in school now, your life could really open up. You put your career on hold for a long time."

"That's true." It was something she'd never really thought

about while in Llandrigg, because she hadn't been able to think about it. There had simply been no opportunities. But now... for a second, she let herself picture it. Living in an apartment in the city, working at a charity, a totally different life than what she had now. She'd always loved the buzzy feel of Manhattan; she and Matthew had lived there for a couple of years before they'd had kids and made the expected pilgrimage to the suburbs. Could they do it again? Did she want to?

For the first time, a small smile curved her lips at the thought.

"I'll think about it," she told Matthew, only to have him rise from the sofa, a look of amazement on his face, as he pointed to the window.

"Snow," Matthew said.

Ellie turned, surprised and pleased to see thick, downy snowflakes drifting past the window and it felt like a benediction. Their guests would have a white Christmas, after all. As for after that... who knew what would happen? But Ellie suddenly felt excited by the prospect.

CHAPTER 20

SARAH

Unexpected snowstorms have blizzarded South Wales and cut off several villages from sources of electricity and water, leaving many in peril for the entire holiday season. Government sources say the disruption may last all the way through Christmas...

Sarah stared at the news article on her phone, hardly able to believe it. It had been snowing for three days straight, and the steep road down into Llandrigg had been completely cut off from the outside world. The morning after it had started, Sarah, Mairi, and Owen had all piled into her trusty Range Rover to head over to the inn; the vehicle's wheels had cut through the scant few inches, no problem, but that had changed now. Now, there was nearly a foot of snow, and school had been canceled through Christmas, and she and the children were stuck at the inn, stranded, unable to get home—and without anyone else able to get here.

Christmas was officially canceled.

When the snow had first started, Ellie had been as optimistic as Sarah.

"Snow for Christmas!" she had enthused, when Sarah had come into the kitchen that first morning, brushing flakes from the shoulders of her coat. "We'll have enough for the children to make snowmen, even! Isn't it wonderful?"

By evening, when the snow hadn't let up, Ellie's indefatigable cheer had started to falter just a little. "It's getting rather deep... I hope the roads will be cleared in time for the guests?" She'd glanced anxiously at Gwen. "Surely they will be?"

"I should think so," Gwen had replied, but she'd looked as worried as Ellie. "But we've never had this much snow before."

The next morning, the electricity had cut out and the roads became completely impassable. There was talk of the government declaring a state of emergency, and a volunteer foodbank had been opened at the church. The guests were due the following day, and Ellie had had to write painful emails explaining the situation.

In any case, most of the guests had been watching the news and realized what was going on—all of South Wales, as well as England from Birmingham to Bristol, had been affected, although not quite so badly as Llandrigg, down in a steep little valley, with treacherous, icy, snow-covered roads. They'd been more than willing to cancel.

"I can't *believe* this!" Ellie had wailed, the night before their guests had been meant to arrive, and now none were coming. "After all our work..."

"We can still enjoy it," Matthew had told her bracingly. "We can have the best family Christmas ever! We've got tons of food, and firewood, we're warm and safe... it could be worse, Ellie."

She'd stared at him in disbelief, and he'd given her a contrite look.

"I know it's a huge disappointment, Ellie, of course I do."

"You could say that," she had replied rather shortly, and Sarah couldn't blame her for her irritation. Ellie had been working flat out for two months, and all now for seemingly nothing. It had been a very bitter pill to swallow.

Sarah slid her phone back into the pocket of her dressing gown as she moved about the kitchen, cracking eggs into a pan on the Aga, which was thankfully oil-fired and so hadn't been affected by the power outage. Everything else, had, though, and they'd been using candles and a couple of oil lamps to light their way, which at least had seemed exciting to the children. Everyone was still asleep, but she thought it would be nice for them to wake up to the smell of eggs and bacon frying, on this day which had been meant to be so important, when their guests should have been arriving.

As disappointed as she was for Ellie's sake, Sarah could acknowledge she felt a little relieved that no one was expected. She'd been more than ready to make the big Christmas push, but the thought of a quiet Christmas with her family—minus Nathan, admittedly—felt like a blessing. Just like their impromptu sleepover, it was a moment out of time, and one she desperately needed. She was still trying to figure out where she went from here, and while she had few vague, barely formed ideas, she could use the time and space to flesh them out a bit more, to let her mind wander, her thoughts coalesce.

"That smells good!"

She turned to see Mairi slouching into the kitchen in her pajamas, and her heart lifted with hope. Her daughter had not been on speaking terms with her since Nathan had moved out, although she'd thawed a little in the last week or so. Sarah hoped it was a sign of better things yet to come.

"It does, doesn't it?" she agreed as Mairi curled up in an armchair in the corner of the room and Daisy jumped into her lap. "I thought everyone could use a good fry-up."

"Is Aunt Ellie still disappointed that no one's coming?" Mairi asked as she stroked the little dog. "She seemed pretty gutted last night."

"Yes, I think it's quite hard for her, after all the work she's done."

"But it doesn't really matter so much, does it," Mairi continued, "if they're moving to New York?"

"Well, it's not definite, that they're moving," Sarah reminded her. That particular bombshell had been dropped on her a few days ago, when Matthew had admitted he'd had a job prospect and they would be flying over in January, assuming the snow stopped by then...!

Sarah had been surprised and unsurprised at the same time; she'd realized she'd never totally accepted her brother running the inn as his career. He'd been too ambitious for that, and yet in an entirely different way from Nathan. It had never been about status or money for Matthew, the way Sarah had come to realize it had been for her husband. He'd simply enjoyed his job. She was not surprised to discover he'd been missing it, but she was saddened to think of them leaving Llandrigg.

"How do you feel about them possibly moving?" she asked Mairi. What with her daughter's sullenness toward her, she hadn't had a chance to talk through it with her properly. "You'll miss Jess, of course?"

"Yes, but..." Mairi hesitated, her head lowered, her gaze on the little spaniel curled up on her lap. "Don't freak out or anything, Mum, but I've been thinking about doing something different for A levels, anyway, so I wouldn't be at school with Jess."

"Oh?" Sarah realized she wasn't freaked out the way she once might have been, but simply intrigued. "And what is that?"

"Well." Mairi took a deep breath as she lifted her head to look at her. "I hate how stressed I get about academics. And it's not because of you or Dad, not really. It's because... I find it all so hard."

"You do?" Sarah couldn't hide her surprise. "You mean, harder than normal? But you've always been a straight-A student, Mairi." She bit her tongue, not wanting to make her daughter think she still had those expectations for her.

"I know, but it never, ever came easily to me," Mairi confessed. "And the truth is, I don't like it. I don't like studying, I don't like trying to get my head around all these complicated concepts... and the thought of doing A levels... of having to stress out about even more exams... I don't want to do it. I'm not sure I can."

Not do her A levels? Sarah thought she'd come a long way from how she'd been, so ambitious for her children, but A levels *were* kind of important. It was hard to get a decent job without them. Still, this was the most Mairi had talked to her in a long while, and she wasn't about to mess up the first proper conversation they'd had in weeks.

"So, what are you thinking of?" she asked as she set a cup of tea down on the table by her daughter's chair and sat opposite her at the kitchen table, smiling in what she hoped was a cheerful and expectant way.

"Well, there's a BTech in equine studies," Mairi ventured rather shyly. "There's a degree program over in Usk that offers it. That's only about twenty minutes away. I know it's not the same as A levels, and it might limit me career-wise, but I've realized how much I like riding Mabel, and just horses in general, and I've missed it this last year. A lot."

"I think Mabel has missed you," Sarah replied. She was glad her daughter had come to this realization, even if part of her was still surprised and a bit worried about what it might mean. Even so, she knew Mairi had to make her own choices. "I think that sounds like an interesting idea," she told her daughter. "We should definitely look into it."

Mairi looked nothing short of completely gobsmacked. "Er... really?" she stammered. "You don't mind me not doing A levels?"

Sarah smiled and lifted her shoulders in a shrug. "I don't

mind, if this is what you think you really want to do. I'd like to find out some more information, of course, and make sure you have a proper think about it, but, like I said... if it's what you want to do, Mairi, then great."

Mairi shook her head slowly as she gave a shaky laugh. "I didn't expect you to say that."

Sarah smiled faintly. "Well, maybe I've changed a little bit, in that regard."

"Yeah." Her daughter gave her a direct look. "You have."

"And is that a good thing?" Sarah asked, managing to keep her voice light, although she knew she cared rather a lot about Mairi's answer.

Mairi nodded slowly. "Yes," she said, her voice firm as a smile dawned on her face like the sun peeking over the horizon. "It is."

They lapsed into silence then, a more comfortable one than Sarah had experienced with her daughter in a long time. Outside, snow heaped the windowsills like mounds of icing; every branch and tree was similarly softly covered, making the whole world seemed hushed and still, a fairyland of ice and snow, perfect for Christmas—guests or not. It was an incredibly beautiful place, she thought with a touch of nostalgia, of gratitude. She'd lived so close to the inn all her life, she'd started to take it for granted, but she wouldn't any longer. She'd try not to.

"What do you think Dad will say about it?" Mairi asked as she picked up her mug of tea and cradled it between her hands. "Me not doing A levels?"

Sarah couldn't keep from giving a small sigh. "I don't know, but I hope he'll be as pleased and proud of you as I am."

Mairi nodded slowly. "You've changed," she said, "but he has, too."

Sarah tensed, not wanting to say anything that would influence her daughter against Nathan. He was still her father, after all, even if he seemed to have—temporarily, she hoped—forgotten that fact. "In what way, do you think?" she asked.

Mairi shrugged. "I don't know. He's just seemed like when he's with us, he'd rather be somewhere else. After a while, it starts to feel kind of... hurtful, I guess." She ducked her head. "I don't really want to be around someone like that, to be honest."

"Your dad is having a bit of a blip, it's true," Sarah replied carefully. "But he still loves you and Owen very much."

Mairi made a face. "Yeah, but you *have* to say that."

"It's true, sweetheart." Sarah knew she had to believe that. And she *did* believe it. Whatever happened between her and Nathan, she believed he would be there for his kids. He'd messaged them several times since the snowstorm, and they'd had a video chat, as well. He was trying, in his own way, and she was trying to let that be enough, for now.

"I know it's true, really," Mairi replied, wrinkling her nose, "but at some point, it's a little bit like, 'what have you done for me lately?'"

Sarah let out a sad, little laugh of acknowledgement. "Yes, I suppose it is," she agreed. "But he'll come around." Especially, perhaps, after spending Christmas alone in a corporate flat in Cardiff. He'd been planning to spend Christmas Eve with the kids; obviously that couldn't happen now. He might be missing them quite a lot.

"You must be feeling that way, Mum," Mairi said a bit hesitantly. "I mean, we're his kids, but you're his wife."

Sarah paused as she tried to frame her thoughts in a way she could reasonably express to her daughter. "Yes, it's hard," she finally admitted, "and it hurts. But we don't know what the future holds."

Mairi raised her eyebrows. "Do you think you and Dad will get back together?"

"I don't know." And, Sarah realized, she was actually okay with not knowing. She was learning to exist in the present, something she had to keep reminding herself to do, but it gave her a certain sense of peace that she'd never had before. Maybe Nathan would decide for certain that their marriage was over, or maybe he would ask her to try again... and maybe she would say yes. "But in the meantime," she told Mairi, "I'm thinking about what I want to do with my life, just as you're thinking about what to do with yours. I'm not sure I want to work as an accountant anymore."

"You don't?" Her daughter looked almost comically surprised. It was hard to understand and accept, Sarah knew, that your parents had dreams and hopes and lives just like you did. She'd felt the same about her mother and John, although she wasn't sure where that was going—if anywhere—now. Still, her mother had a right to her own life, whatever that meant, just as she had a right to hers.

"No, I don't," she replied. "And I was sort of playing with the idea—the really rather crazy idea—of opening my own stable yard."

"*What!*" Mairi looked dumbfounded, and Sarah let out a little laugh.

"I know it might sound like something completely out of left field, but Trina's selling up, as you know, and the Riding for the Disabled program is going to have to go all the way to Chepstow," Sarah explained.

"But... *where?*" Mairi asked. "I mean, would you buy a stable yard? Trina's?"

"No, I don't think so," she replied slowly. "I don't have the money for that, and in truth, I'm thinking of something slightly different." It was an idea that had been sliding in and out of her mind like an elusive shadow for a while now, and this was the first time she'd put it into words, given it credence. It felt both thrilling and a bit terrifying. "I was thinking about here, actually," she told Mairi. "If Uncle Matthew and Aunt Ellie move to New York, and the inn has to close... I could possibly take it over, but not as an inn. I'd run it as a sort of equine center. Granny has space in the barn—not as much, it's true, and we'd probably have to build more out back, in one of the paddocks, to give any horses more stabling. And I was thinking I could use the house as a guesthouse for disabled riders... they could come and stay here, have an intensive week of therapeutic riding. I was reading up on it and it really helps, apparently, especially after an injury. I could run it as a charity, even."

Mairi didn't reply and Sarah let out an embarrassed little laugh. Now that she'd said it all aloud, it sounded rather daft.

"Sorry," she told Mairi with a laugh. "It's just some jumbled thoughts I have. I don't know if it will actually come to anything. It probably won't." It would take a lot of money to set up—more, perhaps, than she'd get from the half of the proceeds from the sale of their house, if it came to that, and she had no idea if it was something that would take off, that would work at all. But she had felt an excitement about it that she hadn't felt about anything else, in a long while, and that was a very good feeling.

Mairi reached over to her, putting her hand on Sarah's, her face alight. "Mum," she exclaimed, squeezing Sarah's hand. "I think it sounds ace!"

CHAPTER 21

GWEN

It was not, Gwen reflected, the Christmas anyone had wanted, but it was, perhaps, the Christmas they'd all *needed*—enjoying each other and the inn, perhaps, at least for the latter, for the last time, which gave it an added bittersweet poignancy.

The week that had been meant to be their Christmas extravaganza had been, in its own way, a celebratory affair, despite the obvious and rather crushing disappointment of having to cancel all their guests. There had been sledge rides down the hill across the lane, and a snowman-building competition that Ava had triumphantly won. There had been epic games of Monopoly by the fire, and then, later, relaxed glasses of mulled wine after the children had gone to bed. There had been cozy suppers in the kitchen, and afternoon tea and scones —someone had to eat them, after all—and full fry-ups courtesy of Sarah, while the snow had continued to drift gently down, blanketing the whole world in white and making the inn its own cozy cocoon.

All told, it really had been a rather wonderful week, and now it was Christmas morning, and Gwen had got up to put her traditional Christmas cinnamon buns in the Aga, feeling very glad and grateful for the life she led, with its many blessings. It was a poignant reminder, she thought as she pottered around the kitchen in her dressing gown, to enjoy life while it lasted, in whatever season you found yourself in. There were ups and downs, beginnings and endings... you couldn't have one without the other, and sometimes you found yourself having both at the same time.

As for the future... well, that would never be a certainty, by its very nature. And like Sarah and Ellie had both had to do, Gwen was trying to live in the peace of the moment, and not worry about what came next. Easy enough to do when life was going well, a little harder when the going got bumpy. And yet here they were, bumping along as best as they could, and managing—mostly—to enjoy the ride.

"I thought I smelled cinnamon buns!" Ellie exclaimed as she came into the kitchen, tying the sash of her own dressing gown. Her blond hair was pulled back into a messy bun, and her blue eyes were alight with enthusiasm, despite the recent disappointments. "I couldn't sleep, but not in a bad way. I was feeling excited about the children opening their presents. Matthew always said I'm more like a child at Christmas than they are... I'm just glad I finished all the shopping before the snowstorm. Ava's getting the dollhouse she's been wanting for ages, and I've managed to keep it hidden, which is a feat in itself."

"Yes, indeed." Gwen smiled at her daughter-in-law, both proud and grateful for how she'd rallied despite the setback of the snowstorm, as well as the potential move to New York. Ellie had had a lot to deal with all at once, and she'd handled it with both grace and aplomb. "How are you feeling about everything?" Gwen asked as she made them both cups of tea.

She was suddenly reminded, rather poignantly, of how she and Ellie had both risen early one morning, soon after Ellie had moved here, and how they'd had cups of coffee right in this kitchen, the atmosphere between them so stiff and awkward as they'd fumbled to understand each other and failed. Two years had changed a lot of things, Gwen acknowledged, for the mood now was comfortable and easy, if more than a little bittersweet.

"I feel... hopeful," Ellie replied after a moment. "Even though I didn't expect to be. I've been resisting this move— again—but I've started to see how it could be a good thing, or at least an exciting and interesting possibility, and in any case, maybe things aren't meant to last forever." She let out a little self-conscious laugh. "That's my deep thinking, anyway. We gave it a good run, though, didn't we, with the inn?" The smile she gave Gwen was lopsided, filled with both sorrow and hope.

"We did." Gwen sat across from her as they both sipped their tea. "And I think you're right with your deep thinking. I was just reflecting how there are different seasons to life, and that's all right. It's nice, really, because you wouldn't want everything to stay the same. Static, as it were."

"No, I don't suppose you would," Ellie agreed thoughtfully. "How are you feeling about the inn possibly closing? I suppose you're due your retirement!"

"Yes, you'd think so," Gwen granted with a laugh, "but just the other day Sarah spoke to me about an idea she had for this place. A reinvention, as it were, although it's just a glimmer of a possibility right now."

Ellie looked both surprised and intrigued. "Oh? What's that?"

Briefly, Gwen explained Sarah's hesitant thoughts about running the inn as a charity for disabled riders. "I don't think I'd get nearly as involved this time round," she finished, "but I'd like to be here, to be supportive and help out where I can, especially with things with Nathan as they are."

"That sounds brilliant," Ellie replied after a moment,

clearly needing a few seconds to absorb this turn in events. "And just the kind of thing Sarah might need."

"Yes, my thoughts exactly," Gwen agreed, and they shared a small, conspiratorial smile before she rose to take the buns, glistening and golden, out of the Aga.

It wasn't long before the children were trooping down, eager for their cinnamon buns and exclaiming over their Christmas stockings, which they opened in a flurry of yet more exclamations and white tissue paper. Then they were heading outside to play in the snow, while Matthew built up the fires and Sarah, Ellie, and Gwen all worked in companionable harmony in the kitchen, making preparations for the Christmas dinner.

The turkey was massive, and had thankfully been delivered the day before the snow began in earnest, taking up a whole shelf of the fridge. Sarah took charge of the Yorkshire pudding batter, while Ellie peeled potatoes and Gwen stuffed the turkey. The mood was relaxed but also jolly, and despite all the recent sorrows and disappointments, Gwen felt as if her heart were overflowing with thankfulness and joy that they'd arrived at this place.

"This is really *fun*," Ellie announced, almost in surprise, when they were having a small glass of sherry to fortify themselves before it was time to open presents and finish the dinner preparations. "I didn't expect it to be, because I was only thinking about the disappointment of not having the guests coming. But now that it's Christmas, I'm not sure I would have wanted it any other way."

"Nor me," Sarah admitted. "It feels a bit of a guilty pleasure, enjoying all the things meant for guests when it's just us—I particularly enjoyed that Baileys you bought, Ellie!—but I think it's just what I needed. I'm only glad I managed to make it over here before the snow got too deep."

"Another day or two and it will probably be cleared

completely," Gwen remarked. "It usually melts quite quickly, but it's lovely while it lasts."

Which was really a sentiment for all of life, she thought with a smile as she finished her sherry. They were all facing new things—Ellie, with her potential move to New York, Sarah with the possibility of starting this horseback riding venture. As for Gwen herself? Well, she didn't know what the future held, only that she was ready for it.

The rest of the day passed in a blur of activity and enjoyment—opening presents by the tree, a massive roast dinner that they brought to the heaving table, and dessert after—a traditional Christmas pudding, raisins and all, flaming with brandy, and an enormous meringue overflowing with whipped cream and fresh fruit.

Afterward, Matthew insisted that the women of the house sit by the fire and enjoy themselves while he did the washing up. Gwen was grateful to get off her feet, and she had the requisite tin of Cadbury Roses to dip into while they listened to a replay of the King's speech and the children lounged around, playing with their presents or content simply to sit in a post-meal stupor.

Gwen was just unwrapping a hazelnut whirl when the lights flickered and then went back on.

"Civilization at last," Sarah exclaimed, and Ellie said with a wry laugh,

"Just in time."

Gwen glanced around at all her grandchildren, her heart overflowing with love. What did the future hold for them all? Mairi had told her about her plans to study equine management, which Gwen thought was brilliant, and Owen was looking forward to getting more involved in the stables, if Sarah's idea did come to pass.

Jess was excited to live in a place where there was high fashion and YouTubers, and Ben had looked up New York City

soccer clubs online and seemed very excited about them. Josh
was also excited, because New York City had a junior chess
league *and* a massive Lego store, and Ava, as ever, was optimisti-
cally looking forward to making new friends. They were still
waiting to hear about whether she indeed had diabetes, but, in
the meantime, Ellie was doing her best to monitor her sugar
intake. The doctors had assured her that if Ava did have
diabetes, it had been caught early, and she wouldn't be in
danger before she could be properly seen, after the snow had
cleared. Ellie had confessed to Gwen that if Ava did indeed
have diabetes, it would be a relief to be in a city with excellent
medical facilities nearby.

It was going to be all right for them, Gwen thought. Maybe
it would be wonderful, but even if it wasn't, they'd get through,
learn through the downs and enjoy the ups.

She rose from her chair to go into the kitchen, where
Matthew was scrubbing the last of the pans.

"The electricity came on," she told him. "Did you even
notice?"

"I did, although it hasn't made as much difference as I
thought," he replied with a smile. "Electricity doesn't scrub out
this pan, unfortunately."

"No, I don't suppose it does. Nothing beats elbow grease."

As she came to stand next to him, he put his arm around
her, and she leaned into him in a way she hadn't in a long time.
"All right, Mum?" he asked softly, and she smiled, her head
against his shoulder.

"Yes, I'm all right."

"New York—"

"Is very exciting. I'm thrilled for you, Matthew. Really,
I am."

He glanced down at her, an expression of concern on his
face. "And what about John?" he asked, and startled, Gwen
blinked up at him.

"What about him?"

"I just... I hope things didn't cool off there because of me. I think I was taken aback because it made me miss Dad, in a strange way. I hadn't felt that kind of grief in a long time. You always carry it with you, but you don't always feel it."

"I know," Gwen replied quietly. "I think it did the same for me. But John and I are just friends, Matthew." Although she found she still thought of him quite a lot. Was he thinking of her? He hadn't messaged her. Not yet, but maybe he would. She realized she hadn't entirely given up hope, just made peace with the idea, either way. "But if I did become... interested... in someone," she asked Matthew, "at some point, would you mind?"

"No, of course not." He looked affronted that she would think so, even though, considering what had transpired before, it was a reasonable question. "I mean... I hope he'd be a good guy."

"He would," Gwen assured him with a laugh. "Although I don't even know who he is yet, or if he exists at all!"

"Oh, he exists," Matthew replied. "Somewhere."

Maybe somewhere nearby, even. Gwen smiled at the thought.

Back in the sitting room, the children were beginning to stir, sleepy from the day's exertions. Ellie heaved herself up from the sofa with a big sigh and started gently chivvying them to bed, while Sarah, with a grin for Gwen, poured herself another Baileys.

"Tonight is for relaxing!" she pronounced, and Ellie laughed as she scooped up a sleepy Ava.

"Save some for me," she told Sarah before she headed upstairs.

Sarah glanced at Gwen, the bottle aloft. "Mum?"

"Oh, why not?" Gwen replied a little recklessly. "It is Christmas, after all."

"Yes, although, in an odd way, it feels like New Year's," Sarah replied. "All change."

"Yes, all change." She paused. "Have you heard from Nathan?"

"He wished the children a merry Christmas," Sarah acknowledged as she sipped her drink. "And he said he'd ring them tomorrow. I think he's probably a bit lonely. He said he missed us, which was new." She paused thoughtfully. "But, to be honest, I'm not holding my breath. If he wants to have a rethink and put in the effort to make our marriage work, that's one thing. But it's got to come from him."

"And if he doesn't?" Gwen asked gently.

Sarah gave a little shrug. "Then I'll be okay," she told her mother. "Maybe not immediately, maybe not for a while. But I will." She smiled at her. "Really."

"Yes," Gwen replied, thinking of John. It wasn't nearly the same thing as Sarah and Nathan's twenty-year marriage—in fact, quite the opposite—but hopes deferred were still just that. She toyed with the idea of reaching out to him. Why not? Why did she have to wait for John to make the first move, especially if they *were* just friends?

"I'd better make sure Owen and Mairi are being sensible and actually going to bed," Sarah said as she heaved herself up from the sofa. "I don't want to leave Ellie with all the work. Don't drink all the Baileys, Mum," she added, with a playful wag of her finger.

"I won't," Gwen promised. "Just most of it."

As Sarah left, she slipped her phone from her pocket. Maybe it was the Baileys, or just the fact that life felt so fleeting and yet so precious, but she wanted to be daring, even reckless.

She typed out a text.

Merry Christmas, John! Hope this holiday season has you counting your blessings. That's what I've been doing, some-

what to my surprise. Life is short, isn't it, when you think about it? Always good to make the most of it. Gwen x

Was that too cryptic? she wondered. Or too overt and even pushy? But Gwen found she didn't care. It was how she felt, what she wanted to say, whatever the consequences. Life was for living, after all. She pressed send.

She remained where she was seated, half-hoping for an answering message, but none came, and she told herself that was all right, let the realization soak into her. It *was* all right. She was content simply to sit here, enjoying the warmth and comforting crackle of the fire, the snow in sweeping drifts outside, the lights on the Christmas tree twinkling like bits of promise.

"Did you save me some Baileys?" Sarah demanded good-naturedly as she came back into the room.

"And me, too," Ellie chimed in as she joined them by the fire.

Gwen gestured to the bottle. "There's still plenty left... I think."

Her daughter and daughter-in-law hooted with laughter just as her phone pinged with a text.

Gwen slipped it out of her pocket and glanced at the screen.

Gwen! I'm so glad you messaged. I've been thinking about you quite a lot, actually, and especially how we said goodbye so abruptly, which was entirely my fault. I was hoping we could...

Smiling, she slipped her phone back into her pocket. She'd read the rest of the message later, but she felt hopeful about it. Quite hopeful, indeed.

Still smiling, Gwen reached for the bottle of Baileys to top up everyone's glasses.

"Merry Christmas, everyone!" she said as she raised her glass in a toast, and Sarah and Ellie raised theirs, as well.

"Merry Christmas," Sarah echoed.

Ellie added with a whimsical smile, "And here's to the Bluebell Inn, whatever may happen!"

"Hear, hear," they all said, and smiling at one another, they clinked glasses and toasted the future—whatever it held.

A LETTER FROM KATE

Dear Reader,

Thank you so much for reading *Christmas at the Inn on Bluebell Lane*! It was so much fun to revisit these characters and lovely little Llandrigg, and I hope you enjoyed their new adventures. If you would like to keep up to date with all my latest releases, just sign up at the following link. Your email address will never be shared and you can unsubscribe at any time.

www.bookouture.com/kate-hewitt

If you did enjoy the story, I would be very grateful if you could write a review. I'd love to hear what you think, and it makes such a difference helping new readers to discover one of my books for the first time.

I love hearing from my readers—you can get in touch on my Facebook group for readers (facebook.com/groups/KatesReads), through Twitter, Goodreads or my website.

Thanks again for reading!
Kate

www.kate-hewitt.com

 twitter.com/author_kate

ACKNOWLEDGEMENTS

Many thanks to all at Bookouture who help to bring my books to light—my editor Jess, copyeditor Jade, and proofreader Tom, as well as those in publicity, marketing, audio, and foreign rights— Kim, Mel, Alba, Richard and Saidah—you are all brilliant! Thanks to the other authors in the Bookouture Lounge who offer such wonderful support, and also to my lovely readers, especially those in my Kate's Reads Facebook group who are always enthusiastic! Writing can be a lonely job, and it's lovely to check in and find some messages of encouragement. Happy reading, everyone!

Made in United States
Troutdale, OR
10/10/2023

13590803R00159